NIGHT & DAY

Sally Miall

Children's books by the same author (Sally Bicknell)

The Midwinter Violins

Chatto and Windus 1973. Paperback: Puffin Books 1976. ISBN 0701150300

The Summer of the Warehouse

Abelard Schuman 1979. Paperback: Beaver Books 1983. ISBN 0200726331

Follow That Uncle

Abelard Schuman 1980. ISBN 020072729X

NIGHT & DAY

Sally Miall

New Media Foundry

First published 2006

ISBN-10: 0-9553751-0-X

ISBN-13: 978-0-9553751-0-1

Published by New Media Foundry Ltd.,
Homefarm Orchard, Threehouseholds, Chalfont St Giles,
Bucks HP8 4LP, United Kingdom.
Phone +44 1494 872751 - email marcus@bicknell.com

New Media Foundry Ltd., company incorporated in Great Britain N° 370 4891

Typeset in Garamond 12pt
Printed by Biddles Ltd. in the United Kingdom

Contents

I

Waiting for Mimsy

1   The End Is In The Beginning

The writer Quentin Jones sits at his desk. It is, in fact, not a desk but an old kitchen table, once heavily stained and scarred with scratches, burns and cuts. It cost him a fiver in the Portobello Road and another fiver to have it delivered to his first independent home, a north-facing basement, in Muswell Hill, advertised as 'A Garden Flat with Potential'. Earnestly he tended his table: cleaning, sanding and waxing, until it became the essential length of smooth woodiness on which he would write his books. The Table.

He was working in television then, just down from Cambridge where he'd written satirical sketches and got a First. Later he joined a big publishing firm where the in-fighting took more time and energy than the production of books. In the space of a few years he was taken over, moved sideways, moved upwards, and taken over again. He enjoyed himself, fought with the best, and earned a respectable salary. But he knew it wasn't for him. He wanted to write, not sell.

By this time he had left his basement and taken The Table to a comparatively luxurious flat in Fulham, where he wrote W*horehouse*. His employers turned it down. It was too long, they said. It asked too much of the average reader. So he sold it to a rival firm. Publication brought instant acclaim, huge sales, a film offer. He'd worked for this, but when it came he felt defenceless, as if newborn. 'Recognition brings meta-morphosis,' he told an interviewer.

The critics loved him. 'A remarkable first novel,' they said. 'A voice for the seventies.' To concentrate his energies he left publishing, helping out occasionally as an adviser, attending lunches and dinners, adjudicating when there were prizes to be given. He became The Writer.

He is fifty now, living in Hampstead in a big house with a well-kept garden. His shoulders are bent forward by long hours of work at The Table. His sardonic but amiable features, well-known on television, show marks of maturity. His dark hair is frosted with grey. He wears reading glasses. But his long legs and arms are well muscled, his stomach flat. He goes jogging on the Heath once or twice a week, swims and practises Tai Chi. As a young man he was proficient in martial arts. He has always enjoyed exercise. Physical fitness, he believes, helps the creative process.

But today there will be no creation. He sits at The Table, thoughtful and sad.

He and his wife Barbara were on holiday in France. The telephone rang at two in the morning. There had been violence, a terrible incident in which people died. One of them was a close friend.

Horror is everywhere these days, a cliché in newspapers and on television. We are distressed. We are full of pity for victims of crime, abused children, refugees, the old, the sick, the poor. In our comfortable homes, with friends and family, we discuss the cause of the latest disaster. We blame the government, the media, the weather. It was ignorance, neglect, global warming, the breakdown of the family. There they go, those poor sufferers, starving, broken-hearted, sick and dying.

The telephone rings. It is our turn.

There was no question of going back to sleep, so they tidied the house, packed up and left. The holiday, three days short, was over. They were needed elsewhere. Not to break the news. It had been on radio and television the same night, in the papers the next day. But they would help, where possible, with consoling words and practical advice. With the funeral arrangements. With fending off the media.

Shortly after sunrise they were in a taxi on their way to the airport, with seats on a plane to Heathrow. The flight was the last leg of a long-distance journey. The cabin crew were exhausted, the toilets dirty, their landing delayed for forty minutes. These were pinpricks, a smaller sort of suffering.

Home at last, they became a help team, sorting letters, taking rerouted telephone calls, passing messages, listening and offering sympathy while people sobbed and wailed. Why, why, do these terrible things happen? The authorities should have done something. I blame the police. There should have been safeguards. If only...

No good, if only. You can't re-write real life.

Quentin sits in his revolving chair, looking for comfort in familiar things. In front of him are his state-of-the-art word processor, and his printer. Out of sight under The Table is the electric typewriter on which he wrote *Whorehouse*, in his Fulham days. Also the battered portable on which he produced television scripts in Muswell Hill. These old machines are important to him. He wouldn't dream of throwing them out.

Two of the walls are lined with shelves, packed with reference books, copies of his own works in hard cover and paperback, files of letters and reviews, his complete set of Dickens, other favourite novels old and new, spare floppy discs, tapes, ribbons, supplies of paper. One day he and Barbara are going to blitz the shelves. She says a lot of the stuff can be thrown away or put on computer, and she is quite right.

He loves Barbara very much, and he's missing her although she's only gone to the post-box on the corner. She is everything to him: wife, lover, mother of his children, his most valued critic. She is a small person, so that when they lie down together her head rests comfortably just below his collar-bone. He tells her she is beautiful, and she denies it. She says she is getting fat. He can't see it. He loves every thing about her, her blue eyes, fair skin and soft blonde hair. Her strong little hands, her perfect feet. Her inside and her outside.

Surprisingly for her size, she has considerable reserves of practical energy. And she has brains, and a sharp wit. She writes verse, which is published in magazines and newspapers. While they were on holiday she started a new poem, called *'Kevin In The Supermarket.'*

> In tee-shirt, jeans and trainers, by the trolley he stands,
> His arms stretched to hold on. Both hands,
> His mother says. Waiting at the check-out he sings his song
> And swings one foot. Oh Kevin, must you go on
> Swinging your foot that way,
> And singing, singing all day!
>
> Children turn their heads to listen.
> They get the message in his endless song.
> They smile, catching sight of him through the long
> Avenues, household cleaners, margarine, cottage cheese,
> Self-raising, soluble, ready-mix, freeze-dried peas...

That's Barbara's poem so far. Now it's on hold.

What with Quentin's table and the shelves there is only just room for another horizontal surface, on top of two filing cabinets, where he has his fax machine and two telephones, which he can reach by swinging his chair round.

On one side of the door hangs a pin-board on which printed ephemera have accumulated. Interesting postcards, lists, reminders, newspaper cuttings. On the other side is a haphazard collection of framed photographs. Himself receiving a literary prize. Barbara in her wedding dress. Their twin daughters, now nineteen, called originally Ariadne and Cressida, now known as Harry and Chris. Beautiful, talented girls, Harry a painter, Chris a musician.

Waiting for Barbara, Quentin re-reads a review of his latest book:

> '*Recycle* takes us into the heart of the inner city, the bottom layer
> of society's rotting pile, where the fomenting detritus of urban

squalor is transformed into nourishing compost. The death of a black schoolboy in a racially-motivated disturbance re-unites a splintered community. Inevitably Quentin Jones turns to Dickens for inspiration, his hero as innocent as Barnaby Rudge, his backdrop the rubbish heap of *Our Mutual Friend*.'

Good reviews, letters about the paperback and American rights, a film offer for an earlier novel, *Purgatory*, which he will turn down. They want their own Oscar-hunting screen-writer, and a director who has a talent for vulgarity. None of that, thank you very much. He, Quentin Jones, gives the orders. He plays God.

Yesterday, a beautiful May morning, flowers blooming, birds singing, was the day of the funeral. The *paparazzi* weren't going to miss this one and turned up in force, hordes of them surrounding the small church, as well as a crowd of ghoulish sightseers, so that friends and relations had trouble getting inside. The police did their best. Finally, nearly an hour late, the service began, hymns, tributes, prayers. The ambience reminded Quentin of his father's funeral, and he began to weep. Barbara was dry-eyed, very pale. Arm in arm they followed the coffin and the packed crowd of mourners out into the graveyard.

Quentin's tears gave way to annoyance when a television producer, taking a short cut over tombstones, caught up with him and tried to start a conversation.

'Hi, Quentin. We met on *Book Talk*, remember? You said Dickens was a realist, his characters and stories are very much of the world as he knew it.. But he was interested in esoteric matters too, wasn't he. I mean to say, do you think he believed in the After Life?'

'For Christ's sake, not now,' said Quentin, blowing his nose.

'Of course, of course. I only wanted to point out that in *Prison Bars* you had a scene in Hell. Then in *Purgatory* you described an After World which was very badly organised, Chaos if you like. You said the lucky ones might get a few minutes of so-called Heaven before total Oblivion, but no more.'

'I can't talk about it now. Please leave me alone. It's not a good moment.'

'I thought it might be worth asking if you'd like to take part in something I'm putting together about spiritualism in Victorian times. Conan Doyle and Wilkie Collins, you know the sort of thing. There's a revival of interest in the paranormal.'

'Just bugger off, would you.'

'Quentin, with respect, you believe in Fate, don't you. Events have a direction, perhaps invisible to us, but it's there all the same. On Book Talk you said that Dickens worked on this same principle. Like you, he had a sense of inevitability. The End is in the Beginning, that's what you said.'

At this point Barbara placed herself firmly between them, saying, 'Excuse me,' as she stepped on the producer's foot with one tiny stiletto heel. No more trouble from him. Round the grave there was singing by a young group, their daughter Chris among them, which reduced Quentin to tears again. He wasn't the only one.

Here comes Barbara back from the post. He hears her closing the front door, and goes to meet her in the hall. She is wearing washed-out blue jeans with matching waistcoat and a shirt in a pink rose pattern. It is true that she is fatter than she used to be. No longer size 10, she takes a 14 and has to turn up the hems.

'Darling, I missed you,' says Quentin. 'Am I ridiculous?'

'Yes,' she replies. 'But I like it.'

She gives him a quick, dry kiss. During this past week they have hardly embraced, hardly touched. Love has been in mourning.

Barbara has been sleeping badly, troubled by vivid dreams, like film sequences. The star is a fair-haired man. She has dreamed about him before, sometimes as a baby, or a little boy. She has heard him singing in church. Once he saved her from falling into an open grave. Last night she dreamed that he was talking to an Angel. She wakes up exhausted, confused. It's difficult to throw the dream off and get on with real life. *'Kevin in the Supermarket'* seems shallow, not important. She wants to write about the death, but can't get the right mood.

> *I saw, or thought I saw,*
> *The bodies lying on the floor,*
> *But I was elsewhere.*
> *I wasn't there.*

This is no good, it's trite and awful. The horror is too big for her sort of verse.

Quentin follows her into the kitchen. ' I can't stop thinking about it,' he says.

'Nor can I.' Barbara has been thinking particularly about an affair she had many years ago, when she was Barbara Carey, known as Boo. The memory fills her with guilt. She wishes it had never happened. She was

13

young and silly, without direction. Then Quentin came into her life and made her happy and fulfilled. A turning point.

He pours her a gin-and-tonic, a Campari and soda for himself. He rattles the ice in his glass. 'Darling Barbara,' he says awkwardly. 'I hope we'll feel better soon. There's been a sort of chill, hasn't there.'

'An ice-cube,' she says. 'It's nothing. And it's melting.'

'That's good news,' says Quentin. 'Then perhaps, when you've finished your drink, you might come upstairs with me. We could make love, for instance.'

Barbara doesn't hesitate. 'It's called bonking now,' she says, straight-faced, suddenly leaning over and kissing him hard, so that their glasses wobble and drink splashes on the floor.

'Ah, ah,' he says, returning her kisses with interest. *'Bonkeremus. Je te bonkerai.'*

'Suits me,' says Barbara.

The healing process has begun.

In a rose-tinted cloud of sex, gin and Campari, they go upstairs together. He unbuttons her waistcoat on the way. The bedroom door is open, showing pale walls, flowery drapes, a king-size bed with a patchwork quilt in delicate shades. She kicks off her pink and blue trainers. He lifts her up and kisses her lips, her neck. She murmurs, 'My love.' With one foot he pushes the door closed.

Quentin and Barbara believe that bonking should be private.

When the twins were old enough to be told about sex, they said they would like to see it being done. They had just had their fourth birthday. 'We'll sit on the edge of the bed,' they said. 'And we won't talk.'

'It's not for watching,' said Quentin. 'It's for two people who want to be alone together because they like each other very much.'

'Grown-up people,' added Barbara. 'Or grown-up animals. Cats and dogs, birds, butterflies. Frogs.'

After that there was talk about eggs, and how they were fertilised, about kangaroos, fish, whales and rabbits. About breast-feeding, and twins. For a while Harry and Chris arranged nursery matings between teddy bears and Barbie dolls, then interest in the subject waned. For ten years or so they were busy with other things: making friends, going to school, reading, painting, making music.

The girls are not identical. Harry is dark-haired and petite, Chris tall and blonde. To Quentin they are miraculous creatures. As young teenagers they were not only pretty and clever but also kind, and amusing, somehow so much better than other people's daughters. Surely

14

they wouldn't fool about with spotty youths, insist on having the Pill, stay out all night? And yet by the time they were fifteen they were doing all these things - except that the boyfriends didn't have spots. Quentin tells himself not to be a jealous old fool. But that's how he feels, jealous, displaced, middle-aged. Secretly he wishes that they had remained virgins until the day when suitable mates, approved by himself, came along. Then they would get married and live happily ever after.

Barbara thinks his attitude is Victorian. She takes an up-to-date view of sex and likes to talk about it, how essential it is, how good it can be and how destructive. The girls confide in her and sometimes take her advice. She is also good at dealing with rejected lovers. 'Go and talk to Mama about it,' says Harry, or Chris. 'And we can still be friends, okay.'

Quentin prefers not to get involved. He wonders if he's a bit of a prude. When he first started writing his publisher suggested that there should be more sex in his novels. Quentin wouldn't oblige. 'I'm not interested in porn for porn's sake,' he explained. 'It's not my style, organ thrusting and cries of joy and frothing sperm, just to give the reader a thrill. It's got to be intrinsic.'

Sex between him and Barbara is intrinsic. This may be the secret of their happy marriage. As for Heaven and Hell, the After Life and Inevitability, these are not articles of faith for Quentin Jones. They are concepts, windows through which he can access characters and scenery. He explores, and is inspired to create. He recognises that he is not an intellectual. If he were his books wouldn't sell so well.

He is The Writer.

The next day Barbara looks at '*Kevin in the Supermarket*' and decides that she must finish it, no matter what. It's a struggle, but she does it, and sends it off to her agent with an apologetic note. 'Hoping for better times ahead.'

Babies crying in the wilderness, upset,
Hungry and unemployed, for a moment forget
Discomfort and lack of job satisfaction.
Do we hear something? Is this the promised action?
Is Christ getting off at the bus stop? Is that the Baptist over there,
Swinging his foot and singing, the boy with the curly hair?

Buying lemon-scented wholemeal soap
Customers ignore the message of hope.
They remember Armistice Day, November.
The flower of England fallen in the mud.
Christ crucified, Caesar dying in a pool of blood.
In the next episode barbarian feet
Trample the Roman Empire. Bank robbery in the High Street,
Saw it on television. They'll get us too at last
With crinkle-cut, non-toxic instant blast.

So cry, children, cry. Fill the precinct with your noise.
Break your battery-operated fail-safe toys.
Groan and bow your heads in the stroller, howl in the pram.
Never another Jesus, carrying a soft white lamb.
But Kevin just keeps hoping, keeps singing,
As he stands by the trolley, foot swinging.
One day the Angel will come with his shining sword.
Bad news will go away. Order will be restored.

2   Entertaining

When Charles Broome-Vivier married Marian Foster everybody agreed that he was a lucky man. She was twenty-two, grey-eyed with dark hair, very attractive. She was also kind, tactful, and a good organiser. 'I adore her,' Charles told his friends. 'And she's wonderful with money. Much better than I am!'

This was a good joke, because he was a banker. She brought a lot of money with her, thanks to her father who had made a small fortune in the textile industry. Charles was grateful for this because he would one day inherit his family place, Broome Hall, which would be expensive to run. Even more important, he had political ambitions. Marian's money would be a great help if he became an MP.

The wedding, in 1967, was a grand affair, reported in glossy magazines. Marian, in a daringly short dress with plunging neckline, was voted Bride of the Year. The honeymoon was in Sardinia, at a friend's villa. The happy couple came back to London and settled into the house just off Knightsbridge which Marian's father had given her as a wedding present. They lived at first on the top floor, which she had made into a studio flat. 'Such fun,' she said. 'Pretending to be artists.'

Getting the rest of the house decorated and furnished took another six months. Then they began to entertain. Her parties were never dull. She could charm even the stuffiest guests into enjoying themselves. And her food was wonderful. They went out a lot, too, to drinks and dinners, charity balls, nightclubs, the theatre. In her spare time she ran a boutique, an exclusive dress shop. Everyone had a boutique in those days. Some lasted six months and then went bankrupt. Hers lasted for years. She sold at the right moment, just before the recession.

Four years passed. They should have had children by now, but none had appeared. The marriage seemed to be going through a difficult stage. A pity, people said. They were such an attractive couple.

'Darling, I'm off. I'll try not to be late,'

Charles stood in front of the mirror, folding his cashmere scarf round his neck and buttoning his overcoat. The middle button was under strain, so he undid it, acknowledging that he had put on weight over Christmas. Otherwise he was not displeased with his appearance. He was thirty-three, well-built, with a healthy complexion and a good head of hair, brown with a touch of gold. He was proud of his hair. It had what his hairdresser called 'a natural bend' and as yet there was no sign of a bald patch. Hair was important these days. One hardly ever wore a hat, except for weddings and Ascot. No more bowlers in the City, though he might wear his fur hat, rather amusing, if the weather got any colder.

He smiled at his reflection, feeling a surge of optimism. There was hope for the future. At last, after five years of Labour misrule, the Conservatives were back in power. How different things were going to be, what a bonus for the City! And what a contribution one might be able to make, given the opportunity.

Marian, slim and beautiful, came out of the kitchen. They were giving a dinner party that night, so she was dressed for action in jeans and designer sweater, her hair tied back in a pony tail. 'People are invited for seven forty-five, darling,' she said. 'I'll open the claret. And we'll need some white for the starter. Is there something in the cellar, or shall I buy?'

She had consulted him about the food, but he'd forgotten what had been decided. Was it lamb, or beef? One had to have a roast, she'd said. Stews and ragouts were out. She would carve, which she did well. He would pour the wine and keep the conversation going. Their daily help would serve and clear up afterwards.

'Did you say soup first, darling?' he asked, picking up his briefcase. 'And then lamb?'

'No, darling. First we have individual salmon mousses, with a shrimpy sauce. Then it's beef, not lamb. And the dessert is *tarte tatin* with cream.'

'Of course, darling. Sorry, you did tell me. There are three bottles of Sancerre downstairs, they'll do for the starter. Put them in the fridge. Then the claret. And I'll produce something to go with the pud when I get back. And you're an angel, darling.'

They would be ten tonight, the guests all important to him in one way or another.

'Goodbye, darling,' she said, and gave him a quick kiss on the cheek. He didn't like being fussed over when he was ready to go.

He kissed her twice, because he felt guilty. He was being unfaithful to her, and it wasn't the first time. Twice before he'd confessed, and generously she had forgiven him. He knew that one shouldn't behave like this, but he found women so tempting, so interesting. And the chase was such fun. In marriage there was no chase, only a certain sameness. He was devoted to Marian, of course. He couldn't possibly manage without her. She organised their social life, paid bills, dealt with correspondence, looked after his clothes, his health. She was practical, nice-looking, even-tempered. In almost every respect she was a perfect wife.

Unfortunately she hadn't managed to produce yet. He wanted a son, particularly, because of Broome. She was twenty-six, she should be getting on with it. She had become a little tense about sex recently, which didn't help. He had heard that tenseness might stop a woman conceiving. And it did rather put a fellow off.

He was seeing Barbara Carey, known as Boo, at least twice a week. He knew he would have to end it soon, before things got out of hand. But Boo was such fun, so desirable, so pink and pretty. And far from tense. Her flat was in Sloane Street, opposite Knightsbridge station, conveniently on his way home. Several times recently he hadn't got back until half-past eight or nine, and Marian had wondered why, naturally. He had a good excuse. The merchant bank he worked for was about to take over a smaller bank, and he did have some extra responsibilities as a result. 'Sorry I'm late, darling,' he would say. 'The merger is keeping me busy. I'll be glad when it's over.' It was so easy, so credible. 'Merging' had become part of the private language between himself and Boo. 'Can we merge on Wednesday as usual?' 'How about a quick merge on Friday before you go away for the weekend?' Boo loved this joke.

'Goodbye, darling,' he said, and gave Marian yet another kiss to ease his conscience. He was opening the front door when the telephone rang, so he hovered, waiting while she answered, lifting his eyebrows to mean, 'Is it for me?' She shook her head and mouthed, 'No, it's Mummy.' So he departed, blowing a further kiss, thinking about the merger he was going to have with Boo that evening. He'd have to leave the office in good time.

Marian's parents were divorced. Her father, William Foster, now retired from Foster Fabrics, Nottingham, lived in Spain with his second wife. Her mother Emily lived in a cottage in the Cotswolds. She had been an actress years ago, pretty enough to play leading roles in rep. She had kept her looks to some extent, but divorce had soured her disposition. She complained continually about her lack of money, and the difficulty she had in maintaining a decent standard of living. Conscience-stricken, Marian helped her out from time to time with special requests: a redecorated living room, a Mediterranean cruise. Birthday presents had to be bottles of gin and whisky, and for Christmas a case of wine. Emily liked to entertain. People were so kind, she said, and asked her to parties. She had to pay them back. Marian found her thinly disguised hints about money infuriating. But she wasn't one for letting off steam. She kept her feelings to herself.

'Mummy, how are you?' She was afraid it would be money as usual, but this time her mother had some other problem, expressed in a roundabout way which was almost incomprehensible, and such a waste of time on a dinner party day when there was so much to do.

'She's old and ill,' Emily was saying. 'It comes to all of us in the end, doesn't it. She must be nearly ninety. You'll have to go and see her, pet, because really I can't. The train is so expensive these days, and driving is out of the question with the car in its present state. I'll have to start saving up for a new one. And it's no good trying to involve Harold.'

Harold? Marian thought of Harold Wilson, who had been Prime Minister, then remembered her uncle, Mummy's brother, who was absolutely boring and had a ghastly wife and children to match. She hadn't seen any of them for years and couldn't give a damn. 'Mummy , who is ill? Do explain, please.'

'It's Mimsy. You know, in Wimbledon. Mimsy Mason. She's my aunt, the last of that generation. Vincent died last year, and Harold's not on speaking terms with Mimsy, and she never took the slightest interest in his children. She's had a stroke, and the hospital says she must have constant care. You're such a good organiser, dear. I know you can manage. Just get her into a decent home, that's all. You do remember her, don't you. She gave you some very nice presents.'

Yes, Marian remembered. Mimsy Mason, her great-aunt, had never married. As a young girl, they said, she had lived with an artist in Paris. Mummy had always disapproved of her. Much to her annoyance Mimsy had from time to time given Marian exotic and valuable gifts. Once it was a pair of *art nouveau* earrings. 'Totally unsuitable for a girl of your age,' Emily had said. Later there was a jade locket, then a string of cultured pearls with a *diamanté* clasp.

As a wedding present Mimsy had given Charles and Marian a pair of enamelled snuff-boxes. Charles thought they might be Fabergé and had shown them to a friend who was at Sotheby's. Not Fabergé, the friend said, but another Frenchman, worth fifteen hundred pounds each and certain to appreciate. After that they had a display case built into the wall, with an alarm, where they kept the snuff-boxes and other *objets*. Charles said they should visit the generous great-aunt. It was the least they could do. So, grateful newly-weds, they went.

Mimsy had moved from a large house overlooking the Common into a two-bedroomed flat. The living room, much smaller than her previous one, was crowded with antique furniture, ornaments, gilt chairs and tables, bronzes, oil paintings heavily varnished, china in glass-fronted cabinets. Oriental carpets overlapped each other on the floor. Others, the finest silk, hung on the walls. Velvet curtains, much too long, swept dramatically to the floor and kept out most of the daylight. There had been an elderly maid, who brought tea. It would have been a dull occasion except that Mimsy was well-informed and found Charles irresistible. She had given him most of her attention. He had been quite impressed with her.

Marian made a face at the telephone. What a bore! 'Mummy dear, we've got a dinner party tonight, so I can't do anything about Mimsy until tomorrow. She's in hospital, did you say?

'She was,' said Emily. 'But she's out now. Somebody telephoned, said his name was Dave. The current boyfriend, I presume. Just imagine, at her age. He's probably after her money, if she's got any left.'

'Well, that's up to her, isn't it,' said Marian sharply. The way Mummy went on about money was really rather repulsive. 'Look, I'll telephone and find out what's happened so far. And tomorrow I'll cope with the somebody called Dave, and I'll make enquiries about a home. Yes, Mummy, I'll let you know, but not until tomorrow evening. Rather busy. Yes, of course, Mummy. Goodbye.'

She put down the telephone with a sigh of relief. So much to do, such fun. She loved giving dinner parties. Tonight was a challenge, because a television presenter was coming, and a woman MP, and someone from the Foreign Office and his very grand wife. Then there was a married couple, old friends who would be supportive. And the Deardens, Patrick and Clarissa.

Seeing Clarissa was always slightly disturbing. She had been Charles's first love, and liked to remind him of their great romance, which had happened ages ago when they were up at Oxford together. Marian found Clarissa self-centred and difficult. She was a journalist now, brilliantly clever. And good-looking if you liked red hair, green eyes with pale gingery lashes, and a pale skin with freckles. At Oxford she had been a revolutionary, down with everything. Her friends, Charles particularly, had been surprised when she married Patrick, who was rich, would one day inherit a title and sit in the House of Lords. At the moment he was at Central Office, which could be helpful for Charles. Tonight he was the guest of honour, and would sit on Marian's right. He would be boring.

Yellow freesias for the table, she decided. Cream candles, matching place mats and napkins. In the hall, on the landing and in the living room she would have yellow roses and bronze chrysanthemums, whatever she could find in warm colours, to help people forget that it was January.

Planning these things kept her mind off certain disorderly thoughts, milling about just below the surface, threatening to break out. If they got loose it would be absolutely awful. She accepted that Charles didn't like being fussed over when he was ready to go to the office. That was understandable. But recently he hadn't wanted her to fuss over him at all, especially not in bed. Last night when she snuggled up to him, hopefully letting her nightie slip off one shoulder, he had said, 'Sorry, darling. Terribly tired. It must be that flu I had before Christmas.'

She knew, because instinct told her, that he was making love to someone else. And she knew who it was. Not Clarissa, that was over years ago. Someone they saw at other people's parties, who was young and pretty, and unattached.

She didn't want to ask him about it. There might be an angry scene. Anger between married people was so uncivilised. And above all their marriage had to be civilised, and affectionate, and fun. The trouble was that it had happened before, and so her trust in him had been slightly damaged. She loved him still, of course, but not in quite the same way. She tried not to let it show, but her body must have told him. Their love-making had become forced, the natural warmth gone.

He'd said, when he confessed about the other times, that the animal in men was very strong. They were made that way. So it's psychological, she thought. I haven't got pregnant, so the animal in him has told him to try another woman.

One day he would become an MP. He was so much the right sort of person. How proud she would be! The supportive wife, helping where she could, making a perfect home for him. And with a family, three of four children, to complete the picture.

If only she had got pregnant before the unfaithfulness started, she wouldn't have minded so much. She would have had her role as a mother. The house would be ideal for children, near the Park, with enough space on the top floor for little bedrooms, and a bathroom. And Nanny's room, with TV.

She would take the children down to Broome Hall at weekends. Charles's father would spoil them. They would have dogs and ponies. Later, when Charles inherited, they would spend most of their time there. She was looking forward to re-arranging Broome, getting the roof mended, putting in new central heating. She would take part in local affairs, committees and so on. Charles would spend two or three days a week in London. He would be a wonderful father, adored by his children. And by his wife.

She wondered if she bored him. She wasn't clever about books and current affairs, although she'd been to Abbey Mead School. 'As good as Eton,' her mother had said. 'You meet the right sort of people. And your father can easily afford it.' The Abbey Mead product was hopefully an all-round person, self-assured, thoughtful of others, interested in what was going on in the world. And fairly well-educated. Marian achieved the Abbey Mead style, but only got two 'O' Levels. She did a typing course when she left, and book-keeping and *cordon bleu* cookery. She worked as a secretary, which was hateful, then as a model. That had been super, but they didn't really want you when you were over twenty. You had to be a skinny teenager. For a while she'd done Directors' lunches. Then, with relief, she'd married Charles. The house had kept her busy for a while. Once it was repaired, re-decorated, elegantly furnished, she found she had time to spare. A baby would have filled it nicely.

To keep her mind off the subject she had bought the boutique, which she ran with her best friend from school, Celia Chase. They called it Marcellina, a mixture of their two names. Marian bought the clothes, and kept the books. Celia was her employee, as manageress. She needed the income. She was so attractive, Marian thought, she could have married anyone. But she had chosen Victor Chase, a publisher, who was rather drear and had no money to speak of. They had two children, Emma, aged three, and Rupert, nine months, collectively referred to as The Adorables. Celia had a series of foreign girls to look after them. Marian helped out in emergencies. She loved doing it. It was ironic that she was well off and had no children while Celia, with the Adorables, found it difficult to make ends meet.

Often, embarrassingly, Marian found herself watching children in the Park, on buses, in the street, so that their keepers stared at her suspiciously. In shops she browsed around the children's departments, considering little sleeping suits, party dresses, cots, prams, small boots, raincoats with matching hats. Today she was imagining a daughter, four years old, called Teresa or Sue, who would have to be a very good girl because there was going to be a dinner party, and Mama was busy getting everything ready.

'Oh, stop it!' she told herself. She could hear her daily, Mrs Briggs, getting things out of the broom cupboard, which meant that the vacuum cleaner would be in action soon. So she had better telephone Wimbledon right now and get it over.

Quentin Jones would not let someone like Mrs Briggs make her entrance without a quick character sketch. She was a small, tidy person, her eyebrows plucked to a fine line, her hair dyed raven black. She cleaned for the Broome-Viviers every weekday morning, and sometimes reappeared in the evening to help with parties. Her personal life, unknown to them, was dominated by religion. She was a regular attender at the Church of the Holy Word, Fulham, where she bore witness on subjects such as Sin and Eternal Damnation. Her husband, whom she described to Marian as 'a fishmonger, and very demanding, there are limits to what a woman can put up with,' had left her for someone else, said to be no better than a prostitute. 'They will burn in Hell, excuse me, madam.' After these revelations Marian avoided personal questions. Mrs Briggs came with excellent references and was efficient and reliable. They couldn't possibly manage without her.

'Briggsie, good morning!' cried Marian cheerfully. 'Just one telephone call I must make. Be with you!' She dialled the Wimbledon number before Mrs Briggs could start talking. There would have to be a cup of tea later on and some chat about the weather, the cost of things these days, and how the buses never came when you wanted them.

The ringing tone went on and on, while Marian waited. She would pop in and see Celia when she went out for the flowers, and tell her what the gynaecologist had said. She might mention her suspicions, too, about Charles. It would be a help to unload.

No answer. 'Oh, come on, do!' she said, tapping her fingers. 'Come on!' No answer, no answer. Then someone took the receiver off and put it down with a clatter. She heard voices in the background.

Man: 'There's no question of that. I'm staying here with her. She knows me, she trusts me. Please go now, just go.'

Woman: 'I'm sorry, but I am trying to help, that's all.. That's what the social services are for. Several people telephoned to say that there was no one looking after her. And the hospital said we should visit. But if you think you can manage...'

Man, snarling: 'I can manage, and I thank you, so please just go. I'll get in touch if I want help. You may not have noticed but someone is trying to speak to me on the telephone, and possibly they have something important to say to me. So go, please. I'm sorry. Goodbye.'

There was the sound of a door being emphatically closed. Marian waited. This must be Mimsy's friend or lover, whatever. He sounded oafish. 'Oafish' was the word you used at Abbey Mead for people who didn't have good style.

'Sorry,' he said at last. 'What is it?'

'Oh, hallo,' said Marian. 'My name is Broome-Vivier, Marian Broome-Vivier. I am Miss Mason's great-niece. I would like to speak to her please.'

'You can't. She's had a stroke. I can give her a message.'

'Oh. Well, tell her I'm coming down tomorrow. I'll take over and get her organised. No problem. I gather she's out of hospital, but she can't live alone, can she. I'll make enquiries and get her into a decent home...'

'You bloody well won't. You're not in charge, Mrs Marian Whatsit. You can come and see her. She would like that. But she's not going into a home, and that's final.'

'I only meant - I'm sorry. I'll come tomorrow at eleven, if that's all right.'

'Okay then. Eleven tomorrow.' He rang off.

Marian hurried out to buy flowers, then went to Marcellina to see Celia. She told her about the telephone conversation, exaggerating to get the full effect.

'You bloody well won't, Mrs Marian Whatsit! I mean, one could at least be polite, don't you think.'

'Absolute oaf!' agreed Celia. She checked her appearance in the nearest mirror, smoothing her hair, which was dark and straight, pinned up on top to give her height. She wished she had Marian's model girl body. She was small-boned, and had put on weight since having the Adorables. Her skirts were tight when she sat down.

They went through to the office, where there were racks of clothes waiting to be collected, special orders and hems to be adjusted, as well as a desk and two chairs and a cupboard full of Marcellina dress boxes and plastic bags. It was small and cramped, the part of the shop that customers didn't see.

'That lipstick is good on you,' said Marian. 'Rose pink.' She felt better already, just being with Celia. They had been girls together at Abbey Mead, shared flats in London, taken holidays together. So important to have a friend who knew you that well. 'Celia, the gynaecologist was super. She was so frank, she seemed really to care. She said there was nothing wrong with me physically, and was I inhibited about sex, and I said No. And had I had lots of experience, so I told her, you know, about teenage adventures.'

'Your first was in Michael's car,' said Celia. 'Then there was Jim.'

'No, Alan was before Jim. Then Jeremy, and really that was only because I felt sorry for him, divorced and lonesome. And it was totally unsuitable because he was my boss at the time. And years older than me.'

'But attractive,' said Celia. 'He was so groomed, Savile Row suits, and grey hair. And you had two weeks in the Scilly Islands.'

'Yes. And he was adventurous. Some things I hadn't done before..' They exchanged an understanding look. In bed, they knew, experience was the best teacher. 'He was good at it. But I didn't enjoy him like one's supposed to, so it was only fair to say, Look, we've had fun but it's not long-term. Anyway, I told her, the gynie woman, how I absolutely adore Charles and I do want his children. And Celia, she said he should come for tests! Can you believe it? He should have a semen count or something. I mean really, I couldn't ask Charles to do that. It's an insult to a man, don't you think? I couldn't do it any more than I could ask him to adopt some little unwanted thing. He's too special.'

'You could try those fertility drugs,' said Celia. Poor Marian, so super in every way. She trusts Charles, she loves him. And he's unkind to her, selfish, deceitful. The absolute male chauvinist pig.

'Yes, the gynie mentioned hormone treatment. I said I would have to think about it. I mean, someone had quads, didn't they. I wouldn't want a whole lot at once, it's like a litter of puppies. She said, did I enjoy sex with Charles? And I said Yes, of course, it's absolutely super. And she said, you won't believe this, to increase chances of conception he must put it up as far as possible! I had to laugh. Celia, I do want to tell you something, cross your heart et cetera.'

'Absolutely.'

'Charles has been a little bit off me recently. It's just a temporary thing, of course. He's overworking, the City is very stressful you know. And there's this merger coming up, and actually I think he's having an affair. I must tell you, because I know you'll never reveal. It's Barbara Carey. Known as Boo.'

'That's ridiculous. It couldn't be Boo Carey.'

'Why not?'

This was complicated for Celia. She would gladly tell a lie to save Marian pain, but it shouldn't be too much of a lie. Thoughtfully she admired her nails, varnished rose pink to match her lipstick. 'Because Victor says Boo's having an affair with Quentin Jones.'

'That's the most disgusting thing I've ever heard,' said Marian. 'Carrying on with two men. If Charles is, and Quentin Jones. What a whore.'

'Absolute whore, if true,' Celia agreed. 'But actually I don't think Charles cares a damn about her, because he adores you and everybody knows it.' The fact was that friends were saying that Charles and Marian were showing signs of marriage fatigue. And that Charles was playing around.

'Oh, to hell with it, then!' said Marian, her cloud of gloom much reduced. 'Swear you won't tell a soul. It's just that he keeps saying we should have her to dinner. I mean, who wants an extra woman? And he has a sort of look when she's mentioned.'

'Honestly, Marion, let's forget it. Boo Carey is pathetic. I feel sorry for her. She's divorced, she hasn't got any friends, and no brains, too boring for words. Anyway, she's having it with Quentin.'

Positive untruths, since Celia knew that Boo had lots of friends, and was said to be clever and interesting. As for having it with Quentin Jones, nobody knew for sure whether they had started yet, but he was obviously lusting for her.

'I've just had a super idea,' said Marian. 'I could invite her and Quentin together. Wouldn't that be fun? Celia, you won't breathe a word.'

'Absolutely not. Want a coffee?'

'No, I must rush. I want to get everything super organised, then it's easier to face the dreaded Clarissa. I mean, at least I give good dinner parties.'

'Clarissa is so affected,' said loyal Celia. 'I don't know what people see in her.'

Two potential customers had come in, a bride-to-be and her mother. They walked slowly along the racks, picking out garments and holding them up, frowning and murmuring to each other.

Daughter: 'Please, not beige or cream, Mama. I'm in white, remember.'

Mother: 'Oh yes, of course. How about blue then? Can I have blue?'

Daughter: 'I'd much rather not, Mama. It's such a cold colour. Look, here's a suit and blouse, really lovely. This would be perfect, don't you think. Just try on the jacket.'

Mother: 'It is quite nice, isn't it. I wonder – *(dropping her voice)* But just look at the price, dear! I can't possibly spend that much. All I need is a pretty dress, and a coat. And a nice hat.'

Daughter, quiet but very firm: 'Mama this is my big day and you're part of the show and you can't wear just a pretty dress. I mean, there will be photographers from *Queen* and so on. It has to be a good label, Mama. And just look how beautifully it's made, the material is lovely and look at the buttons. You'll be able to wear it next summer as well, with a different blouse. Please Mama, it's so important to me, I know you won't regret it.'

Mother, defeated: 'Well, I might just try on the jacket…'

Celia joined them offering alternatives. 'We can get a hat made to order,' she said. 'If the wedding is in June, you should have straw, trimmed with ribbon. This is an elegant ensemble, dress and coat, but the suit is a better colour for you. What about green? This is attractive, a jungle print. Excuse me a moment.'

Marian was collecting her flowers and handbag. 'Celia Chase, you are wonderful. Thanks for everything. Wish me luck for this evening. And

Wimbledon tomorrow.'

'Goodbye, Mrs Whatsit,' said Celia.

Charles left the City in good time and went to Boo Carey's. They merged, and he felt wonderful, so strong, so male. She was such a sweet little thing.

'Boody-doo,' he said, lifting her blonde hair and nuzzling her neck. 'Lovely Boody-doo. Thank you.'

'Mmm,' she murmured, thoughtfully

They were lying in her four-poster bed, which had curtains in rosebud chintz held back by two plaster cherubs. The wallpaper matched the curtains. The chairs and dressing table were painted pink. She was pleased with the effect. It was romantic, rather French.

What she wasn't pleased with, not any more, was being divorced. At first it had been a relief, because she had been so unhappy. The wrong sort of life, with the wrong man. He was rich, her ex-husband, and had paid up to get rid of her as quickly as possible. So she had enough money for the flat, and her clothes. The trouble was that she was lonely, and sometimes very depressed

She was just twenty-one. So far, she told herself, her adult life had been a series of painful negatives. She'd dropped out of university, her marriage had failed, and now she was having an affair with Charles, who wasn't available long-term, being married to the beautiful Marian. Not a good way to behave.

Part of the trouble was that she had nothing to do during the day, She knew she ought to get a job, but hadn't done anything about it yet. Charles had suggested she take a typing course. He'd been kind and helpful, and he was amusing. He made her laugh when he wasn't clambering over her puffing and blowing. He was too fat to be good in bed.

Just a few days ago something had happened which she hoped might change her life from a negative to a positive mood. She had actually met Quentin Jones. She had seen him before, in a crowd, and heard about him. He'd been brilliant at Cambridge, was now a publisher, and said to be writing a novel. Meeting him, talking to him for a few precious moments before someone else butted in, had been an extraordinary experience, like sunshine breaking through clouds. She had fallen in love. She longed to see him again, wondering if he would be at this party or that, or if she could manage to meet him, as if by coincidence. To become his friend, then his lover. To embrace his slim, angular body.

She lay with her arms round plump, pink-faced Charles, dreaming of a future in Paradise with Quentin Jones. Bodies together, thoughts shared, days and nights spent caring for each other.

'I've got to go,' said Charles, extricating himself. 'People coming to dinner.'

Boo sat up and wrapped herself in the eiderdown. She'd just had a wonderful idea. 'Sweetie, I've been thinking...' He'd gone to the bathroom and she had to wait until he came back. 'Charles, wouldn't it be fun to meet in daylight for a change? Just lunch or something on Saturday when you don't have to go to the City. And come back here afterwards.'

'Complicated, ' he said, pulling up his underpants. 'I have to go down to Broome to see my father. One has a duty.'

'Of course, sweetie-pie. But why don't you just say you have some extra work, and won't be down until later?'

Balancing on one foot then the other, Charles put on his socks. This was Wednesday. Lunch on Saturday might provide the opportunity he was looking for to tell Boo that they must ease off. They would go on seeing each other, of course, but less often. No risk of a scene, tears and so on, because they would be sitting at a table, eating and drinking, people all round them. It would be civilised, the kindest way. She was so young, and cared about him. Perhaps too much.

'That's an attractive thought,' he said. 'Marian has a horse at Broome, she's going down early to exercise the beast. I was going with her, but I've got to work instead. I'll go down later, in time for dinner. Having done some merging during the afternoon.'

They exchanged meaningful looks. Boo giggled. 'Charles, you are a naughty, naughty boy,' she said. 'I know, let's have lunch at that place where we went once before, when we were just getting to know each other. Down at the bottom of the King's Road.'

'Perfect!' He kissed her goodbye, realising that he hadn't entertained her for weeks, in fact hardly at all since their affair started. Girls liked to be taken out, it was only natural. A drink in a pub, a decent meal in a restaurant. 'You mean The Welcome Sole, don't you. Right, I'll book a table. See you there, twelve-thirty on Saturday.'

As soon as he had gone, Boo got up, showered, dressed, and made the bed. She ate a little supper of bread and marmalade, washed down with several cups of tea. Then, in creative mood. She sat down at her desk.

After several false starts she produced a poem, which was also an acrostic:

Q uite
U nexpectedly
E verything has changed
N ight is a sunny day
T roubles melt away
I nstead of misery
N ow love has come to stay

She made a fair copy, writing in italic with a black pen. Round the edge of the paper she drew a necklace of hearts and flowers. With water-colour and a fine brush she coloured the hearts red, the flowers pink and blue. Carefully she put her work in a big envelope, sealed it with a kiss, and hid it in her make-up drawer.

In the morning, she told herself, I will go out and get a job. And please God, if you exist and have the Power, let Quentin Jones be lunching at The Welcome Sole on Saturday.

The feeling that life was good and her suspicions groundless lasted Marian right through the day. She went home, finished laying the table, arranged the flowers and had a salad by way of lunch. Then she washed her hair, put it up in rollers, and went down to the kitchen to make final preparations. Everything was perfect, orderly, ready for action.

She had a new dress. It was red, the sleeves long and narrow, the skirt short with fullness at the back. 'It's provocative,' the designer had said. 'There's something devilish about it.' She put it on twenty minutes before the guests were due, with high-heeled sandals and her gold necklace, earrings and bracelet. Her hair rippled round her shoulders. She knew she looked good.

Charles was home in time for a shower and change, just. Then people started arriving, punctually, as if eager to start enjoying themselves. The dinner was near perfection. The beef carved like a dream, the *tarte tatin* was just right, not too sweet. Mrs Briggs served and cleared efficiently, and went home in a taxi.

The conversation was lively, most of it above Marian's head. She didn't mind that. At this sort of party she listened more than she spoke, in case she said the wrong thing. Patrick Dearden, on her right, had been less pompous than usual. She asked him what his spare time interests were. 'If you have any spare time, I mean.' It turned out that he was keen on guns and shooting, and had a collection of antique weapons, as well as various modern ones.

'How fascinating,' she said. 'Does Clarissa shoot too?'

'No, she's useless. It's not her sort of thing. We shoot hare and pheasant for the pot at Dearden, and rabbits to get rid of the little buggers. But what really interests me is marksmanship, Bisley and so on. You shoot at all?'

'Yes, I go out with Charles's father, at Broome.'

'Come down one weekend. I could give you a few lessons.'

He was smiling, looking at her cleavage, her shoulders, her neck, then into her eyes, as if judging her potential. She felt giggly at the thought of his giving her a few lessons. He had aristocratic good looks, large brown eyes and dark curling hair, perhaps like Lord Byron. She was slightly disappointed when he suddenly switched his attention away from her to a discussion across the table about Europe and the Common Market

Clarissa was wearing dark blue, which didn't suit her. But you had to admire the way she talked. She set her sights on the television presenter and by the end of the evening had persuaded him to have her on his panel. During dinner Charles divided his attention fairly between the woman MP and the Foreign Office wife. Afterwards he circulated, talking to each guests as if he had been particularly looking forward to the opportunity. Marian could see that Patrick was watching him, sizing him up as a good host, someone who would both talk and listen.

One way and another it was a successful evening. The Deardens stayed until after midnight, Patrick finding he needed a few more words with Charles, so that Marian had to make conversation with Clarissa, which she found difficult. She told her about Marcellina, and what fun it was having this mini-career.

'I'm not very bright about literature and politics,' she explained. 'But I enjoy the financial side of things. Oh, and I love opera, we're going to Glyndebourne this summer. And I go to art galleries...'

'And you're a wonderful cook', said Clarissa, expressionless. 'Such a good dinner. Come on, Patrick.'

When they had gone Charles put the drinks away in the Victorian cabinet which they used as a bar, while Marian cleared away glasses and ashtrays.

'You were in good form, darling,' she said as they went up to bed.

'You too,' said Charles. 'Patrick couldn't take his eyes off you. Sporting weekends, do I gather?'

'No thank you! I'm not the Bisley type. Darling, do you think I should have got someone extra to serve? Was it all right, just Briggsie?'

'Perfect. Not too formal. You're wonderful to do this for me, darling. Contacts, knowing the right people. So important if one wants to get into politics. And the new dress,' he remembered. 'You looked stunning.'

In the bedroom - thick white carpet, Regency-striped curtains in white and gold, white satin quilted coverlet over lace-trimmed sheets and pillow-cases, Recamier sofa upholstered on blue and gold brocade with two matching chairs - he kissed her briefly, undressed and put on his pyjamas. He sighed heavily as he got into bed.

'I'm worn out,' he said. 'It's been a tiring day.'

'Darling...' It was no good. He had turned over away from her and closed his eyes.

She dreamed she had sex with Patrick Dearden. He was dressed as Lord Byron, in velvet knee breeches and a white ruffled shirt, open down the front to show his hairy chest. He had an antique pistol tucked into his belt. She was laughing, running away from him at first. Then she let him catch her, lay down and pulled up her petticoats. He was big and heavy, and so beautiful, so satisfying. 'You'll go no more a-roving, my pretty one,' he breathed. 'You are mine, mine!'

'Ah, ah!' she cried, waking in orgasm, then floating down into a peaceful valley.

Charles slept on, snoring.

Clarissa Dearden made her fist television appearance a few weeks later. She spoke with confidence, dominating the discussion. And she looked elegant. She had been to Marcellina, taken Celia's advice, and bought an emerald green suit which showed off her white skin and flame-coloured hair. 'She's a natural for television,' the girl from make-up said.

One of the questions under consideration that evening was proper care for the mentally ill. There had been recent scandalous revelations of neglect and cruelty in a National Health institution where, as Clarissa said, sufferers could be dumped by their relatives. She had personally visited the place, researching for a newspaper article.

'The building was a crumbling Victorian mansion,' she said. 'The rooms were cold, dirty and crowded, as many as twenty beds so close together that you could hardly walk between them. It was Hogarthian. It was Bedlam. And this is the twentieth century! The toilets were filthy. There were rats in the kitchen. The food was inedible. Places like this should not exist. They should be, they must be, replaced by smaller units where sufferers can be properly cared for. With modern medication they can be helped to lead useful and dignified lives. Society has a duty towards them.'

'I agree that one should not pass by on the other side,' said a clergyman. 'Something must be done.'

Stimulated, the audience bombarded the panel with related questions.

What about old people's homes? What about children in care? What about prisons? The discussion was animated. The presenter had to deal briefly with the next two questions because time was running out.

Clarissa was invited to take part again, and was subsequently seen quite often on television. Her career in journalism also took off at this point. Patrick was thrilled at her success, although her views were far from orthodox. 'My wife is a shocker!' he would say proudly. 'Should never have given women the vote!'

Mimsy Mason sat in an armchair wearing a nightdress and her paisley shawl. It was too much trouble to pull her stockings up, so she had them only as far as her knees. David brought her slippers and put them on for her. He had brushed her hair. Since the stroke she didn't like walking alone in case she fell down, so she had to call him if she wanted to go to what she called the WC.

She lifted her teacup and took a sip. Her hands were steadier today. 'You're a good boy, David,' she said. Then she felt foolish because, of course, he wasn't a boy any more. He was forty. His hair, which had been blonde, was going grey. There were wrinkles round his eyes. 'Person, I mean. Good person.'

He sat down next to her and held her hand, putting on what he hoped was a relaxed air. He was short of sleep, tensed up, feeling hopelessly inadequate. 'You've got Marian coming today, Mimsy. Your great-niece. She's coming at eleven.'

'Marian,' said Mimsy carefully. If she spoke too fast nonsense words came. 'Her mother...' A pause while she concentrated. 'A treble. A treble. A treble grumbler. No wonder he left her.'

'I told Marian that you'd had a slight stroke.'

Mimsy nodded. 'Stroke' was a difficult word. She couldn't get it right, not yet It had been a shock to find herself lying on the floor. She had called for help. Someone must have heard her because the porter came. He had a key. Then they put her in an ambulance and took her away, though she screamed. The time in hospital had been a nightmare. All the faces were strange. Nobody told her what had happened. Doctors and nurses came and talked round her bed as though she wasn't there. She kept asking for her own doctor, and they said he'd been there yesterday, or was coming tomorrow. But she never saw him. They were lying to keep her quiet, of course. Then David came.

'How did you know?' she asked him. 'The hoss. You came to the hoss.'

'The porter cabled me in Saudi. I'm working there, building a dam.' He had told her this several times. Poor Mimsy, usually so attentive, so bright.

When he'd left six months ago she had been well-organised and confident. There was regular help, a cleaner, a health visitor who came to bath her three times a week, and some local do-gooders who came to visit and do her shopping. Unfortunately these arrangements had broken down. The cleaner had dropped out. The porter's wife had taken on the job temporarily, but didn't fancy it long-term. A different health visitor came. 'Clumsy and common,' Mimsy had said. 'I'll wash myself in future.' Local ladies had stopped calling because the flat was so squalid.

Dave didn't know where to start. There were dirty plates and cups in front of the television set and by her bed, old newspapers gathering dust, unwashed clothes on the floor. The place stank of dirt and neglect. The toilet wasn't flushing properly, which partly accounted for the smell. Plumbing was something he could cope with, however. He borrowed tools from the porter and fixed it in a few minutes.. At least she's still using it. She might become incontinent, the doctor said. She might have further strokes. Her heart was tired. She was eighty-five, after all.

She smiled at him apologetically. 'Remember. Building a dam. You are a stuck. A stuck. A structural engineer!'

'Right! But you wanted me to be an artist. Sorry to disappoint, Mimsy.' He smothered another yawn. So tired, so frustrated.

'A good boy, David. The hoss, the hoss. I don't want to go. And not to a home. Die in my own bed.'

She was trembling at the thought of being taken away again. He said quickly, 'There's lots of life left in you, Mimsie. You're not dying, and you're not going into a home. I'm going to get you a private nurse, full time, living in. And I'm not leaving until I've go it all fixed up. Like another cup of tea?'

She shook her head, and he took the tray away. She wasn't eating. Tea with milk and sugar was all she could manage. He wondered if he should get some invalid food from the chemist.

She had looked after him since he was ten. She had sponsored him at the orphanage, got him to the grammar school, later to university. She wanted to adopt him, but she wasn't married. 'Ridiculous,' she used to say. 'A marriage licence is only a piece of paper.' She didn't give up, and won her battle to foster him. He remembered the day when they told him he was going to the big house on Wimbledon Common. Not just for a visit, to live there. To have good food, and his own room.

Now he was the parent, and she the child. To put her in a home would be base ingratitude. Also, she was used to getting her own way, and would make a hell of a fuss if she was ordered about. Her behaviour in hospital had been 'extremely disruptive', they said.

But to get help, to find these private nurses, was not easy. He had tried the numbers the doctor had given him without success. A representative would have to visit first, to assess the circumstances. They would need references. There was no one free at the moment.

He had telephoned her niece Emily and her nephew Harold. They were not prepared to help, which was hardly surprising. Mimsy had chosen to live her life without them. He had spoken to her solicitor, who was reassuring about finances. Mimsy had medical insurance, and bills not covered by this would be met. She had put funds aside. That was good news.

Then the bloody social worker had come again, the great-niece had telephoned, and he'd lost his temper. Building a dam in Saudi Arabia was easy by comparison.

Before her stroke Mimsy had watched a lot of television. There had been programmes which she looked forward to, the News, horse racing and old films. But now the voices and the flickering screen conveyed no message. And she had forgotten how to read.

By way of compensation, she had made an interesting discovery. If she sat quietly, with her eyes closed, memories of the past came back to her in the most orderly fashion, as if someone was telling her life-story. The quality of this programme, available only to herself, gave her great pleasure. She was able to recall scenes, events and characters which she hadn't thought about for many years.

The flat was pleasantly warm. The heat came up from below, the porter was in charge of it. The sitting room was small compared to the one she had had previously, in a house not far away. She couldn't remember the name of the road. The house was cold in winter. There was central heating but it was not efficient. There was a beautiful drawing-room with French windows looking on to the lawn, the herbaceous border on one side and on the other the cedar tree and shrubbery. The gardener came three times a week. There had been a cook and a maid before the War. The Second War, because of Hitler. The maid had come with her to the flat but wasn't much use. Poor old thing, she died. She was called Agnes or Gertie or some such name.

I have had a stroke. A stroke.

There was no central heating when I was a little girl, only coal and wood fires. We were not allowed fires in our bedrooms unless we were ill. We had to wash in cold water. In winter there was often a layer of ice on top of the jug. There was a matching basin, soap-dish, tooth-mug and slop-pail. I remember a pattern of violets. Sometimes there was a matching chamber-pot.

People do not use chamber-pots any more.

There were five children in our family. My sister Katie was the eldest, then came my brother Tom. He was four years older than me, and I loved him more than anyone in the world. He was a kind, clever boy, with blue eyes and light brown hair. The rest of us had dark hair and brown eyes. He was the only fair one. It was he who gave me the name Mimsy, which I have kept ever since.

I was born in 1886 and christened Mary Isabelle Mason. 'M for Mary, I for Isabelle, M for Mason,' said Tom as soon as he learned his letters. 'And that makes Mim.' Soon everybody called me Mim, or Mimsy.

After me came another girl, my sister Rose, then Vincent, the baby of the family. Mama died giving birth to Vincent. I did not know this at the time. I only knew that she had gone away forever to the churchyard down the road, and that a new baby had come. We were all so sad, especially Papa. To add to his troubles, his business was not doing well and he had to borrow money to pay for a nursemaid. Vincent was a strong baby and after his first year Katie took charge of him. She was fifteen. She was nursemaid, mother and sister to him.

When I was older, Katie told me that babies came from their mother's bodies. She said that Mama had had several miscarriages and one stillborn baby. She died because of Vincent. I was very upset. I felt unshed tears inside me for days afterwards. I was a big girl by that time. It was when Katie told me that my monthlies would be starting soon. She said that I was nearly a woman now and it was important to behave in a proper way with men. Some women allowed men to embrace them before they were married. It was sinful, and a woman who did this would certainly lose her reputation. She might get in the family way and have an illegitimate child as a result of the sinful embrace. No decent man would want to marry her if this had happened.

Katie never married. She was a good woman, unselfish, practical and kind, but not attractive, being plain and thin. In those days a thin figure was not fashionable. Katie had no bust to speak of and the dresses we wore did require a good bust. She didn't care enough to pad her bodice. She just went on looking flat, like the spinster she was. She said she had no time for men, though I believe she had hopes of a young curate at one time. Certainly no man ever gave her a sinful embrace.

She devoted herself to the family. She did the housekeeping and she made and mended our clothes. She taught me and Rose how to sew and knit. We helped her mend sheets and make flannel petticoats. We knitted woollen socks, scarves, vests and gloves. We ironed shirts; we sponged and pressed Papa's suits. She taught us how to cook, how to make white sauce and a good brown gravy.

We did not do housework. That would have been unsuitable for people of our class. We had a cook-general and usually a housemaid as well, depending upon Papa's finances. Katie saw to it that the servants kept the house in good order, the kitchen floor scrubbed, the stairs brushed, all rooms regularly swept and dusted. And every year in March or April, as soon as the weather was right, she would supervise the spring cleaning, which meant taking the rugs and carpets out into the garden and beating them, taking down the curtains and cleaning them with Fuller's Earth, washing the windows inside and out, thoroughly cleaning the whole house to remove all traces of the smoky grime which had accumulated during the winter.

My sister Rose was a big girl with a good figure and a well-developed bust. Her face was plump and pretty, with a natural bloom. She had many admirers. My attractions were of a different sort. I was not as tall as Rose, nor as well-covered. I was slender, and my bust was not well-developed. I had to pad my bodice when I first started going out. Later, in the Jazz Age, flat chests became fashionable, so my slim figure and elegant legs showed to advantage. I was already in my thirties but could easily be mistaken for a young flapper. Rose had heavy legs, and the short skirts of the time did not suit her. In middle age she put on too much weight, which had a bad effect on her heart. I never let myself go in that way. I took good care of my figure. My health has always been good.

My brother Vincent was spoiled from the beginning by Katie's obsessive care. She let him have his own way in most things, which is not good for a child. He was seldom reproved or punished, and as he grew older his behaviour became an annoyance to me. I was a dignified young lady; Vincent was a noisy small boy with muddy boots, going out of his way to upset me with rudeness and practical jokes. Surprisingly he grew up into a serious young man with a capacity for hard work. He passed the examinations to become a chartered accountant and joined a reputable firm, advancing from the lowest position to become the senior partner. Accountancy being a dull profession, it suited Vincent very well. He died a few years ago. I can't remember when it was. I never liked him as much as I did my brother Tom.

Tom was only nineteen when he died. So many young lives are wasted in war.

Papa was a fine figure of a man, tall and handsome, with a rosy face and curling whiskers and moustache. His waistcoat spread generously outward to that special button which held his watch-chain. He had a certain dash in his manner, which suited his profession. He was a theatrical costumier. This was profitable in the summer when orders came in for the Christmas pantomimes but slow in the spring, when there was little ahead except pierrot shows. Papa despised that trade because it was not legitimate theatre. 'Tupenny-ha'penny sing-songs at the seaside,' he used to say. And they were miserable customers. They wore their costumes until they were threadbare. The same was true of the music hall artistes of the time.

But Papa persevered, and his hard work was rewarded in the early years of the twentieth century when London theatre reached a peak of excellence. He took over a smaller enterprise and created Mason Gough & Company, a firm which is still well-known in the West End. He became comparatively wealthy, making costumes for successful productions, meeting famous actors and actresses and members of society. He used to boast that he had met Edward VII at a supper party. He was often out late at night, enjoying good company, wine, brandy and cigars. Men were like that, Katie said. Ladies did not smoke, and should drink only sherry or sometimes a glass of wine or port. Over-indulgence made one flushed and excitable. Women of the lower classes often drank to excess.

When I was older, much older, I learned that Papa kept a lady friend, one of his seamstresses, in rooms in Covent Garden. She was not publicly acknowledged. The theatrical world was notorious for moral laxity, and it was no doubt for this reason that Papa was determined that his children should not follow him in his profession. He wanted the boys to do better, as lawyers or doctors. Katie had already found herself her mission in life, replacing Mama, and Papa was duly grateful to her. Rose and I should certainly not become actresses. We had no idea, he said, what temptations and dangers threatened young girls who went on the stage. To sit in the audience was one thing, To be in the glare of the footlights was another.

We lived in Lambeth, in a semi-detached house. We were a better sort of people than those who lived in terraces. We had water-closets: they had outdoor privies. Our kitchen was in the basement, at the front of the house, and next to it was a housekeeper's sitting room, on the same level as the back garden. I used to play in that room and in the garden when I was a little girl. The dining room was on the ground floor, above the kitchen, with a dumb-waiter in a cupboard in the corner. This was a useful contraption. Cook, down below in the kitchen, would put the food inside the dumb-waiter and Katie, in the dining room, would wind it up. Papa being so often out, Katie would carve the meat and put vegetables on our plates. In those days the greens were very pale and tasteless. Possibly they were overcooked. We had to eat everything we were given, or there was no pudding. The puddings were hot and steamy in winter, served with custard. In summer we had trifle and jam tart. Katie knew all about cooking, she never wasted food and we were always well fed.

Once, when I was small, Tom put me in the dumb-waiter and wound me down to the kitchen. Cook told Katie and there was a terrible row. Tom promised never to do it again, and Katie said she wouldn't tell Papa, just this once. Tom would have been beaten for that.

Papa's study was next to the dining room. He had a desk there and his books. There were leather chairs. He did not use it often and we children seldom went into it. On the same level was the morning room, where Rose and I did our lessons. Katie taught us reading, writing and arithmetic. Tom taught us history and geography, which he learned at his grammar school. Katie had not had much education, only two years at a day school before Mama died. Later Rose and I went to a boarding school as pupil teachers, where we were permitted to study with the older girls and in return looked after the younger ones, supervising their meals, helping them with reading, writing and sewing, settling them in their beds at night. Many were homesick and cried themselves to sleep. We did what we could to comfort them, though we were homesick ourselves and often wept in our attic bedroom and wished we were at home. The girls at this school came from the best families and as a result we were able to improve ourselves. We dropped the Lambeth accent which was our habit and learned to modulate our voices pleasantly, and to express ourselves in a clear and unaffected way. We acquired good manners and deportment. In later life these things were to our advantage.

Rose married well, a gentleman with an estate in Gloucestershire. She had three children. Her younger son died in the last War. He was a fighter pilot in the Royal Air Force. Poor Rose, it was a sad loss. The two remaining children, Harold and Emily, are still alive. I never got on with either of them. It must be said that Rose was a narrow-minded, conventional woman. She took a censorious attitude to me because I lived with my dear friend and lover Cecil Jeffries, unfettered by the bonds of matrimony. Rose's criticisms affected her children's view of me, Harold's especially. He has never visited me and does not write. At Rose's funeral he was barely civil.

Emily, to give her her due, writes to me occasionally and sends me Christmas cards. But such a grumbler, always complaining about something. I was not surprised when her husband left her for another woman. Her daughter Marian, however, is charming. I have given her small presents in the past and I am leaving her a few more things in my Will. Some of my furniture is to go to the Victoria and Albert Museum, which may save Death Duties.

David gets the rest of my estate, this flat to keep or sell as he thinks fit, and my investments. I am not making any other bequests. I have expressly forbidden my solicitor to read the Will after the funeral, with people waiting to hear who will get this or that, and no doubt arguing about it afterwards. I am to be buried in the churchyard at St George's, next to Cecil.

It is curious how likenesses appear, often missing a generation. Marian takes after me, that is to say she looks very much as I did when I was a young girl. I first noticed it when her mother brought her to the house, some years ago. I think she must be in her twenties now. She is married to a handsome man, well-bred and intelligent. He came to see me once, I can't remember when it was. He was most interesting about the politics of the day. We had a Labour government at that time. I have always voted Labour, being a supporter of the Fabian Movement. Now I am beginning to wonder if the working people want that sort of condescension on our part. That is what it amounts to. The gulf between the classes was taken for granted in the old days. Now Labour requires us to be of one social level.

Marian's husband is a Conservative and hopes to get into Parliament one day. His name is – I can't remember. It will come back to me. I hope he comes again, I would like to ask him about Edward Heath, the new Prime Minister. It is odd that I can't remember his name. He is Marian's husband. Never mind.

I have had a stroke.

Marian parked her Mini in the forecourt and collected the things she had brought with her, some of the flowers from last night, a box of perfumed soaps and a bottle of Amontillado. The porter put her into the lift and told her which button to press. She found Mimsy's flat and rang the bell. The door opened.

Marian, thinks: 'He is not what I expected. Not a muscular type with a red face. He is of medium height, lean, sunburned, good-looking. Blue eyes, high cheekbones. Ash-blonde hair cut much too short. Wearing light trousers and a bush shirt, all wrong for London in the middle of winter. He is looking at me in a very unfriendly way and I'm not going to stand any nonsense from him. Absolutely not.'

Dave, to himself: 'She is much younger than I thought. Quite pretty, dressed like a tart. Skin-tight jeans, black shiny boots reaching almost to her crotch, a padded jacket. Dark hair. The face brightly painted, lipstick, eye-shadow, mascara. Has a challenging look, one foot ahead of the other, as if to take the first step. We'll see about that.'

They glared at each other for a moment. Then she started, 'I hope this is all right. I don't mean to interfere or anything…'

He began at the same time. 'I'm sorry about yesterday. I wasn't very civil…'

That broke the ice. He waved a hand to show her in, the gesture slightly affected as if he were play-acting, sending up the idea of good manners.

'Thank you,' she said, smiling politely, stepping into the hall to be met by a wave of hot air carrying a smell of drains, stale food and unwashed clothes. He noticed that she had mouthed a sort of 'Phew!' He said, 'Sorry. I know it stinks. The place got into a bad state before she had the stroke. I'm keeping it warm because the doctor says there's a risk of pneumonia. And I've come from abroad, so it doesn't seem hot to me.'

'Oh, you're quite right to keep her warm. Absolutely. Just tell me what I can do to help. I really don't want to interfere. Anyway, I'm Marian Broome-Vivier.'

'Dave Mason.' They shook hands, Marian awkwardly, because she was still holding the presents.

'Oh, Mason,' she said. 'Then we're related.'

'No, long story. To cut it short, she fostered me, and I took her name to simplify things. Here, let me take your coat. Nice flowers, very kind of you.'

He led the way into the living room, apologising again for the heat and the disorder. He'd only been here two days, hardly started on the tidying up. He'd got Mimsy out of hospital, the idea being to find a nurse or someone to live in. He was occupying the spare room at the moment, he could stay with friends when the nurse arrived. The Council kept sending a social worker and there was really no need. He was in touch with Mimsy's lawyer and her doctor, it was just a question of getting a good system going.

'Absolutely,' said Marian. 'I'd very much like to help, if I can. Anything, cleaning and so on. Organising.'

Mimsy was dozing in an armchair. She opened her eyes, saw Marian, patted her thin white hair and held out one hand in a regal manner. 'Welcome,' she said slowly. 'Welcome, my dear.'

Her hair had been auburn last time, Marian remembered. She looked smaller, her body foreshortened into a curve, the arms and legs drawn up close. Her dark eyes protruded from a tiny pointed face. She looked like a nocturnal animal shyly facing a television camera. Marian took her hand and bent down to kiss her cheek. There was a smell of stale urine.

'Mimsy, I'm Marian. I hope you don't kind my turning up like this. I've brought you some flowers, and these French soaps are nice, aren't they. And some sherry to cheer you up.'

'Kind, so kind. Your...' Mimsy searched for the word. Hub, hum, humdrum.

'Oh yes, Charles sends his love. My husband Charles. He couldn't come today, he works in the City, you know. I'm so glad to see you, Mimsy. Just tell me what I can do to help.'

'Like a bath,' said Mimsy. 'Soap.'

Dave was in the kitchen filling a kettle. 'A good nurse is what we need Someone not too starchy, more like a companion. But I haven't had much luck so far. I don't like to leave her alone. And I'm running out of supplies, I've had to ask the porter to get things for me. Coffee, okay? I'm sorry about all this.'

'Nice bath,' murmured Mimsy in the background.

'If you want to go shopping, I'll stay,' said Marian. 'Absolutely no problem.' She followed him into the kitchen looking for a vase for the flowers. Every horizontal surface was crowded with cans of food, open packets of biscuits and cereals, half-finished pots of jam, bits of stale bread and dirty crockery. She could hardly wait to create order out of this chaos. She arranged the flowers in a jug and put them in the sitting room where Mimsy could see them.

'You go out, Dave. And I'll make a telephone call if you don't mind. About nurses, I know someone who might help. And could I stay and have a sandwich with you? Get some cold meat, bread and butter, cheese, lettuce, tomatoes. I hope you don't think I'm being bossy.'

'I do, and I like it. Write it down. Here.' He gave her his notebook and a pen.

'I want a bath,' said Mimsy, loudly and slowly.

'What a super idea,' said Marian. This was fun, unexpectedly. 'Dave, our lunch materials, and for cleaning, this and this.' She scribbled a list for him. 'Something for the loo, whatever you think. You've got English money, okay?'

He went out, wearing a thin jacket and one of Mimsy's scarves round his neck. Marian rolled up her sleeves and started collecting things to be washed up. She found an apron, filled the sink with hot water, at the same time telling Mimsy about Charles and the merger, and his political hopes, about last night's dinner party and what they'd had to eat. Mimsy listened and nodded, smiling slightly, while Marian put dirty dishes in to soak, threw away mouldy bread and jam, and wiped the worktop which was horribly stained.

'Mimsy, I'm going to telephone a friend, she's called Celia. She's absolutely super and she has a lot of contacts. She'll help me find a nurse for you. We run a boutique together, and her husband is a publisher. They've got two heavenly babies.'

Mimsy looked up. 'I had a baby once,' she said.

Marian stood in the kitchen doorway, wiping her hands on the apron. A baby? Did Mummy say anything about a baby? Could be wishful thinking, in retrospect. 'Oh, I didn't know that,' she said casually.

'Little boy. In Paris. He died.'

'Well, I'm so sorry. Now, I'm going to clean round you. And we need some fresh air in here, don't we. Only a few minutes.' She spread a blanket over Mimsy and flung open two windows, letting in a delicious ice-cold breeze, while she went round the room with a cloth, removing deposits of dust congealed with spilled food and drink. 'What lovely furniture you have, Mimsy. This table is French, isn't it? Walnut. So pretty, beautifully made.'

'French, the father. A writer. Penniless. Love in a garret.' Mimsy waved her hand as if to dismiss the memory. Then she closed her eyes and rested, with a satisfied expression.

The telephone was in the hall. Marian looked for an extension in the bedroom, but there wasn't one. She would arrange that later. She dialled Marcellina.

'Celia, it's me. I'm in Wimbledon with the great-aunt and it's absolutely vital to get her a nurse. Who is that girl, ex-Abbey Mead, who runs a nursing agency? Has an absolutely vast bosom.'

'Golly, yes,' said Celia. 'Beatrice King, madly worthy. I'll get back to you, give me your number. And tell me about the oaf situation or I'll never speak to you again.'

'He's called Dave, he's gone out shopping. Not absolute oaf, he apologised as soon as I set foot inside. He's come from abroad, somewhere absolutely tropical. He's heated this flat to boiling point. Well, not exactly good-looking, but all right. Rather strange manner, possibly poofter.'

'Still in the closet?'

'Could be. Anyway, you never saw such a mess. Absolute squalor. You'll ring me back? Super.'

In Mimsy's bedroom she stripped the bed which was damp in the middle. Luckily the mattress had a plastic cover. She collected the clothes which lay in heaps on the floor, put them in a plastic bag, cleaned the bath, ran the water, and scented it with Miss Dior from her handbag.

Dave, not absolutely oafish, possible poofter, came back with the shopping and dumped it in the kitchen. Then he followed her about, saying 'I'm really so grateful. What can I do to help?'

'Find some clean sheets and make her bed. And while I'm washing her have a look at the armchair. I think she's peed in it. Remove the cushion if necessary, put a piece of plastic there in case it happens again. And find a clean nightie.'

In the bathroom, stripped, Mimsy clung to Marian's shoulder.

'Come on,' Marian urged. 'One leg up and over. Now the other. Good girl, isn't that lovely and warm. Whoops!' She grabbed Mimsy as she began to slide the length of the bath, just in time. Her body was pale and slack, just a skin with the bones loose inside. The knees, elbows, wrists and ankles were swollen and knotted. Her back was rounded into a curve so that the vertebrae stuck out.

With a sense of familiarity Marian washed the hands and feet, the neck, the ancient torso and emaciated limbs. She would be like this one day, and so would her little dream daughter, Teresa or Sue. Old and weak, needing help in the bath. The same body, inherited, understood.

She had to call Dave to help get Mimsy out. Covering her private parts with trembling hands, Mimsy murmured, 'Venus. Rising from the waves.' They wrapped her in a towel and Dave carried her to the bedroom, helped dress her in a clean vest, long knickers, stockings and nightgown. Marian noticed that he was gentle and efficient about this. He had good hands. He would be good with animals.

Lunch was festive, eaten in the dining room, which was warm and uncontaminated by the general smell. Dave had been using it as a study, so his briefcase and a pile of papers, mostly Mimsy's neglected correspondence, covered half the table. They sat Mimsy at the other end. She ate a small piece of toast and some tinned soup flavoured with sherry. She said it was delicious. Marian and Dave, on each side of her, had sandwiches and salad, with a bottle of white wine. Then they put Mimsy to bed for a nap and sat talking over coffee.

Marian felt relaxed with him. So many men tried to impress you on first meeting, to establish superiority. She hated that. Perhaps homosexual, perhaps not. She couldn't quite figure him out. But he was good company. She told him about the boutique, Charles, Broome Hall, the horse she would be riding on Saturday. He said he'd been riding a camel recently, going out with a survey team. He explained about the dam, a major project. Eventually there would be houses, shops, offices, a small town developing. The site would be landscaped. Trees and plants would create an oasis. It would have its own micro-climate. In a few years' time, he said, the Arab countries would be enormously rich because they had a monopoly of the world's oil. The British had good relations with the Saudis. He liked the place and the people.

'Building a dam is creative,' said Marian. 'Like gardening. The desert shall rejoice and blossom like the rose.' Shades of Abbey Mead, the duty prefect standing at the lectern reading from the Revised Version. She could see the empty dam, the group of temporary buildings surrounded by sand. Later a miraculous transformation, the emptiness filled with a shimmering expanse of blue-green, life-giving water. A town of many houses, shaded by palm trees.

'Exactly,' said Dave. He smiled at her, so that she noticed the space between his front teeth, which made him look like a pirate.

Come back to earth, she told herself. The wine's gone to your head. 'Oh, and I meant to say, I'm sorry my mother was unhelpful on the telephone. She's divorced, and it's made her unhappy. And difficult.'

'Mimsy can be difficult too,' said Dave. 'She's unconventional.'

'She had lots of lovers, people say.'

'Only two she talks about. When she was very young, in Paris, she lived with a writer. Then she lived with an artist, Cecil Jeffries, first in Paris. Then here. He was a Catholic, they don't divorce. She didn't mind that sort of thing, went on calling herself Miss Mason and outraged her family. Cecil was twenty years older than she was. They had no children, got me from an orphanage.'

'I never met him,' said Marian. 'Mummy took me to the house once, I was still at school. I suppose he was dead by then. Mimsy was absolutely weird, floating draperies and amber beads. And her hair was red.'

'She used to dye it, with henna. Yes, she liked to dress in pre-Raphaelite style.'

Marian couldn't remember a Dave-like boy at the house. 'Were you there when we came?' she asked. 'I can only remember Mimsy.'

'If you were at school, I was at university. Or I'd gone abroad.'

Celia telephoned while they were washing up. 'You won't believe this, the agency's called Queen Bee. I mean, she looked just like one, didn't she. There's a New Zealand nurse, super qualified, she can start on Sunday. She's called Kiwi.'

'Celia Chase, you're a genius.'

'You have to go in and register. It's expensive, can the great-aunt afford?'

'Yes, she can. Absolute thanks. Love to Victor and the Adorables.'

She told Dave the good news. 'Wonderful,' he said. 'I'm really grateful.'

Then she collected the things she would take home to wash in her own efficient machine, put on her sweater and jacket, and slung her handbag over her shoulder. She said goodbye to Dave, and to Mimsy, who had woken up fretful. Perhaps there was too much sherry in her soup.

Driving home in the mini Marian felt elated, proud of herself. She would go back tomorrow, and Sunday if necessary. See the Queen Bee first thing tomorrow, then back to Wimbledon to carry on with the cleaning. Get the flat into a decent state for the nurse called Kiwi.

That evening, waiting for Charles, she telephoned her mother. 'Mummy, hallo. I've been to see Mimsy and she's not going into a home. I'm getting a nurse, it's all fixed, The stroke wasn't serious. But she does have difficulty speaking.'

'How clever of you, pet. She's lucky to be able to afford it, isn't she. As I say, I can't take on other people's troubles. I've got enough of my own. And it's not as if I ever got on with her.'

'You took me to her house once. There was a big garden. Her lover was an artist.'

'Yes, he used to paint. Not a Picasso, dear. And what about the boyfriend?'

'He's not a boyfriend. She fostered him from an orphanage. He's quite old, his hair is going grey.'

'Oh. Yes, I remember now. There was talk of a foster child. One didn't like to enquire in case it was hers. Father unknown, you know what I mean. I suppose he'll inherit what she has.'

'Could be,' said Marian, very cool. 'The important thing is that she should be properly looked after, because this Dave character has to go back to Saudi Arabia. He works there. I'll keep in touch, Mummy. Goodbye.'

What had been good about her day was that she hadn't once thought about Barbara Carey, known as Boo. She had been too busy thinking about the Mimsy problem. When Charles came home she was still riding high. They ate cold roast beef and drank leftover wine. She told him about Wimbledon. He stayed up late , working on papers which he had brought home. She put Mimsy's laundry in her machine and made a list of things to take to the flat tomorrow.

She went to bed and fell asleep before Charles came upstairs.

Stroke. I have had a stroke. My great-niece Marian came today. She bathed me and gave me lunch. She has gone home now.

David is here. He brought me home from the hospital. He is watching the News. Television is in colour these days.

My memories are better than television. I can remember Queen Victoria's Diamond Jubilee. I was still a young girl, I had not put my hair up. Four of us went to see the procession, my sister Katie and my brother Tom, my younger sister Rose, and myself. Rose was such a trouble. Her boots were hurting, and we had to walk slowly on her account. We crossed by Vauxhall Bridge and made our way towards Buckingham Palace. The crowd was so great that we were afraid we would altogether miss the show, but a policeman kindly let us through to the front just in time. We could hear the band. People were cheering and waving flags as the head of the procession came into view. There was a mounted escort and for several minutes I saw nothing but the legs of the horses going by.

Suddenly the royal carriage was in front of me. I shall never forget that moment. I saw the Queen, exquisitely small, dressed in black because she was still mourning the death of her beloved husband, Prince Albert. Her face was pale, her expression calm and happy. For a fleeting moment I thought she smiled at me.

Her carriage went by, and after it came many other carriages. We saw the Royal Family, followed by Crowned Heads from all over the world, also many uniformed officials and persons of distinction representing foreign states and the Empire. Many soldiers and sailors marched with them. Tom was particularly interested in the soldiers because he had already decided to join the Army.

It was several hours before the crowd began to disperse, everyone in a most friendly mood. We walked home full of enthusiasm for our Queen, who had ruled over us for Sixty Glorious Years. On the way back Rose began to cry, saying that her feet were blistered, which was tiresome of her. Tom had to give her a piggy-back, although she was a big girl, nearly nine. Katie was bothered that she was showing too much leg and petticoat, which was not done in those days.

I often think about dear Tom. A few years later he went to South Africa to fight the Boers and I never saw him again. He was too young to die.

In those days we did not have the telephone, although the machine had been invented. We had telegrams. In time of war casualty lists would be compiled by Army headquarters in London, the names having arrived by various means, overland or by fast naval vessel. Relatives were informed by telegram from their nearest post office, where the message was transcribed from Morse Code and written out on a special form, to be delivered by a boy on a bicycle.

It so happened that Katie was at the window and saw the telegraph boy, in his serge uniform with red piping, his pill-box cap perched on one side of his head, pedalling slowly along our street looking at the numbers. She was hoping that the message would not be for us, because telegrams usually brought bad news. But the boy stopped at our gate. He leaned his bicycle against the fence, and came up the front steps.

Katie had already opened the door. She took the envelope, read the message, and called for me to fetch Rose and Vincent and bring them to Papa's study. We children hardly ever went to this room, and afterwards I avoided it because it was there that I heard the tragic news that Tom had been killed and was buried in a strange country far away. Katie remained calm. She told us we must be very brave, our brother had died fighting for Queen and Country. Rose and Vincent were already in tears. I did not cry at first because I did not believe that this terrible thing had happened. Surely God would not have allowed it. I had prayed for Tom's safe return every single night since he went away.

The front door was still open, the boy standing on the step. 'Please wait,' said Katie. 'I wish to send a telegram to Covent Garden.' She wrote out the message and gave him a florin, which included a good tip, closed the door quietly and went to pull down the blinds in the front rooms. Then she broke down in tears, and so did I. We sat in the darkened hall with Rose and Vincent, trying to comfort each other.

Papa took a hansom cab and was with us very soon. Weeping, he embraced his children, now only four. It seemed that our sadness would never be over. For many weeks afterwards we continued to receive

Tom's letters, because the mail steamers were so slow. Seeing his handwriting and reading what he had to say would make our tears flow again.

I was fifteen years old at that time. I wish that Tom had lived, to help me with the problems of adult life. As it was I broke away from my family and suffered what was then a disgraceful fate. At the age of twenty-one I took a post as governess with a family in Paris. I spoke some French, having learned it at my boarding school, and rapidly improved my knowledge of the language. I had three children in my charge. I taught them arithmetic, reading and writing, often in English, so they learned that at the same time. It was my misfortune to meet in my employer's house a young man, a writer, with whom I fell in love. François swore that he loved me but could not marry me before he was twenty-five, or he would lose his inheritance. Fool that I was, I believed him. I left my employment and went to live with him in the artists' quarter, on the Left Bank.

The shock to my employers, and even more to my family, was considerable. I wrote to Papa and Katie, explaining my action, telling them of François's talent, the novel he was writing, and his love for me. I reminded them that I was now of age and free to do as I wished. Papa did not reply, although I wrote again and again. Katie took a charitable view. She wrote to me regularly with family news, and said she prayed for me daily. I was grateful for her generosity of spirit, then and always.

It was ironic that Papa should have taken this attitude to my love affair. We did not know it at the time, but he had already installed his mistress in comfortable quarters and was spending much of his time with her. Katie continued to keep house for him in Lambeth, and looked after Rose and Vincent.

My beloved François, I soon discovered, was penniless. We had hardly enough money for our daily needs. I became an artists' model to improve our situation, and sat for students at the Beaux Arts, and for many established painters in their studios.

A year later I became pregnant. François left me at this time of need to live with another woman, whom he subsequently deserted as he had me. My body became unsightly as my pregnancy advanced and I was unable to pursue my career. I found shelter in a convent, where my son was born. He was a feeble child. He contracted influenza in the first month of his life and died. I was distressed. But young people are resilient, and as soon as I was strong enough I returned to my profession.

I had several lovers in the next two years, men who enjoyed the company of an attractive and intelligent young woman and were generous in return. It is true that they sometimes helped me with money, but that is not to say that I descended to prostitution, certainly not. I survived, living from day to day. There were good times, especially in the summer. I dreaded the winter. My lodgings were often very cold, and I could not afford proper food and warm clothing. However, I have a remarkable constitution and I was seldom ill.

I was rescued from this uncertain way of life by the English painter, Cecil Jeffries. He was almost twice my age, an artist of the old school unaffected by the Modern Movement. He was working in Paris at that time, and I modelled for him for some months before he declared his love for me. There was no question of marriage since his wife was a devout Catholic and would not divorce him. After my experience with François I was at first suspicious. But Cecil was a man of honour. Once he had won me he never changed his attitude of loving respect. I became his mistress, keeping my own name, Mimsy Mason. We had no children. I was lucky enough to foster David. He is a good boy.

I owe Cecil eternal gratitude. He made me a wealthy woman, introduced me to a new world of comfort and sociability, and educated me in art and literature. His studio was a place where the intelligentsia met to discuss subjects of interest, most stimulating to someone like myself. In 1914, at the beginning of the Great War, we returned to England and established ourselves in a comfortable house in Albert Gardens, Wimbledon.

I am so glad to remember the name of the road. That is a sure sign of convalescence.

On Friday Marian went to Kensington High Street to register at the Queen Bee Agency. The office was small, only two desks and a row of filing cabinets. A tall, elegant woman wearing an expensive model suit, high heels and a lot of pearls, came to meet her.

'I'm Beatrice King. And you're Marian Foster, you were in C House with Celia Watts. Let's go into my den, then we can talk.'

She led the way and Marian followed. What a transformation! The big boobs had been reduced to medium size, the fat face was a shapely oval with no double chin. The hips were firm, the legs shapely.

'Yes, I was Marian Foster, now I'm Broome-Vivier. It's such fun to see you again. You're looking absolutely wonderful.'

Beatrice King laughed. She was attractive, almost beautiful. 'I know, I know,' she said. 'I used to be a fatty. To tell you the truth, I hated Abbey Mead. I was absolutely miserable, and the food was ghastly, wasn't it.'

'Absolutely,' Marian agreed, remembering watery potatoes, thick gravy and starchy puddings.

'I started eating sweets,' said Beatrice. 'Obsessively. I smuggled them in.'

'But you were a School Prefect!'

'Yes! It was absolutely oafish of me. I got fatter and fatter, my parents couldn't understand it, the doctors said it was glandular. I fooled everybody! Then when I left, I couldn't get a job. Except here. It was very run-down and old-fashioned, they didn't mind my looks. It was called Clark's Nursing Agency, which was sort of unimaginative. Then the boss lady got ill, and gradually I took over. When she died I changed the name. And then something marvellous happened.'

'Yes?'

'I started going to a health farm. I lost a stone the first time. Then another stone. Then I fell in love.'

'How absolutely super!'

'Derek was a patient there too. We started having sex together, and that did the trick. I'm stabilised now, so is he. He used to drink too much, mostly because women didn't fancy him. He was simply too fat. And too heavy, if you know what I mean. When he was on top... Anyway, once we'd found each other, and we were both losing weight, everything was wonderful! And he's intelligent, and quite well off. Look.' She held out a manicured hand to show a glittering solitaire diamond..

'You're engaged! Wonderful! Can I tell Celia?'

'Of course. It will be in *The Times* on Monday!'

They got down to the problem of Mimsy's nurse-companion. Beatrice gave Marian details of Kiwi's background, education, training and experience. Since Marian was Old Abbey, they would waive home inspection. Presumably the premises were of an acceptable standard. And there's a cleaner.

'There will be,' said Marian. 'No problem.'

They parted like old friends, swearing to meet again. Marian telephoned Celia as soon as she got home. 'The whole event was such a revelation. It was just so romantic. Two people find each other by chance, and love blooms.'

'Marian, I've got three people in the shop, and two of them are serious. They're trying things on.'

'Super. Telephone you Monday.'

What fun it had been. She found she was smiling as she packed the Mini with Mimsy's clean clothes, French bread and salad, two bottles of wine, and some pâté. Driving to Wimbledon, she told herself that she was really enjoying looking after Mimsy. And she liked Dave. He'd been oafish at first, overwhelmed with it all. Now he was being positive and helpful.

She parked in the forecourt and went up in the lift. He opened the door, smiling, with positive news. He was going to stay until the nurse-companion came, Kiwi or whatever, and leave for Saudi Arabia on Monday. He'd booked his flight. He would spend Sunday night with his friends who lived in Pimlico, handy for getting the coach to Heathrow. The doctor had been. Was Mimsy taking her heart pills? He suspected not. Marian said she would check.

They fed Mimsy and put her down for a nap. Over their own rather late lunch he asked her to say, sincerely, if she was going to find looking after Mimsy too much of a burden. And she said, very sincerely, that she was going to love it. She wasn't good at politics, and she didn't read much. Charles was the brainy one. But she did feel confident about fixing things, making arrangements, seeing that people got what they wanted in the way of food, drink and comfort.

'What would life be without them,' said Dave.

Boldly she invited the porter's wife to come up for a cup of coffee. She soon found out what had gone wrong between her and Mimsy. The poor woman wanted paying, that was all.

'I'll come in daily if there are proper arrangements,' she said, as Marian obliged with back payments in cash. 'I don't like awkwardness about money. And she'll need full-time nursing now, won't she. They tell you it's a minor stroke and that means the big one is on its way. I'll be off now, and thank you very much.'

'Cheerful, aren't we,' said Dave as the door closed after her.

'Never mind,' said Marian. 'We've got a cleaner and we've got Kiwi. I'll come in tomorrow morning, and do a final tidy-up. And I'll bring lunch .'

'I wouldn't have thought it possible,' he said. 'I'm so grateful to you, bossy Marian.'

He was finding the combination of her good looks and practical energy unsettling. These things didn't usually go together. He wanted to touch her, to put a hand on her shoulder or stroke her hair, to make sure she was real. He wondered, casually, what she would be like in bed.

'And talking of bossy,' she said. 'You must, simply must, telephone Mimsy's solicitor about paying bills. A Power of Attorney.'

'I'll do that right now. And thanks again. See you tomorrow.'

Hurrying home against the rush-hour traffic, Marian thought she might be slightly in love with Dave, in a school-girlish way. Just a day dream, not at all serious. She liked the shape of his head, his tanned skin, his dark blue eyes. And his profile was good. He wasn't handsome in a conventional way, but when he smiled - Help! She nearly drove through a red light.

Mustn't get silly. It's an amusing thought, that's all. I like being with him, I feel relaxed. He isn't hunting me. He's strong, and independent. He works in the desert building a dam. There will be an oasis there one day, with its own micro-climate.

She had cleaned the spare room for him, though he protested. The bed unmade, a zipper bag lying open on the floor, shirts and socks half tipped out. She didn't unpack for him; that would be going too far.

Home again, she showered and dressed. She and Charles were going to dine with friends, informally. One didn't give real dinner parties on a Friday because most people went away early for the weekend. Thanks to the Wimbledon adventure she was in high spirits, bubbling over, wanting to talk about it. The others roared with laughter when she described getting Mimsy into the bath. 'One skinny leg over, then the other, and off she went! Whoops! She tobogganed along on her bottom, I had to grab her. Then she clung round my neck, nearly strangled me!'

She was tempted to tell the Queen Bee story, but decided against. It would be oafish to make a joke of Beatrice's transformation, fatty to fiancée. You couldn't send it up, just for laughs. Oh, that awful food at Abbey Mead! It was so understandable, hating the place and taking refuge in guzzling sweets.

In the Mini on the way home Charles said casually that he'd probably not be ready to start for Broome first thing. He'd got a load of papers to go through. He would make it in time for dinner. But she should go ahead, because of the horse.

'Take the Bentley,' he added generously. 'I'll come down in this.' The Bentley, second-hand, was his precious totem, a symbol of all that was good. Marian was an expert driver, possibly better than he was. He knew he could trust her with it. Now he held his breath in case she should offer to wait for him.

'Oh darling, really not,' she said. 'I don't want the Bentley. I like my little Mini.' She patted the dashboard. 'Actually I think I'd better spend the morning with Mimsy and give her lunch. So why don't we say No to lunch at Broome, but we'll both be there for dinner. I'll telephone Ted first thing tomorrow.'

Ted Broome-Vivier, Charles's father, now a widower, lived alone at Broome Hall. The gardener's wife did some cleaning and brought him cooked meals which he could heat up. He insisted that he was perfectly well-fed and looked after.

'You're sure that suits you, darling?' said Charles. 'I must say you're being a very devoted great-niece. Lucky old Mimsy.'

He heaved a sigh of relief. The lunch with Boo at The Welcome Sole could go ahead as planned.

A stroke. I have had a stroke, that is all. The doctor has prescribed pills for my heart, which is ridiculous. My heart is strong. It always has been.

When I returned to England with Cecil, my first thought was to see my old home and my sister Katie. She invited me to visit her a few days after my arrival. I was so happy to see her again. She was as thin as ever and very wrinkled, although she wasn't yet forty. After an emotional and affectionate embrace we settled down to talk, to tell each other of those many things which had been left out of our letters. I told her the whole story of my years in Paris, my hopes of marriage to François, his leaving me when I was pregnant with his child, my eventual happiness with Cecil. She wept when I told her of the death of my baby son.

I asked Katie if Papa would see me now that I had returned to England. She said she had urged him to show Christian forgiveness but he was obdurate. Vincent was of the same mind. He was now working in the City, but still living at home with Katie to care for him. Rose was married, and had two young children, Emily and Harold. I wrote asking her to come and see me in Albert Gardens. She replied that she would like to see me again, but would not introduce me to her husband and children. I found this deeply insulting. And I was hurt by Papa's refusal to see me, and Vincent's.

But dear Katie was all forgiveness and understanding. She never once reminded me of the warnings she had given. She never said, 'I told you so. That's what happens if you allow a sinful embrace.' She accepted me as I was and remained my loyal and loving sister. She came frequently to see me and Cecil. She enjoyed our style of life, our interesting friends and the comforts of our home. Later, when Vincent was married and Papa deceased, she was left alone in Lambeth. The house was much too big for her, and the tone of the neighbourhood had gone down since we were girls. Cecil and I persuaded her to sell the place, and she moved to a smaller house, near Albert Gardens, where she lived for the rest of her life. She interested herself in the local church and in charitable works. After the Second World War we took her with us on some of our foreign travels. She had never been abroad before and had seldom taken a holiday, except for trips to the seaside.

It was not until Papa was seriously ill that he relented and invited me to come and see him. I went immediately and sat by him and asked his forgiveness. I did not honestly feel that I needed forgiveness, it was rather he who should apologise to me for his cruel neglect. But a show of humility was clearly what he wanted. He said he still loved me dearly, although I had let the family down. My elopement had been a terrible shock to him. Rose and Vincent also came to say farewell to Papa. We were together round his bedside at the last, and together round his grave, giving an appearance at least of family unity.

In later years Vincent seldom visited me. I never met his wife and children. Rose changed her mind, apologised and asked me to forget what she had said, which I was glad to do. She came to see me often, sometimes with her children, once with her husband. She was no doubt impressed by my new circumstances, and the fact that Cecil was in every way a gentleman.

Many people connected with the theatre attended Papa's funeral, among them his mistress, though we did not know it at the time. She stood, heavily veiled, with the other employees from Mason & Gough. It was not until later that we discovered that Papa had kept her for the past twenty years. She came to Lambeth and confronted Katie, saying that she had given Papa her youth, she had helped make his business successful, he had promised to make provision for her in his Will. No doubt, she said, we his children had persuaded him against leaving her a legacy. Eventually, with Cecil's help, I settled the matter. We gave her an annual allowance and were eventually rid of her. It was all most unpleasant.

There is nothing wrong with my heart. The doctor is a fool.

5   Saturday

The Welcome Sole seemed to have become a very popular place. As Charles settled into a corner table he looked round to see if there was anyone there he knew. Fortunately there was not. He didn't usually mind being seen out with a pretty girl, but this was Saturday after all, when most fellows were at home with their wives.

Boo arrived a mere twenty minutes late, punctuality not being one of her strong points. He noticed at once that she had changed her usual frivolous style for something more serious. She was wearing a dark suit with a white shirt and a miniature bow tie. Her golden locks were swept into a neat plait. She looked enchanting, he thought, like a dear little schoolgirl. Getting up to give her a welcoming kiss, he noticed a new perfume.

'Hallo, sweetie,' she said. 'I do hope you're not furious with me. I had to go for a beastly interview.'

'Interview, what on earth for?' He had already looked at the menu and was planning to have *sole bienvenu* with a salad. His father would have a meal waiting at Broome, and would expect him to eat a large share of it. So a light lunch would be preferable. And he didn't want to waste time with Boo in a restaurant. He wanted her naked, and to himself. 'What sort of interview?'

'You'll never guess, but I'm going to get a job. In Horrids.' Several people claim to have invented this name for Harrods, but it was actually Boo Carey who said it first. 'Sweetie, they loved me. They said I could start on Monday week, and the hours are awful but the wages are not bad. And so handy for me, I'll be able to walk to work. It's in the handbag department, really gorgeous things especially the beaded evening bags. And the expensive ones, crocodile and so on, are kept in glass cases so the customers can't pinch them.'

'Good Lord.' He hadn't thought about it before, but now it struck him that her awful ex-husband had probably given her an inadequate settlement. Poor little thing, standing behind the counter in Harrods. 'Well, clever little Boody-doo. And what would she like to eat?'

Boo ignored Fish of the Day and examined the *à la carte*. 'It's a special occasion for me, sweetie. Oh, yum-yum, do I dare? Charles, could I have the lobster thermidor as a special treat, and just an avocado to start with? And can we have champagne?'

'Of course. I think I'll have the same.' He pressed her knee under the table. 'Shellfish is good for it.'

'Good for what?' said innocent Boo.

'For what we're planning to do this afternoon.'

'Charles, you are a very, very naughty, boy.'

He loved it when she said that. He decided to enjoy the meal, never mind what he would have to eat at Broome that evening. And perhaps he would put off the business of telling her that they must see less of each other. It was so touching, the thought of her going out into the world to earn money.

He drank more champagne than he meant to, and had a brandy with his coffee while she ate a chocolate ice cream. He felt as if he'd rescued a little beggar girl and was giving her the best meal she'd ever had. In their secluded corner he relaxed his rule about public display and took her hand and kissed it, while she chattered on about this and that, people she knew and parties she'd been to. She'd be able to get a discount on clothes, she said, when she was working at Horrids.

Then a man came up and stood by their table, a face Charles knew but couldn't immediately place.

'Hallo, Boo,' he said, handsome in a lean and hungry way, wearing a ridiculous high-collared suit with floppy tie and striped waistcoat, quite unsuitable for lunchtime on a Saturday.

'Hallo, Quentin sweetie,' said Boo.

Charles half rose. Quentin Jones, of course, a publisher. 'I'm Charles Broome-Vivier. We've met.'

'Yes, we have,' said Jones unsmiling. 'With Victor and Celia Chase. Well, see you, Boo.' He went back to his own table, where he was sitting with a large and noisy group in which he seemed to be the only one not having a good time.

Boo sat silent, which was unusual for her.

'Extraordinary clothes,' said Charles. 'A bit of an exhibitionist, wouldn't you say.'

'I don't know,' said Boo in a small voice. 'Actually I think he's rather nice.'

'And you are adorable and wonderful,' said Charles quickly. No question now of cooling her off. If he did he might lose her forever to the lean and hungry Quentin Jones. 'Boody-doo, you know how I feel. I really care, my darling girl.' He took her hand and pressed it warmly. 'The married man's usual story. I adore you, and at the same time I'm devoted to my wife.'

'Charles, don't apologise, please. I accept it, and I admire Marian so tremendously.'

'And I admire you, Boody. And I want you so much. Shall we adjourn now and discuss the merger?'

The bill was huge, but it was a special occasion. He paid, left a suitable tip, collected his overcoat and Boo's fox fur jacket. She kept him waiting, which was annoying of her, hovering at Quentin Jones's table and chatting. Perhaps it had been a mistake to come to such a popular place.

Finally she caught up with him. He helped her with her jacket, and gave her a quick squeeze as they went out on to the pavement. The sky was heavy with cloud and an icy wind was blowing. There were no taxis in sight. He wished he'd managed to get the Mini for the day. He could have parked in a side street, for a quick getaway. Minis were everywhere these days, no one would have noticed it. The Bentley on the other hand would have been conspicuous. And it was too valuable to be parked in the King's Road on a Saturday. Its normal habitat was a rented garage.

'Hi, Charles! Hi, Boo!' It was Celia, pushing a big old-fashioned pram loaded with the Adorables and several carrier bags of weekend shopping.

Charles winced. God, what bad luck! A taxi drew up and he grabbed the door handle. If only the bloody thing had come a few minutes earlier! 'Hallo, Celia! Hallo, Emma and Rupert!' he cried enthusiastically. 'I'm giving Boo a lift. Sorry there isn't room for you too, ha-ha!'

'Hallo, Celia,' said Boo. 'I must tell you, such fun. I've got a job in Horrids, in the handbag department.'

'How absolutely super! When do you start?'

'Monday week. The hours are dreadful, up at dawn.'

'Come on, Boo. Can't wait all day.' Charles ushered her into the taxi, wagging his head merrily as if to say, 'You women!' He waved as they drove away. He thought he had carried it off pretty well. Celia would tell Marian, of course. He would have to have a cover story ready.

Once he was safely in the four-poster with Boo he forgot about it. What a lover he was, better than ever! Her squeals of delight were music in his ears. After a suitable interval he took her a second time, not such an energetic performance, naturally enough, but excellent in its way. He fell asleep after that, and woke to find that it was already dark. That was January for you. It must be four o'clock at least.

'Sweetie,' Boo breathed in his ear. 'It's half-past five. Time for you to go.'

'My God.' He sat up and rubbed his face. He felt awful, a bad taste in his mouth and a bit of a headache. 'I'll have to fly, adorable Boo. All right for Wednesday evening? Thanks a million.'

The Bentley would get him to Broome in time for dinner. He had meant this afternoon to be a quick one, but Boo had been particularly amorous. It was good of her to wake him. No nonsense, begging him to stay and that sort of thing. And getting a job in Harrods, poor darling. She really was quite a girl.

Mimsy ate a good lunch, poached fillet of plaice washed down with a glass of wine. Dave and Marian helped her to bed, where she fell asleep and snored.

They settled in the dining room, like grown-ups after a fractious baby has been fed and is quiet at last. Marian sat at the head of the table, acting hostess. He was on her right, her guest of honour.

'You're spoiling her,' he said. 'And she loves it.'

'I love doing it,' said Marian. 'Here, finish this, do.' She put the last of the cheese on his plate. He cut it carefully and gave half back to her. They divided the remaining grapes between them, and the rest of the wine.

'Cheers.' He emptied his glass and smiled, looking at her. A friendly pirate. 'I'll miss you, bossy Marian.'

She felt her face going red, and hoped he wouldn't notice. She'd had several glasses of wine, as well as sherry before lunch. 'And I'll miss you, Dave. Look what we've managed to get done together.'

He said, 'Do you think we should try a kiss as well? Just one.' Then he made a comical face, as if to say, Have I said the wrong thing?

'Of course.' She smiled, to keep things light. But inwardly she was frantic. She desperately wanted to kiss him, and more. She wanted to hug him, to lie down with him, to have him inside her. Was that what he wanted? He seemed so cool, as if not wanting to get involved.

But now he took her hands, leaned forward and kissed her. The smell of him, the feel of his lips, made her dizzy with urgent need. She had to have more, all of it, as soon as possible.

'Oh Dave,' she said, trying to breathe normally. 'If you want - that's what I want too. It's a *coup de foudre,* isn't it. I knew as soon as you opened the door.'

Coup de foudre was the 'in' phrase for knowing that you wanted sex with somebody as soon as you'd met them. She'd never used it about her own feelings before, only other people's.

Holding her hands, looking into her eyes, he said in fluent French that he, too, had known as soon as he opened the door. Now he hoped she would open her door to him.

'Oh Dave!' she gasped. She'd suddenly realised what *Au Clair de la Lune* was all about. Not just an innocent little Pierrot, but a man wanting to go all the way. 'Oh Dave!' She kissed him again and kept her mouth pressed to his while they got up together and stumbled awkwardly

60

through the hall to the spare room.

'Take it easy, there's no hurry,' he said when his mouth was free for a moment, before she silenced him with another blast of kisses. He got some of her buttons undone meanwhile, then she let him go, unzipped her boots and kicked them away, tore off her sweater, blouse, jeans, socks, briefs and brassière. He managed to take off his shoes, and she helped him off with the rest, quickly, efficiently. They collapsed together on the narrow bed, Marian on top at first, then he rolled her over so that he could kiss her neck and shoulders, her nipples, her navel, running his hand down to the fork between her long, strong legs.

Their bodies were easy together, rolling and twining, his sun-tanned to the waist, hers winter-pale. She didn't want much foreplay, which came as a surprise. She made it clear that she just wanted him to penetrate and get on with it. He had thought of her as conventional, maybe inhibited, needing to be gently persuaded..

'In!' she cried. 'Please! Go, go!' She wrapped her arms and legs close round his body and urged him on.

'You're a wild girl!' he panted. 'Is this okay? Okay for you?'

'Yes, go on! On! Now!'

He took her and she moaned with satisfaction. Then they lay quiet, looking at each other. He wanted to tell her, but could not immediately find the words, that sex was nothing in itself. It could be so dull, so trivial. But with her it had been miraculous, a few moments of blessed recognition. Ourselves, together. Unfortunately there would be no further moments, no development.

He said, hoping that she wouldn't think him elderly, or patronising, 'It's unusual, to feel like this. For me.'

'Absolutely,' she said. 'We're in a different place now.'

He stroked her hair. She told him she'd thought he might not be interested in women, which made him smile. He said he'd been married, ten years ago. It hadn't worked out, partly because Mimsy didn't like his wife.

'Why?'

'Said she was suburban.' He frowned, remembering unhappy times. 'Which was unfair. Mimsy's background was suburban. But she travelled and met interesting people, which broadened her mind. Sorry, I don't mean to go on about it.'

'But do, if you want.'

'Briefly.' he began. God, how stuffy I sound. 'Well, it turned out that my ex-wife's idea of marriage conflicted with mine. She wanted us to live in a nice house and have nice friends. Catch the same train to work every day. I wanted to take her abroad, to show her the world. She wanted stability, she said. And a family.'

'You had children?'

'Yes, a daughter. I'll see her tomorrow in Pimlico. She's nine, quite bright. Nice-looking. It's always wonderful seeing her, and hell at the same time. There's a stepfather now. I gather she likes him well enough.'

Marian studied his profile, the straight nose, the lips she would kiss again soon, his forehead. His hair, such a beautiful pale colour. His arms, his hands. She said, 'Dave, you must get married again one day. Honestly, one can't go on moping for the rest of time.'

'I know.' He had a girlfriend in Saudi, an Australian called Robyn, a cheerful blonde, with a good body. He stayed with her in Riyadh, in the flat she shared with some other Ozzie nurses, whenever he had a few days off. So far the relationship had been the way he liked it, without commitment. 'I promise you I don't mope, wild and bossy Marian. I've decided that I'm just not the marrying type.'

A moaning voice reached them. 'David, where are you? Come, David! Potty!'

He was out of bed in a flash, throwing on a dressing gown. Marian sat up and said, 'You can't go like that.' But he was gone.

Whoops! She dressed as quickly as she could and hurried to Mimsy's bedroom. Dave hadn't made it in time, though he'd carried Mimsy to the bathroom. The bed was wet, a trail of pee ran through to the loo, where Mimsy sat wailing. 'I called, and nobody! I called, I called!'

'Okay,' Dave was saying. 'It's not a disaster. Might happen to anybody.'

Marian mopped up, following the trail to the bathroom. 'Mimsy, why don't you have your bath now that we're here,' she said, turning on the taps. 'Look, I brought you this bath oil. It's so good for dry skin. Let's get your nightie off, and this, and the panties. That's better. Dave, could you come back later and help me get her out?'

She looked up at him and he wrapped his dressing gown closer and said, 'Anything to oblige, but anything.' She had to smother a fit of the giggles. What a hoot, an absolute bedroom farce!

'Nice bath,' said Mimsy, feeling more cheerful. 'Smell nice.'

An hour later, order restored, clean sheets, Mimsy bathed and changed, Dave dressed, they sat quietly drinking tea. 'David is a good boy,' Mimsy told Marian several times. 'Go away. Stuck. Stuck. Structural engineer.'

'Yes, he has to go away,' said Marian. 'But we've got a nurse coming, and I will visit once or twice a week. I'll do the shopping and laundry and make sure you've got everything you need.'

'And your hub. Your hum.'

'Yes, my husband Charles and I are going down to Broome tonight, Mimsy. That's where his father lives. It's a lovely old house, with acres of land. I have a horse there, so I have to exercise it. Then tomorrow night Charles and I will come in on our way home, to see how you are, and say hallo to Kiwi. And Dave, you'll be in Pimlico.'

She smiled brightly. It hurt. She didn't want to leave him. She wished they could have had more time together.

'See hub, Charles,' said Mimsy. 'Clever man.'

'Charles is super,' said Marian. 'Now I'll just get out some sheets for Kiwi, and make sure her room is ready.'

Dave followed her. They tidied the spare room together and made up the bed. They kissed, and he said, 'I suppose you couldn't cancel the horse and come here in the morning, before I go. Before Kiwi comes.'

She said, 'No, Dave. I couldn't possibly. But it's been super knowing you.'

'Me too,' he said. 'Chin up.'

She smiled, but she felt like crying, and he must have noticed.

She said goodnight to Mimsy. Dave wanted to see her downstairs and into the car, but she said not to bother. He came with her into the hall, helped her with her coat, put his arms round her and kissed her several times. She managed to get outside the door, smiled and waved, then ran down the stairs, crying all the way.

Outside sleet was falling, blown about by an icy wind. She looked up, just in case, and saw him leaning out of the sitting room window, three floors up. She shouted merrily, 'Bye-ee!' He waved, she waved back, struggled with the Mini's door, got in. Headlights, ignition, windscreen wipers. She was off at last, tears streaming. The forecourt was slippery with sleet, so she had to concentrate on that, and then on getting out through Wimbledon to the A3. Stopping at traffic lights, she wiped her eyes with the Mini's duster. The sleet had turned to snow.

You said I was a wild girl and really I'm not usually like that. It was just that this irresistible need came over me, and I let it happen, and you made me so happy. It's not as if I'm inexperienced, Dave. I mean I'm a married woman and I lost my virginity ages ago. But this time it was a revelation. It was a bit silly of me because I'm not on the Pill and had no protection, but if I'd said so it would have spoiled the mood, and we would have had to have *coitus interruptus*, which I don't much like. Anyway I'm a week off ovulation. I know all about it because I've tried often enough to get Charles interested on the right day, mostly without success. Especially recently.

Real snow, getting heavier. She decided to stick to the A3 because of the weather, though the mileage to Broome was less if you cut across. She was only just past Esher, so another thirty miles to go. Charles's father would be busy heating up a meal for them. She really should have started sooner, to help him in that dreadful old-fashioned kitchen. She would like a shower and a change of clothes before dinner, if there was time.

Just then a car came up on the outside lane and overtook at high speed, spraying her with muddy slush. The rear lights disappeared into the gloom ahead, but she'd had time to recognise the Bentley. Charles was driving like a demon, really not a good idea on a dark winter's night, with snow maybe freezing on the road. There was no chance of keeping up with him, she would just have to battle on in the inside lane. He was much later than he'd said.

If he'd spent the afternoon with Barbara Carey, good luck to him. Because I, Marian, his loving wife, spent the afternoon with Dave Mason. And I would normally tell Celia how it was, how he seemed so unconcerned and remote, and suddenly he sprang like a tiger. But this time I can't tell Celia. What happened is deeply private, between me and Dave. I was a wild girl. And he was my lover.

She had to slow down. Cars ahead were creeping along, headlights showing a swirling mist of snowflakes and exhaust fumes. Suddenly, and quite by chance because she was thinking about Dave, she saw the Bentley pulled into the side, and managed to brake, swerve and skid to a halt just behind it. She'd hit the bank but no matter. God, was it an accident? She jumped out and ran.

'Charles! Darling, what's happened? Are you all right?'

'Marian! Christ, I'm glad to see you, darling. It's a bloody fucking puncture, just why it had to happen in this bloody awful weather, and the RAC takes hours to come and where's the nearest telephone, you might bloody well ask. Darling, what shall we do, this is too bloody much!'

The lights of passing cars lit them fitfully, through curtains of blowing snow. He was almost crying, standing there in his sheepskin jacket and grey trousers, his good shoes deep in slush. Poor Charles, it was rotten of the Bentley to let him down like this.

'Darling,' she said. 'Get out the jack and the spare. And we might need the instruction book. Put something behind the wheel so that the car doesn't move. Brake on? And tools, Charles. Loosen the nuts first because you can't do it once the car is off the ground. Won't be a minute.'

She ran back to the Mini, got in and edged nearer the Bentley, so that her headlights lit the flat tyre. 'Spanner, darling,' she said, while Charles stood gazing at the tool kit in a muddled way. 'Charles, spanner. Thanks. Gosh, these nuts are tight! Whoops!' The first one gave way so suddenly that she collapsed on the ground with a bump. Charles pulled himself together and did the others.

They got the jack out and were wondering where to put it when an AA van suddenly appeared in front of them. The driver didn't even wait to ask if they needed help. He got out, jacked up the car, removed the flat tyre, put on the spare and replaced the nuts. He said the snow was something terrible on minor roads, beginning to freeze, inches deep in places. Charles wanted to give him a fiver, but he wouldn't take it. He said this was his job, there were worse ones. He'd never changed a Bentley tyre before, funny thing. Well, goodnight. Mind how you go.

Charles, suddenly protective, told Marian she might have trouble getting through to Broome in the Mini. It was much too risky. She should come with him in the Bentley, they would pick up the Mini on the way back tomorrow, in daylight. So she collected her overnight bag, locked the Mini and left it. It looked very small, the snow drifting up against its wheels.

Inside the Bentley it was soon wonderfully warm, so that their sodden clothes steamed. Charles, driving slowly and carefully, said it was super the way a car like this held the road, even in extremely difficult conditions. Not only nice to look at, also a magnificent piece of engineering. Then Marian told him how Mimsy had wet the bed just when she was getting ready to leave, and how she'd got the flat into reasonable condition for the nurse who was coming tomorrow.

Charles, eager to get it over, said in the most casual way that he'd seen Boo Carey at a lunch place down the Kings Road. He'd gone out for a break to get away from his papers, given her a lift home in a taxi. Incidentally, he'd bumped into Celia and the Adorables, out shopping.

He was glad he was driving, on the last stretch now, off the A3 and along a stretch of what had been a Roman road, and therefore straight, which would soon give way to a winding country lane, easy enough in fine weather, but very tricky on a dark night in deep snow. He hoped that if he seemed awkward, explaining how he came to be in a taxi with Boo, Marian would put it down to difficult driving conditions.

Then she said something which upset him very much indeed. 'Oh, Boo Carey? Yes, she's having an affair with Quentin Jones. Let's ask them to dinner sometime. They would fit in with the arty people, wouldn't they.'

He couldn't immediately think what to say. God, this just couldn't be true. It was idle gossip, surely, based on speculation. Then he remembered the way the man had stood by their table, with a possessive air. Yes, possessive. 'See you, Boo,' he'd said. See her in bed, did he mean, the bastard? What a vile thought. And what a revelation.

Little Boo, sweet and innocent? He was the one who'd been innocent! She was nothing but a tart after all, with her pink frilly bed, the flat so conveniently near Knightsbridge station, furnished in such deplorable taste. Christ, how had he ever got involved with the woman! What a ghastly mistake, and how lucky he'd found out before he got further embroiled. A man could ruin his life. Scandal, blackmail. The end of everything one cared about.

He said after a while, 'Marian, I want to tell you, I was going to anyway. I got into a bit of naughtiness with Boo, I don't know how it happened. But it's over, completely finished. Darling, can you forgive me? I feel so ashamed of myself.'

'Of course. Actually I thought there was something, darling. I'm so glad it's over. No problem.'

'Darling.' He took one hand off the steering wheel to squeeze her knee. 'You're so good, so understanding. We can have them to dinner if you like, but not on my account.'

'No, I'd really like to. I think she'd suit Quentin Jones rather well, don't you.'

'Yes. Of course.' Charles gripped the wheel, trying to see through the swirling snowflakes. He found this shocking news totally incomprehensible. How could she have had that awful fellow? Surely she wouldn't have sunk so low.

It was nearly nine when they got to Broome Hall. Snow lay deep in the drive so that the Bentley skidded from side to side, coming to rest at an angle in front of the house. Charles doused the headlights, took Marian in his arms and kissed her, gratefully and with some passion. She noticed that he smelled of sweat and alcohol. She said, 'Darling, not now! There, kiss, kiss! Don't worry about it, because I'm not going to.'

'You're an angel, darling,' he said. 'You're so generous, so good to me.'

Ted Broome-Vivier had been anxiously looking out from the dining room window, and now he opened the front door and stood, tall and upright, with arms outstretched, saying, 'At last! Welcome!' They collected their bags and hurried indoors, where it was not quite as warm as it had been in the Bentley. Lack of adequate heat was one of the

66

things you had to put up with at Broome.

The house, Ted's mother's dowry, was Victorian Gothic, a miniature fortress with castellations, mullioned windows, and a tower at each end. Subsequent Broome-Viviers had made haphazard alterations, adding a mansard roof in the 1920s and later a pseudo-classical porch, so that the original front door was now inside a cramped hall. Charles's mother, in spite of mild protests from Ted, had replaced some of the windows with modern ones.

'Dolly wanted more light,' Ted would explain. 'Couldn't bear what she called the mediaeval gloom.' He had been in the Army and was used to giving orders, but never stood up to his wife. He didn't like the windows, which made the place colder than before. When he suggested that it was time they improved the central heating, Dolly said it wasn't worth the expense. She was Scottish by birth and believed that fresh, cool air was healthy and invigorating. It was ironic that she had died, a year ago, from a lung infection.

Charles and Marian took off their wet coats and shoes and began, both at once, to explain why they were so late.

Ted joined in, so that there was a three-sided conversation, typical of many family communications, everybody talking and nobody really listening.

Marian: 'Absolutely ghastly weather. It wasn't too bad when I left Wimbledon, my great-aunt seems quite happy, she has her ups and downs of course, but I've managed to get a super New Zealand nurse for her. I started out in the Mini rather late, what with one thing and another, and found Charles in a lay-by with a flat tyre! Would you believe it, such bad luck. The AA came to the rescue...'

Ted: 'I was afraid you might have met with an accident. People drive so fast these days, they don't take the weather into account. I was particularly worried about the lane, where the ditch must be hidden under snow. On the Continent and in the States they are better prepared for this sort of thing. Snow ploughs and chains. And the American Jeep was a great invention of course. And now we have the Land Rover and other heavy-duty vehicles.'

Charles, as Ted picks up Marian's suitcase, finds it heavier than he expected and puts it down again: 'I'll take that, Father. The Bentley didn't do too badly, road-holding being a strong point. But Marian was in the Mini. What with the snow and the short wheel-base she would have been skidding all over the place. So I decided to play safe. Left it in a lay-by, we'll pick it up tomorrow.'

Ted: 'Dinner is in the oven. You must be hungry after being out in the cold for so long. You'd like to change, of course. Charles, you might like to take a drink upstairs with you. And Marian. No hurry, I'm very glad that you're here at last.'

Marian: 'I'll just take off my wet things, Ted. Then I'll come down and help you.'

Charles poured himself a neat double whisky and took it upstairs. In the bathroom, under a shower which dribbled tepid water, he remembered other things about Boo, her tenderness, her loving ways. She cared for him, no doubt about that. 'Sweetie, don't go just yet.' He could hear her voice, see the expression on her little face. She was so young, so vulnerable. He couldn't cut her out of his life without hurting her. One didn't know the truth, and one shouldn't condemn a girl just because other women gossipped about her. It was highly likely, and he blamed himself for not realising this before, that she was short of money. Perhaps the loathsome Jones had helped her financially. And perhaps there were others. God, what a rotten world.

Marian pretended she was going upstairs, then slipped into the estate office, next to the hall, where there was a telephone on a separate line. It was even colder in there, so she took the handset as far as the cord would allow and wrapped herself in the long curtains, which were thick and heavy, passed on from a grander room. Snow whirled about outside. She dialled, and Dave answered immediately, as if he'd been waiting for her.

'It's Marian. Just checking that Mimsy's all right! Dave, it was an awful drive, I caught up with Charles and he had a puncture, and we decided to leave the Mini and go on in his car. It's an old Bentley, he adores it. Yes, it is absolutely beautiful. And Dave, there's a blizzard here. We've only just arrived. This telephone is all right, I mean it's not an extension. Nobody can hear us.'

'Okay then. I'm missing you. I've never met anyone quite like you. I wish I could kiss you again, just once.'

'Just once! That's what you said last time!' They laughed at their secret. 'I'm missing you too. I'll ring at twelve tomorrow, to check that Kiwi's arrived. Then after that you'll be in Pimlico.'

'Yes. I'll be tied up. And you, you've got Charles. He's a good bloke, is he? Doesn't beat you?'

'Charles is super, Dave. I mean honestly. I'm not telling him about us, of course not. Because it's private. But I do love him really. I've never told anybody before. But really I do.'

'He's a lucky man. Tomorrow please telephone me here, beautiful Marian. And on Monday morning I'll telephone from Heathrow. And if

68

the weather gets worse they'll delay my flight, and we'll have time for another kiss.'

'Dave! No, honestly, it was a one-off occasion. It's been so good talking to you. Actually I'm in a corner, behind a curtain. It's quite cosy.'

'I wish I was there with you. Goodbye, Marian.'

'Goodbye, Dave.'

She slipped back into the hall and went upstairs to change.

Dinner, a chicken casserole with potatoes and sprouts, was dried up and tasteless. There was a jam tart to follow, and cheese and biscuits. Charles drank a lot of the claret, which was good, and had a large brandy in the living room afterwards. There was a good fire there. He was beginning to feel warm, at last, and slightly drunk. No harm, it would help him sleep. By the time he went upstairs he was heady with fatigue, food and alcohol. Stumbling about as he got undressed, he remembered the lobster thermidor and the champagne, the huge bill, the taxi ride. What a fool he was! Boo Carey was nothing but a greedy little tart, a gold-digger and a slut. The next time they met she'd be asking for money, wheedling and cajoling. 'Charles sweetie, I'm ever so hard up, they don't pay all that well at Horrids.' And so on. How revolting! And that pathetic publisher, standing there making sheep's eyes at her. Poor misguided fellow, he'd learn!

Wearily climbing into the big cold bed with sagging mattress and lumpy pillows, Broome Hall's double spare, he felt a dim sense of obligation to his darling wife, so loyal, such a decent girl. He wanted to reward her, to show his gratitude by making passionate love.

She said, as he moved over and pulled her towards him, 'Darling, really not tonight. We're so tired, aren't we.' But he persevered, like an aged stallion, clumsily mounted her and got his organ inside, but that was all he could manage. Hardly awake, he slipped out and off, and relaxed into a drunken sleep, while she giggled because everything was so funny, so enjoyable.

Dear old Charles, he had confessed about Boo and it was over, thank goodness. What a day it had been, what a farce! People running about in dressing gowns, and having punctures, and sharing taxis when they shouldn't, and the AA man covered in snow, and the Mini abandoned on the A3.

Why worry? She felt wonderful, and so happy, and so full of love for everyone.

'What day today?' said Mimsy. 'What day?'

She knew that David had said goodbye and gone. He was building a dam far away, overseas. Never mind the name. Then the woman from next door came to call. Fortunately Kiwi, the nurse from New Zealand, managed to show her out after ten minutes. Kiwi was a nice-looking plump girl. Being a colonial she had an accent, of course, and a way of raising her voice at the end of a sentence, as if she were asking a question

'Today's Sunday?' she said.

'Thank you. You are kind. From New Zealand.'

'That's right? Now I'm going to get your tiffin?'

Mimsy closed her eyes and waited for the past to come back. Unfortunately the memories she had enjoyed so much, even the sad ones, were less frequent now. Others, some of which she would rather have forgotten, were claiming her attention. She remembered seeing, during the second War, a graveyard which had been bombed. There were gravestones overturned and earth thrown up in heaps as if by some mad grave-digger, and here and there parts of skeletons exposed, a skull, a femur, little bones from hands and feet long dead.

Yes, bad memories were rising to the surface now, like those poor remains. They were naked, stripped of flesh. And a voice kept sounding in her head, accusing her, naming mistakes, faults, accidents, things she wanted forgotten. You know what really happened, don't you? Why pretend? You did this. You did that. You thought you could hide the truth. But it's there all the same, isn't it.

I have had a stroke, that is why these things are bothering me. They are not important. I must keep calm, then they will go away and the pleasant memories will come back. My past as I like to remember it.

One of the bad things was the birth of that baby. It was delivered after a long and painful labour, which terrified me. I remembered the death of my poor Mama. And I hated the little creature, my son by François, whom he so much resembled. I hated feeding him. The responsibility was too much for me. I was too young, too lonely. There was no room in my life for a child.

He died. The nuns said it was because I had neglected him. I felt guilty and miserable, of course. But I had lost a burden. I was on my own again with nobody to look after but myself.

It was a severely cold winter. I had no money. I needed food, clothes and shelter. There was only one thing to do. Yes, I went on the street. I became a prostitute. It was easy for me, I have always been attractive to men. I was young and good-looking. But how degrading it was. And how difficult to operate freely, to save one's earning from the hands of some filthy *maquereau*. I fought, I struggled for independence. Eventually I escaped from that slime, that loathsome gutter of existence. I became an artists' model once more. And I met Cecil.

I am so grateful to that dear man. He made me what I am today. We were so happy together. And I was fortunate in finding David. If I was guilty, I purged my guilt in befriending him. He wasn't like that wretched baby, a source of shame and misery. He was a lively boy, with blue eyes, light brown hair and a friendly smile. I saw him by chance at the orphanage, a charity which Cecil and I supported, and he reminded me at once of my brother Tom at the same age. I remembered being a small girl, Tom my companion, my protector, the most loved person in my world. David has not disappointed me, except that he married the wrong woman. I told him so at the time. Otherwise he has been a good boy.

I often wish that I could have had my youth today, in this more tolerant society. There has been a general loosening of morals here and in America, particularly since the 'fifties. Young people no longer wait for marriage, they 'shack up' together, enjoying sex and sharing their finances. Sometimes these arrangements become permanent. The couple may or may not finally marry. Some women have children by several lovers and move from one household to another, sometimes with their offspring, sometimes without. This sexual freedom has been made possible by the contraceptive pill. I have heard of young girls, hardly old enough to be called women, taking the Pill as a precaution, so that they can enjoy sex at short notice, casually and without commitment.

On the other side of the argument, there was a play on television a few years ago about a girl who had several children, nowhere to live and no man to support her. With the Pill being so easily available it seemed ridiculous that she should have had a family when her circumstances were totally inadequate. I forget the details of the plot, there was not much to it. She went on producing, like an animal, with no thought for the children she pretended to love. A very stupid type of woman. And yet the play produced a furore, such people should be helped, they should be given homes. I have no patience with those who refuse to look after themselves in this modern age, grumbling and blaming their troubles on society. This is perhaps one effect of social reform in which housing, medical care and schooling are provided by the state.

In the old days one was ashamed to take help of this sort. We remembered the workhouse, the stigma of poverty. I despise women who remain stupid and cow-like when reliable birth control is available. If

I were young now I would use the Pill. I would choose my sexual partners with care. If I got pregnant by mistake I would not hesitate to have an abortion. When I found a suitable mate, I would exchange personal vows with him, or get legally married if he insisted. We would produce only as many children as we could support.

It was partly as a result of the new morality that my sister Rose became less critical of me. She came to stay with Katie in Wimbledon, and I invited her to Albert Gardens, and we were friends again. On one occasion, in the last year of Katie's life, Rose suggested that the three of us went to see our old home in Lambeth. I was still driving a car. While Cecil was alive he depended on me to get him from place to place, because he had never learned. So I had had plenty of experience. I must admit however that it was difficult finding the way from Wimbledon to Lambeth, and when we got there the traffic was considerable and going very fast. The map I had was an old one, and we wandered for some time, getting lost and attracting attention from other drivers, who hooted impatiently when we stopped to look for street names. We had difficulty also in getting into the correct lane in a complicated one-way system, which we circled several times before we found the route we wanted. On all sides there were tower blocks, council flats, offices, garages and shops which had not been there before.

Eventually we found our road, and our house, and a sad sight it was. The plaster was peeling away and there were cracks in the brickwork below. The window frames had hardly a scrap of paint left on them. The front garden was a jungle of weeds under which rubbish lay half buried, old prams, motor tyres, children's toys and heaps of rags. I parked the car at the gate, which hung from broken hinges. Katie was not well, since she had just had an operation, unsuccessful as it turned out. She waited in the car with Rose, who was very overweight and moved as little as possible.

I got out and went to the front door, passing an overflowing dustbin which smelled very badly. I rang and nobody came, presumably because the bell was not working. So I knocked. There was no knocker, so I used my fist. After a long wait the door was opened a few inches, being held on a chain, and a dirty-faced young girl looked through the gap and said, 'Watcha want?'

I could see that she was looking at my clothes, my hat and gloves, my smart overcoat. She eyed my handbag and for a moment I thought she might open the door and snatch it from me. I said, in a clear and polite manner, 'Would you allow me to come in and look at your house? I am interested in it particularly, because I used to live here when I was a little girl.'

72

She looked at me a while longer. Then she said, 'You fucking never,' and shut the door. I was not shocked. I knew what this word meant. It appeared in Lawrence's novel *Lady Chatterley's Lover*, which had recently been published in this country, without expurgation. But I could not repeat what the girl had said to my sisters. I went back to the car, and when they asked me what had happened I simply said, 'She was a very rude young thing. Dirty too. I feel sorry for her.' We went home somewhat disappointed.

What upset me was that when I was young the working classes showed respect for their superiors. I had seen the rough side of life in Paris, but I had lived through that time and recovered my position in society. But this ignorant, foul-mouthed girl, a little more than a child, had no idea of manners, how to behave to strangers, how to address an elderly woman, nicely dressed, who meant her no harm.

The world has changed so much.

Charles woke up with a hangover and the beginnings of a cold, neither of which surprised him. He'd had a lot to drink yesterday, and he'd been soaked to the skin. Getting dressed, he felt unwell and remorseful. Yesterday's snow was thawing rapidly and the sky was clear, so Marian had gone out with her horse. Thoughtfully she had put out eggs and bacon for him to cook if he wanted them. His father, in good spirits, joined him in the kitchen.

'Good morning, Charles. A better day! Now let me fry you a couple of eggs. I'm rather good at it. Old campaigner, you know. Dolly always admired my expertise with the frying-pan.'

'No thank you, Father. Coffee, if you have it. Perhaps a piece of toast.'

Dolly had been an indifferent cook. In her young days one was not expected to learn. Her first experience had come during the War, when there was rationing, and very little domestic help. Looking back, Charles realised that she was just not interested in food. It was nourishment, no more. Ted had never complained. But surely now, in his seventies, he needed something more in the way of staff, a married couple perhaps, living in. There was plenty of room.

'We've been wondering if you shouldn't have more help here, Father.'

'Not necessary, Charles. I like the simple life. I miss Dolly's company, of course . But local friends have been extremely kind. They come and see me, and ask me out to dinner and drinks. I've got Morgan to look after the garden, and Mrs Morgan to clean, and cook me one hot meal a day. I don't need anyone extra, except when I entertain, which is not often. One hears of people who engage foreign couples. They eat you out of house and home, and steal your silver. It's simply not worth it.'

'As long as you're reasonably comfortable,' said Charles.

The food wasn't the only thing that could be improved. Marian had remarked this morning that the bedroom was dusty and the bathroom hadn't been touched since their last visit. Mrs Morgan, without Dolly to chivvy her, was getting slovenly. But it would be no good passing this on. Ted was unworried about domestic standards. Eager to get outdoors and see what damage the blizzard had done to his garden, he was now putting on his boots, a woollen scarf, a felt hat and an ancient Burberry.

Charles excused himself on account of his incipient cold. Sitting alone at the kitchen table, he remembered how pathetically grateful Boo had been for her meal. It had been a treat for her, a banquet, and she had shown her gratitude in the most natural way, in love and kisses. She had been so exciting in bed yesterday, so adventurous. He was prepared to admit that he had led her on. It had been his best performance with her so far, perhaps his best ever. How cuddlesome she was, how soft her golden hair!

Poor darling. Because she was young and pretty and unattached, people gossipped, of course they did. Other women were naturally suspicious of her. Not to put too fine a point upon it, he thought it highly likely that Celia Chase was responsible for this idle rumour. Having an affair with Quentin Jones? How utterly ridiculous!

He drove to the village to get the newspapers, and spent the rest of the day indoors. Marian took the horse out again after lunch. Charles made up the living room fire and dozed in an armchair. The afternoon dragged on. He was longing to get away, back to London and the comforts he was used to. At last, when they'd had tea and biscuits which Ted said would keep the cold out, they were on their way, safely inside the Bentley with the blessed heating full on. It was getting dark as they headed cautiously along the Roman road, where the snow still lay deep.

'Ted is a dear,' said Marian. 'I wish I could help him. I mean, to get the house properly cleaned and have decent food. But I don't want to upset anybody.'

'Yes, darling.' Driving faster when they got on to the A3, where traffic had dispersed the snow, Charles went on thinking about Boo. She was facing the world on her own, at the mercy of such unsatisfactory specimens as Quentin Jones. Unfortunately he himself could do nothing about it, he was married and that was that. He didn't much like the picture of himself as the opportunist lover, having it off with a pretty girl and contributing to her problems rather than solving them. Fortunately no one knew about his involvement except Marian. And she had been angelic about it. He'd told her that it was over, and she'd believed him. This was not completely honest on his part. He was going to drop Boo, of course, but not immediately. The affair would end by a process of gradual disengagement, seeing less of her and finally not seeing her at all. Not in bed that is to say.

'I think we've passed the place,' said Marian, jolting him out of his reverie.

'Ah, the Mini. I hadn't forgotten. darling. We'll double back at the next roundabout.'

'But I looked, and I didn't see it.'

'It's probably horribly dirty, splashed with mud. Camouflaged.'

'But it was white to start with. You'd think it would show up, wouldn't you.'

It was a dual carriage-way section. They reached the roundabout, turned round and drove southwards again. The Bentley's headlights lit up the lay-by. They drew in and stopped. There were a lot of tyre tracks in the slush, and footmarks, but no Mini.

'I don't believe it,' said Marian. 'Darling, do you suppose the police towed it away?'

'We'll have to find out, won't we,' said Charles. 'What a bore.'

'I'm sorry, darling. Whatever happens, I must get to Wimbledon and see that Mimsy's all right with the new nurse. I don't want her to get miserable and confused. I must check, darling. I promised.'

'As you say. But I've got a bloody awful cold coming on, and I want to get home and get to bed so that I'm fit tomorrow. We'll report the Mini to the police, and hope for the best. How long will we have to stay with the great-aunt?'

'Fifteen minutes will do, darling. I'm sorry if it's a bore.'

Mimsy had clung on to the fact that Marian would be bringing Charles to see her on their way home. She couldn't remember where they had been, but it was for the weekend. And now it was Sunday. She said 'Sunday' to herself several times, so that she didn't forget..

It was a long wait but at last they arrived. She was delighted to see Charles again. She held out her hand and he kissed it. Then Marian began a long story about leaving her car in the snow, and the car was a Mimsy. How confusing! The Mimsy had been stolen, Marian said. The snow had melted, and when they got back to where they had left it, it simply wasn't there!

A little later Mimsy realised that the car was a Mini, of course.

Fortunately she hadn't said anything and made a fool of herself. Charles and Marian had gone to the nearest police station and reported it. It wasn't a valuable car, but it would be inconvenient not having it. This sort of thing happened far too often these days. Charles put it down to six years of Labour misrule.

Marian poured glasses of wine for everyone, then she and Kiwi sat talking. Mimsy was glad of the wine, because it had been a tiring day, what with Kiwi arriving and David saying goodbye, and that stupid woman from next door coming in when she wasn't wanted. She wondered if the tiredness was a side-effect of the pills she was taking. She was quite relieved when the visitors left.

He was called Charles, Marian's husband. A good-looking man with nice manners. They had looked for the Mini and it wasn't there. Mimsy smiled, thinking about her mistake.

'Not a Mimsy,' she told Kiwi. 'A Mini.'

'That's right,' said Kiwi. 'Someone took their car? One day my Dad and my brother had this real strange thing happen?' Off she went with a long story about sheep, and what nice animals they are, the wool is the best thing for warmth because it is natural. New Zealand has this temperate climate so sometimes your sheep can be grazing under palm trees, imagine that. One day her Dad and her brother left the truck in this grove of palm trees and went down to the beach for a swim, and when they came back the truck had disappeared, they never saw it again. The police watched out for it all over New Zealand, they had no luck.

Mimsy enjoyed the story. 'Thank you,' she said. 'I like.'

She closed her eyes and fell asleep for a moment, then woke with a start. How horrible! She had just had a vivid dream about something quite disgusting, which she wanted to forget. It was her dead baby, motionless, very pale, floating in a wintry mist. His eyes were open, looking at her. His mouth was open, screaming.

'Kiwi!' she cried. 'I fright! Fright!'

'All rightee?' said Kiwi, coming to hold her hand. She had seen this sort of thing before. Her cases were mostly geriatric terminal. They often got like this towards the end. 'Tell you what, when it's bedtime I'll bring my stuff and sleep by you, right here on the floor? Then you won't be lonely?' She smiled in her friendly way and took the patient's pulse. The doctor was coming first thing in the morning. She'd got his number by the 'phone just in case.

'I fright,' moaned Mimsy. 'Don't like.' She would stay awake all night rather than see that miserable little ghost again. He didn't exist, he didn't matter. She rejected those shameful memories of her life in Paris, the baby and afterwards, when she sank into the depths of poverty and despair. She went on the street. She was a fallen woman, a prostitute. A piece of flesh that didn't matter.

There had been better times since. She remembered the early days with Cecil, the strong attraction she felt for him the first time she went to his studio. She had introduced herself as Mademoiselle Mimi Masson, which was her professional name. he didn't know that she was English and had addressed her in French. She had replied in English, to his surprise. Over several sittings she had confided in him, telling him about her affair with François and how she had born a child who died of influenza. What a horrible memory!

Cecil had intelligence, humanity and good looks. Yes, he was a handsome man with a fine profile, beautiful hands and feet, the body of a Greek god. He practised healthy exercise and ate fresh fruit and salads every day, long before the general trend started. She had learned so much from him. He had introduced her to well-known artists and writers, advanced thinkers, people of intelligence and distinction. He had given her books to read, surrounded her with fine paintings and furniture, dressed her in beautiful clothes.

I am so grateful to Cecil.

I have had a stroke.

'Poor old thing,' said Charles as they got back into the Bentley. 'Not making much sense, is she.'

'But Kiwi is capable, don't you think,' said Marian. 'And Mimsy seems to like her. And thank you for being so super about everything, darling.'

They drove away, heading for Putney Bridge. Neither of them said anything for a while. Marian was thinking about Dave. She had telephoned him at midday, from the privacy of the estate office, and caught him before he left for Pimlico. He was so good to talk to. She felt warm all through afterwards. Tomorrow he'd be gone, she'd be back to ordinary life again. Charles had confessed to a naughtiness with Boo Carey. He'd been honest, that was the important thing, and it was over. And she did adore him actually. Things would be better for them now.

Charles was still thinking about Boo. It was difficult to decide where the truth lay. Had he been deceived by her, or had she been maligned by irresponsible female chatter? He'd be seeing her on Wednesday anyway, a day which had become something of a fixture in their affair. It might be an occasion to mention to her that people were gossiping. Oh, sweetie, she would say. What on earth can they be saying about little me? Well, they're saying that you are having an affair with Quentin Jones.

That was as far ahead as he could reasonably plan. He rehearsed it several times. My affair with you is completely secret, Boo. I haven't divulged it to a soul and don't intend to. It is a private matter between the two of us.

This would be a white lie. Boo would be far from pleased if she knew that he had told Marian. There was no need to upset her unnecessarily.

'Darling. I'm going to need a car this week,' said Marian. 'And for the foreseeable future. I have to visit Mimsy, that's a family duty. And anyway I'm rather fond of her I don't want to use this. No, really darling.' They both smiled at the thought. The Bentley wasn't an everyday car, for going shopping and visiting the sick. Today had been an exception. It was for driving to the country for weekends, for Ascot, Henley and Glyndebourne.

'We'd better get you a new one then. But not another Mini. There are too many of them about, that's the trouble. The yobboes take them off to their secret garages, re-spray, new number plates, put them on the market in some grotty suburb, cash on the nail, no questions asked. You wouldn't recognise it as yours unless you got a chance of looking at the engine serial number.'

'Well, I'll work something out, darling. I don't want you to bother. I'll hire a car if necessary. Who knows, the police might telephone in the morning to say they've found it. I could go to Mimsy's by public transport. But such a waste of time, it would take hours, and I'd have to walk up from the station in this ghastly weather. They say we might be having more snow.'

Charles thought of Boo, snow falling, walking to work at Harrods in her high-heeled boots and short fur coat. Poor girl, it was really rather pathetic.

Mimsy sat upright in her chair. She blinked rapidly now and then, to keep her eyes comfortable. She mustn't go to sleep in case the dead baby appeared again.

Kiwi brought her soup and toast, but she wasn't hungry. Kiwi had a proper meal. There was a smell of bacon, and coffee. Later Mimsy could see her in the kitchen, clearing up. She was a capable girl. She had asked if she could watch television afterwards, because it was so good in the UK, better than in New Zealand. Mimsy thought she might stay up and watch with her, rather than going to bed. It would be easier to keep her eyes open.

This was a comedy programme, Kiwi said. After the News, some of which was unpleasant, there was a film about a detective. Mimsy couldn't follow the story, the pictures moved too fast. By mistake she fell asleep briefly, but it was all right. When she opened her eyes the baby was disappearing over to one side. Having Kiwi there had scared him off. Then Kiwi said it was getting late, time they went to bed.

'Sleep by me,' said Mimsy.

Kiwi went and fetched a pillow and blankets and arranged them on the floor.

'Pretend we're camping in New Zealand?' she said. 'We can see the Southern Cross, because we're in the southern hemisphere? The birdies are singing themselves to sleep? You know in New Zealand we have this bird called a Tui, he says Too-ee, too-ee! He is black and white, sometimes we call him the Parson Bird. Too-ee, too-ee, he says?'

Then she took Mimsy to the bathroom, washed her and helped her clean her teeth. Mimsy was proud of her teeth, all her own. She had always had good teeth.

'I'm going to sleep in my clothes?' said Kiwi. 'I often do when I'm camping? We'll leave this light on? Pretend it's the moon?'

A sudden fearful thought struck Mimsy. 'Snakes?'

'Not in New Zealand,' said Kiwi. 'We don't have them, not a single one?' Then she lay down and made herself comfortable. She looked up at Mimsy from her place on the floor and smiled. 'I'm right here if you need me? Goodnight.'

'Night,' said Mimsy. She felt peaceful and unafraid with the strong Kiwi lying by her bed like a faithful dog.

Thinking about the Parson Bird, she remembered that she had not prayed for a long time, so she put her hands together and said the Lord's Prayer.

Time passed, and perhaps she had been asleep. She thought, but perhaps it was a dream, that Kiwi was walking about, going out to the hall, then coming back and standing quietly at her side. She wanted to say something, but she couldn't make her voice work. It was that sort of dream. It was most inconvenient. Then something else happened, like a violent storm all over her body. It reminded her of her stroke, when she had found herself lying on the floor. But this time it was much worse, such a terrible headache and a painful punch in the ribs, as if something had hit her. Probably what had happened was that she had turned over in her sleep and fallen out of bed. That was how it had been before, she remembered it clearly now.

No, that was wrong. She was still in her bed, not on the floor. Kiwi was there. She said in her cheerful voice, 'The doctor will be here soon? And I phoned Dave?'

Mimsy wanted to say, 'I'm sorry to be such a trouble. My head is sore, and my chest.' But it was too difficult. She knew the words, but she couldn't say them.

The doctor came, and she was afraid he was going to knock her out with an injection and send her away to hospital. She thought she heard him telling Kiwi that she would be better off in hospital, and she tried to shriek and kick her feet but nothing happened. She tried to speak to Kiwi with her eyes, to say she didn't want to go. Kiwi was an intelligent girl, she just said, 'Don't you worry? Dave's here now, don't you worry?'

David walked straight in and put his arms round her and said, 'Okay, Mimsy. Nobody's going to take you away. Okay now.'

The doctor didn't dare argue with Dave. He was a good boy. He went on talking to her, though she couldn't understand him very well. His voice was getting fainter.

Soon afterwards there was an explosion in her head, without pain and wonderful to watch with curtains of colour changing from ruby red to orange, yellow and green, then violet and deep, deep blue. How beautiful that deep blue was, unlike anything in the northern hemisphere. Cecil would have been so interested. She could see the Southern Cross now and many other strange stars. Finally came a dazzling white light, which was the moon rising over New Zealand, where she had never been before. She couldn't move, but there was no need. She was safe now. They couldn't take her anywhere.

It was just a question of finding the person she knew, she couldn't remember the name but it would come back soon. There were other people with her, waiting patiently, trying to remember names, looking at each other as if to say, 'No, it's not you. Nor you.' She was tired, of course, and she was beginning to wonder if she had the strength to wait for the person whose name she couldn't remember, and who was perhaps looking for her, wondering where she was and why she was so late.

Then suddenly she heard his voice.

'Mimsy, here!'

She turned round and there he was, her brother Tom back from South Africa. It was a miracle that they'd found each other, because there was such a crowd, soldiers, sailors, children, wives and sweethearts. All of them were young, strong and cheerful. There were no old people here, nobody sick, or sad or poor.

'Mimsy!' He was waving his cap. As he made his way through the mass of people she could see that his khaki uniform was as smart as the day he first put it on. He was sunburned and fit, and his eyes shone with

80

happiness. People stood aside for him.

'Let the young man pass,' they said, good-natured and smiling.

He thanked them, came towards her and took her hands in his.

'Together again, Mim. Just like old times.'

'Oh Tom, how glad I am to see you!'

It was the day of the Diamond Jubilee, a beautiful day, cloudless and bright. She was wearing her Sunday muslin with a pink sash, white stockings and white kid boots. Her hair, well brushed, hung down her back, and her straw hat had a wreath of daisies. They knew the Queen must be very near because there was a stir of excitement in the crowd. Boys and girls started waving their Union Jacks, and fathers held up the smaller children so that they could see over the heads of the crowd. The band began to play, and the noise of cheering swelled to a magnificent roar, almost drowning the music. The beginning of the procession came into view, first a troop of horse, stirrups and spurs catching the sunlight, then the heralds in scarlet and gold, and then the royal carriage, drawn by six big grey horses. Everybody cheered and shouted. 'The Queen! God save the Queen!'

Her Majesty sat calm and dignified in the carriage, bowing to this side and that. How splendid she looked in her black silk dress embroidered with jet, a tiny bonnet with a veil of lace on her white hair. The carriage was abreast of them now, and Her Majesty ordered the coachman to stop. Tom bowed and Mimsy made her best curtsey.

'Tell those two young people to join me,' the Queen said to the postillion.

The door was opened for them, and the step let down. Tom signed to Mimsy that she should go first, and he followed, bowing again before he sat down. They were facing the dear Queen, and she was looking at them with a gentle smile. Her skin was pale and very fine. Her eyes were bright blue.

'Drive on,' she ordered. And together they passed through the crowds, away from the noise, to a place where all was peace.

God save the Queen.

It was three in the morning.

'Mercifully quick,' said the doctor. 'Such determination, one had to admire her. I'll just make out the certificate.'

'She was no trouble?' said Kiwi.

They left Dave alone. He sat by the bed, holding Mimsy's hand, which was still warm and soft. He kissed her cheek, stroked her hair.

Goodbye, you wonderful woman. Such style you had, such humour and generosity. You were mother, best friend, counsellor. You opened doors for me. You gave me daylight and fresh air. And you introduced me to Marian. We had an affair, Mimsy, something I will never forget. I know you will understand. Passion is a creative force, you used to say. Thank you for everything, Mimsy.

II

Changes In Format

1   Monday to Thursday

The telephone was ringing. Marian's first thought was that they had overslept. Celia always rang at nine on Monday.

Green numbers shining from the bedside clock said five past seven, which was much too early. Something was wrong.

'Hallo?'

Charles turned over, red-faced, nose stuffed up. 'Probably the police. They've found the Mini.'

Not the police. It was Dave, so sad, so flat. Mimsy had died in the night, or rather early this morning. Mercifully quick, she seemed not to suffer. He was in Pimlico now, he'd cancelled his flight. There were a lot of things to arrange. If Marian was free, if she could give a hand with the organising, he would be so grateful.

She managed to say, 'Dave, I'm so sorry. So.' Then she began to cry, which was oafish of her, and not helpful.

Charles took the receiver. 'Hallo. Charles Broome-Vivier. I gather it's bad news. Massive stroke, I see. We were there last night, she seemed cheerful though not saying much. Marian is upset, naturally. She'd become very fond of her great-aunt.'

Marian recovered and took the telephone back. 'Dave, I'm ready to help. We'll have to contact the relations, and organise the funeral.' Just a body now, which had been Mimsy. 'But I don't have a car any more. Stolen, such a nuisance.'

'Chin up,' said Dave. 'My friends here are just the sort you need when life gets difficult. They've lent me a car. I'll pick you up at nine, if that's all right. The undertakers don't open till then anyway.' She wondered if he was giving the pirate smile. 'Sure you can spare the time?'

'Of course. It's family, isn't it. She was my...'

'Okay, see you later.'

She felt like crying again, but only because she was so happy. Dave wasn't leaving for Saudi Arabia after all. They would have more time together. He was coming to fetch her at nine.

Charles's cold was worse. He couldn't take the day off, because he was due to chair a meeting at ten, code-named Mer/FCE. This was one of several sub-committees set up to deal with problems related to the merger, in this case Foreign Currency Experts. They would inherit twice as many as they needed. Some, at the higher level, could be offered alternative posts. But what to do with the surplus? You couldn't boot them all out.

Marian offered him breakfast in bed, since there was time to spare. He accepted without hesitation, arranged all the pillows on his side of the bed and sat up, waiting for the treat. 'It's my one weakness, darling,' he said. 'As you know.'

She knew. She went down to the kitchen and prepared orange juice, cereal with cream and brown sugar, two softly boiled eggs, toast, butter, marmalade and coffee. She had to make two trips to get everything upstairs. They had an invalid table which Charles had bought specially for this sort of emergency. She spread it with a lacy cloth and set out the goodies. Then she went downstairs again and brought up the newspapers and letters.

She blew him a kiss and went into the bathroom. She had a hot, perfumed bath. She powdered and deodorised herself. She still had, in a cupboard of soaps, creams, scents and depilatories, a diaphragm left from the days when she didn't want to conceive. She inserted it, with spermicidal ointment, because she was going to spend the day with her lover. She dressed, not in jeans which might seem disrespectful to the dead, but in a tweed skirt, black sweater and tights, black boots.

Eight o'clock. Everything was going to happen at nine. Mrs Briggs would arrive, Dave would come to fetch her in a borrowed car, Charles would leave for the City, and Celia would telephone.

Charles finished his breakfast and spread out the newspapers. Threats of industrial unrest all over the country, and Heath perhaps not the right man for the job. Someone would have to clobber the Unions, the sooner the better, or the bloody Reds would bring the country to its knees. And that wouldn't help the working classes much, would it.

'You'll have to put an entry in *The Times*, darling,' he said. 'In the Deaths section.'

'Oh yes, darling. I hadn't thought.'

'And you'd better put it in the *Telegraph* too. First speak to your friend Dave, get the funeral fixed, Putney Crematorium or whatever, then ring me at the office, leave a message if I'm not available. Date of birth, died peacefully, much mourned et cetera. Place and time of funeral, where to send flowers or donations. I'll do the rest.'

'Thank you so much, darling.'

She felt quite fluttery at the thought of seeing Dave again. She wished Charles would hurry up, get dressed and go. She hoped that Briggsie would come early, and Dave a little late.

Five to nine, she could telephone Celia and get that done. No answer for quite a while. The Adorables must be playing up, or the *au pair* had gone out on a date and stayed the night. Let's hope Celia wasn't ill. The part-time assistant didn't come in till eleven on a Monday.

Celia answered at last, breathless. She must have just got in.

'Celia, it's me, Marian. Something rather sad has happened, and I want to talk to you about something else anyway. Oh dear, my great-aunt who was really rather sweet...'

'Oh, I am so sorry, Marian. You mean she...'

'Yes, she died in the early hours. The Dave character was there and the doctor and the nurse Kiwi, who was absolutely super. And I'll have to arrange the funeral, telephone the relatives, goodness knows. I can hardly think where to start. And Celia, about...' Charles, dressed and ready to go, was coming downstairs. She lowered her voice. 'What you said about someone, it's all settled. I'll tell you later. Anyway.' Louder now, for Charles to hear. 'I won't be able to come in today. It's awful really, I didn't think I cared, but somehow...' She sniffed a bit. 'I'll ring you later, if I have a moment. Charles sends his love, he's just off to the City. He's got an absolutely ghastly cold, poor man.'

Celia, thinking serves him bloody well right, said, 'Poor man. Marian, telephone me any time, I mean it. So sorry about the death and absolutely fascinated about the other, you know. Bye.'

At that moment, enter by the front door Mrs Briggs with Dave. They had introduced themselves on the doorstep. Briggsie had heard the news and put on a long face. The Lord giveth and the Lord taketh away.

Dave, in a borrowed winter coat which hung loosely on him, shook hands with Charles. Charles, through his nose, said he had to go to the City, deepest sympathy, anything he could do to help, please let him know. He waved goodbye and went.

Marian gave silent thanks. 'Dave, come into the kitchen. You found a parking place? Super. Excuse the mess. Coffee?'

He took off the overcoat. He was wearing a dark suit, a grey shirt and a black tie. The suit was well-made, a perfect fit.

'Coffee, please,' he said. 'I do apologise for involving you. But I have to admit I don't know where to start, and you're such a good organiser. I could say bossy.'

Mrs Briggs shared the joke, adding that bossy or not Mrs Broome-Vivier knew how to get things done. Privately she had noticed her employer's extra pink cheeks and eyes shining like stars. Behold, Satan enters the Rich Man's Castle. Spurn Temptation. Follow Ye the Way of the Lord. She took herself off, with a selection of brushes, dusters and polish, saying she would start upstairs.

As soon as she was out of sight, Marian heaved a big sigh. 'Oh Dave!'

He said, standing close while she poured the coffee, 'We might have time for another kiss after all.' Her hands trembled as she took the two mugs to the table. They sat down close to each other and were kissing passionately when they heard Mrs Briggs coming downstairs again. They separated abruptly.

'Just getting my Hoover,' said Briggsie, adding to herself, since she'd seen what kind of a kiss it was, 'Whore of Babylon. Thou shalt perish in Eternal Fire.'

'We'd better get organised,' said Marian when they were alone. 'But it's going to be difficult. Difficult to concentrate, I mean.'

Mimsy had made some arrangements in advance. Dave knew about these in a general way, her solicitor would have the details. She had reserved a plot in the churchyard at St George's, where Mimsy's sister Katie and her lover Cecil were buried. She had chosen the hymns for her funeral service, and a poem to be read. She had asked for a reception in the flat afterwards, and no public reading of her Will. She wanted family flowers only, and donations to the West Wimbledon Children's Home, which was where Dave had spent the first ten years of his life.

Kiwi was still in the flat. She had told Dave that she didn't mind being alone with a body, it was part of the job. She would stay until midday, which was what the contract said. Marian said they'd let her sleep a while. Dave should telephone Mimsy's solicitor first. He tried, but it was too early. He left a message with the secretary.

Then he telephoned the vicar of St George's, who was distressed to hear of Miss Mason's death. She had been such a positive person. He had visited her during her illness, and his wife had arranged some voluntary help for her, which unfortunately was misunderstood, though meant in the most Christian way. Ah, the funeral. Yes, he could bury her on Wednesday at midday. The organist would be available and would get the choir together. Rather short notice, but he would do his best. Details of music and readings to be discussed later, this evening perhaps. Dave thanked him. Yes, it was indeed a sad loss. He would be flying back to Riyadh on Thursday.

'So telephone and book your flight,' said Marian.

'Yes, wild Marian.' He gave her the pirate look.

She got her clipboard, made a list and was soon crossing things off. Did the porter know? Yes, he did. What about service sheets? Dave knew of a local printer.

'Try the solicitor again, Dave. Or should I start on the relatives? No, I think I'd better telephone Charles's office first, he'll put notices in *The Times* and the *Telegraph*. If that's all right.'

Charles, excusing himself briefly from the Mer/FCE sub-committee, came to the telephone to get the details he needed. 'Wednesday morning will suit me very well. Yes, of course I'm coming. I may not be able to stay for the coffee afterwards. Oh, a buffet lunch. Well, I'll grab something, then get back here. I've got a lot to do, and this bloody cold. *Times* and *Telegraph*, leave it to me.'

'Bless you, darling,' said Marian.

Her mother was next on the list. 'Mummy, it's Marian. I'm afraid I have some bad news. Poor Mimsy died in the night, a massive stroke .'

For once Emily didn't grumble. It wasn't that she was rejoicing at Mimsy's death, in fact she seemed genuinely sorrowful. Possibly she was looking forward to the funeral, followed by a lunch organised by her daughter, who had helped her eccentric great-aunt up to the last while others had ignored her and left her to die, unattended for all they knew or cared. She undertook to telephone Harold, who would spread the news and might offer to drive her up. Her own car was, of course, too old, she would get a new one as soon as she could afford it. She wouldn't stay the night in London, thank you. She had a bridge party the next day, she couldn't let her friends down.

'Thank goodness that's done,' said Marian, crossing Mummy off.

Eleven o'clock. Dave's parking meter was running out of money, and Mrs Briggs was set on doing the kitchen. They decided to pack up and continue the operation in Wimbledon.

Let not Evil enter into your heart, Briggsie said to herself. Trust in the Lord.

Marian collected things for lunch, including a bottle of wine, and went away with Dave in his borrowed car. It was an old MG with wire wheels. He drove as if he were racing, weaving in and out of traffic, getting to Wimbledon faster than she had thought possible.

They found Kiwi having a large breakfast. She was all packed up, ready to go back to her digs in Clapham. Then the undertakers arrived, followed by the porter and his wife, who seemed to feel obliged to see Mimsy off the premises. The woman from the flat next door wasn't going to miss anything, and came in as well. She would certainly come to the funeral, Miss Mason had been such a character.

After her came a man with a briefcase, who was greeted by Dave as an old friend. This was Mimsy's solicitor, John Keble. Marian had a stereotype solicitor in mind, elderly and dry as dust. John was certainly no more than thirty-five, agreeable and very efficient. He went through the arrangements with the undertakers, and cleared up some points with Dave. Marian asked him if he'd like to stay and share their lunch, but he said Thank you, no. He had an appointment with a client at twelve-thirty, they would be having a sandwich together. She couldn't help thinking that if he had said Yes it would have meant less time alone with Dave.

The chief undertaker emerged from the bedroom to ask if the deceased had made any special requests. Dave produced an oriental embroidery which was to cover her, and a prayer book which had belonged to her brother Tom. Later Dave and Marian, as relatives, were invited to view the deceased, and were accompanied by Kiwi, the porter and his wife, the neighbour, and John the solicitor.

The bedroom curtains were closed. In the subdued glow of the bedside lamp Mimsy's face was like ivory. Her hands were folded over the prayer book. They stood and looked, then the undertakers drew the embroidered cloth up and over her face, covered the stretcher on which she lay with some of their own wrappings, and took her away.

John Keble put his papers back in his briefcase and said goodbye. Kiwi's luggage was in the hall, ready to go, so the others had to shuffle round it to get to the door, expressing condolences, asking to be allowed to help if help was required, bumping into each other, apologising. Dave and Marian gave Kiwi some warm hugs and kisses, thanked her and said goodbye. They had ordered a taxi to take her to Clapham. It was now waiting for her in the forecourt down below. They saw her into the lift, waved as she sank out of sight, went into the flat and closed the door.

They were alone at last. He kissed her, a kiss of sadness and gratitude. Then, like people who have settled into a habit which suits them, they had drinks, and lunch, and wine. Afterwards they arranged the spare room for serious love-making, the mattress on the floor, pillows spread around, blankets and sheets loosely laid over the top, for warmth without constriction. He noticed that her urgency was less than at the weekend. There was time for adventure, in which she was at first the leader. Then he took the challenge and flew with her, so it seemed, into the pearly white sky of the desert, just before dawn. So strange, so convincing.

Resting, he wanted to say, 'I love you, I always will.' But this would be a burden for her. There was no usefulness in his love. He said instead, 'You're smiling.'

'Just happy. Enjoying getting to know you. You were a mystery at first. The Dark Horse from Saudi Arabia.'

'I was terribly rude to you on the telephone. Can you forgive me?'

'I already have. Tell me more about yourself, Dark Horse.'

Holding her contented body close to his, he told her about his life with Mimsy and Cecil, a strict upbringing with emphasis on art, good books and healthy exercise. He remembered walks on the Common and in Richmond Park, Cecil wearing a flowing cape and a wide-brimmed hat,

Mimsy in a tweed coat with fur collar and cuffs, a Liberty scarf wrapped round her head. He felt embarrassed by them, especially at school. They were not like other parents, and he perhaps was not their ideal son. Mathematics was his strong subject. He was numerate, not creative. He liked music, which was something neither of them enjoyed. He sang in the choir, and taught himself to play popular songs on the piano. They would have preferred him to spend time drawing and painting. In his teens, inevitably, he argued with them, refused to go to art galleries, went out with friends they didn't like. He wanted a motor-bike. As soon as he was old enough he bought a second-hand one and spent days taking it to pieces and putting it together again. They protested, more and more feebly. He was clever, he worked hard. It was just that his interests were different. The tension eased when he went to Cambridge, to read Mechanical Sciences. His spare time, which was limited, he spent singing, in large groups and small, on stage, in college, wherever.

'I like singing,' Marian said. 'I was in the choir at Abbey Mead. We did part songs, like "The Silver Swan". And bits from "The Messiah". And productions of Gilbert and Sullivan.'

'One day we'll sing together.'

'Not one day. Now. Just a minute.' She got up, put on her black lace brassière, wrapped his shirt round her lower half, and tied his black tie round her forehead. 'Oompah, oompah, stoof it up your joompah!' she chanted, wriggling her hips and making Egyptian gestures with her hands. 'Oh Pharaoh, what is your command?'

Dave lay giggling on the mattress. 'You know any Cole Porter, slave? Or Gershwin?'

They sang *Night and Day* together, then *Smoke Gets in Your Eyes*. The slave invented beautiful sinuous dances to please Pharaoh, and joined her clear soprano with his fairly high baritone. Mummy had all these old records, the slave said, she and her friend Celia used to play them in the holidays. Such fun. Then they sang *The Silver Swan*, the slave as soprano and Pharaoh putting in a base line. Then Pharaoh begged the slave to lie with him again, so she took off her dressing-up clothes and joined him. They had more sex, then they talked.

'Did you ever go looking for your real parents?' she asked.

'I tried. I was in my late teens, maybe sixteen. Mimsy and Cecil helped me, but we got nowhere. I was a foundling. That's old-fashioned, isn't it. Okay, somebody left me outside the orphanage. It wasn't actually snowing, but it was very cold. I might have died. But I'm strong.'

'I know, I know.' She kissed his strong arm.

'I couldn't get over the fact that I wasn't wanted. A man and a woman copulated and produced me, didn't care what happened afterwards. Perhaps my father didn't know of my existence. And my mother, had she come from abroad, perhaps? There were no documents, no birth certificate, no record of a missing baby. I was warmly dressed. The clothes were new, from shops in SW1. So I was a Knightsbridge child, abandoned in Wimbledon.'

'Poor little baby.' She pulled the blanket closer round him, considering the word 'copulate'. She remembered 'Birth, copulation and death' in *Murder In The Cathedral,* which they had performed at Abbey Mead. According to the dictionary, 'copulation' meant a conjunction. 'To copulate' meant to have sexual intercourse. It had an animal sound, degrading, brutish. She and Celia usually said 'made love' or 'had sex', or 'had it with'. Like Boo Carey and Quentin Jones. Mummy said 'had an affair', or 'went to bed with'. Men said 'fucked' when they were with other men, particularly if they didn't like the people they were talking about.

Dave had fallen asleep. She looked at him carefully so that she would remember him. It had been such an adventure, so very special. After a while she slipped away and went to telephone Celia.

'Celia, can we talk? I'm in Wimbledon. It's been so emotional, I'm absolutely shattered. I never saw a dead person before. They've taken the body away, she looked so peaceful. The funeral is on Wednesday in the local church, and I'm doing lunch here afterwards. It will be about twenty people, hot soup, something cold to follow. And Celia, I'm not worried about Boo Carey, not any more.'

'But honestly, Marian, you've got to do something. Boo and Charles had lunch on Saturday at The Welcome Sole. I know, because Quentin Jones saw her there, and he's ever so much in love with her, and he could hardly bear it. Charles was kissing her hand, and then they went off together in a taxi, and I saw them and they saw me.'

'Celia, I know all about it. He told me about seeing you and Emma and Rupert, and he confessed about Boo. And it's over, thank goodness. He's promised. And we were absolute lovers on Saturday night, it was super.'

Whatever made her say that? Covering up for Charles, or for herself? How strange.

'I'm so glad then,' said Celia doubtfully.

'And Celia, the girl from Queen Bee was absolutely super, she was so relaxed. She was with Mimsy when she died. It was three in the morning.'

'What about the Dave character?'

'He's asleep. Worn out, poor man. He's flying back to Saudi Arabia after the funeral. I'm taking over the organising. Charles has been absolutely super, he did the announcements, and he's coming to the funeral. And Celia, I forgot to tell you, in that snowstorm on Friday I had to leave the Mini, I would never have made it to Broome. And I'd caught up Charles, because he'd had a flat tyre, luckily the AA fixed it. So we went the rest of the way in the Bentley, and when we came back last night and got to the lay-by the Mini simply wasn't there! Absolutely vanished!'

'Golly!'

'I was absolutely stunned. We reported it to the police, Charles says I must get a new car, but I might hire one just while I'm doing the funeral.'

'Marian, you must have mine. Honestly, I don't need it until the weekend.'

'I wouldn't dream of it. Absolutely not. Look, I've got to go now. I'll do tomorrow morning as usual. A rest cure by comparison! Bye for now.'

'Bye,' said Celia. Later, closing the shop after a successful day, two cocktail dresses and a suit and three silk shirts, she felt that something wasn't properly explained, but she didn't know what. As for Charles saying his affair with Boo was over, that simply couldn't be true. From what Quentin had said it was still sizzling hot, absolutely steamy.

Poor Marian, this really shouldn't happen to such a nice person.

Dave woke up and Marian made tea. She had dusted the dining room, found a cloth for the table, and set out plates and cutlery for up to twenty-five people. The silver wasn't very clean. She said she would bring flowers tomorrow, and some of the food.

'And we'll have our last kiss,' said Dave.

'Not till the afternoon. It's my morning in the boutique. Then I have shopping to do. Oh, bother the Mini. I don't know how I'll manage without a car.'

He looked better after his sleep. Now he became animated. 'You want a car, what sort? How much do you want to spend? Do you mind second-hand?'

'Anything. It's just for every day. Something reliable,'

'Okay. Tomorrow morning I'll find you a car. I'll come and pick you up. Not till after lunch? What a pity. Two o'clock then. This friend of mine is in the car business. I've known him for years, he was at school with me. Any colour preference?'

'Dave, I don't mind. Something bright.'

'Okay, I'll do some research in the morning, and in the afternoon we'll make passionate love.'

He drove her home in the MG with wire wheels. They kissed goodbye like old friends, and he went on to Pimlico.

It was awfully late, she had to hurry to get dinner ready. Poor Charles, with that dreadful cold. He'd want a whisky as soon as he got home.

Tuesday, Marian's morning at Marcellina. She telephoned Celia, who was at home.

'Celia, he drives like an absolute maniac! One hand on the wheel, the other changing gear like mad. Brrm, brrm! And he says he has a friend in the car business, he's going to find me a second-hand car.'

'Super. Is he a bit of an oaf after all, second-hand cars and that sort of thing?'

'Well, yes. I suppose he is.' Why was she lying like this, to her best friend? What was she trying to hide? 'But he's my foster second-cousin, or something, so you have to be nice about him.'

'I wish you'd produce him.'

'I would, but he seems to be tied up most of the time. Probably goes to pubs with his car-dealer friends. I'll be in touch. Love to Victor and the Adorables.'

Trade was brisk that morning. Marian sold several dresses and a suit. The part-time assistant arrived at midday to relieve her, and she went out to shop for food, took it home in a taxi, and ate a sandwich. Dave arrived punctually at two.

'How about a Renault?' he asked as soon as she opened the door. 'It's basic, very seventies. My friend says it's going to be the car of the year. Demonstration model, low mileage, not on the market generally as yet.'

He told her the special price he was getting, as an old friend. She was amazed, it was so inexpensive. 'It's not stolen or anything?' she asked.

Of course not, he said. It was just a question of knowing the right people. Was she going to ask Charles if it was okay to go ahead?

She didn't want to tell Dave that she was the one with the money, lots of it, to spend as she liked. She telephoned Charles. When he heard what car it was, and the price, he said Dave was a genius and could he speak to him. Marian stood by while they talked about cubic centimetres and fuel consumption. Charles spoke to her again. Surely this was a bargain, too good to miss. She said she supposed it was. 'Go for it, darling,' he said. 'You're a lucky girl.'

The lucky girl and her lover drove to a garage in Kennington, where she bought a red Renault. They drove in convoy, Renault and borrowed MG, to Wimbledon, where they unpacked the provisions for the post-funeral lunch, stowed them in the fridge, checked the arrangements in the dining room. Then they went to bed together, made passionate love, talked, kissed, copulated, rested and began again.

It was one of the happiest days Marian had ever spent. He would be gone soon, her darling Dave. But she was so glad, so grateful for what had happened. He had helped her forward into being a better individual, with a deeper understanding of sex. She was a real person now. He had done that for her.

Driving back to Pimlico, Dave felt very low. His body was limp with post-sex fatigue, and he was emotionally stressed by Mimsy's death. She was old, her time had come, and mercifully she died before she completely lost her dignity. But she was the only mother he had ever known.

He was also going to lose Marian. She had been his on a temporary basis only. That was understood. She had her house in Knightsbridge, her husband, her boutique. There was no room for him in her life. He didn't belong.

This was extremely painful, and there was nothing whatever that he could do about it.

Poor Dave. He will never meet Quentin Jones, Barbara Carey known as Boo, the influential Patrick Dearden and his red-haired wife Clarissa. He will never meet Celia Chase and her husband Victor. He will never meet the Adorables.

The window will close. He will be alone, without access.

Wednesday was dry and icy cold. The ground sparkled with frosted snow. The grave-diggers had been busy the previous day, breaking through the frozen topsoil with pick-axes, then digging deep into softer earth, dark and peaceful.

Marian had come down early in the Renault to finish preparing the lunch. Dave collected the service sheets and had last-minute consultations with the Vicar and the organist. He was going to sing with the choir, and read a sonnet by John Donne. Charles came in the Bentley, in time to accompany Marian up the aisle to the front rows, reserved for relatives. The church was otherwise rather empty, mostly old people sitting together in small groups.

After the service the congregation followed the coffin out to the graveyard and gathered round the grave, which was edged with sheets of plastic grass. Dave stood near the Vicar, ready to throw in a handful of earth. Dust to dust. Marian scattered some loose flowers. Her posy was with the other family offerings, which included a bunch of laurel and bay leaves from her mother, who said that buying flowers in the middle of winter was a waste of money. She had picked what she could find in her garden. The label read, 'For my aunt Mimsy Mason. Her memory is evergreen. From her loving niece Emily Foster.'

Afterwards there was a general move towards the flat, which was only two streets away. Nobody said goodbye, regretting that they had to get home, or back to work. Some walked, some took their cars so that they didn't have to come back later. Several local friends who had shunned Mimsy when she was confused and ill, poor old thing, had turned up to say goodbye to her.

With these, Emily, Uncle Harold and his wife, and some of Vincent's family who knew Mimsy only by hearsay, Dave and two friends who had helped swell the choir, Charles and Marian, the solicitor, the doctor, the Vicar and their wives, nearly thirty people crowded into the flat. They came up in the lift, lined up in the corridor waiting to get in, then queued in an embarrassed way outside the bathroom (Ladies), or the cloakroom in the hall (Gentlemen). Their coats and scarves covered Mimsy's bed and the bed in the spare room. They introduced themselves and edged forward, encouraged by the sight of wine bottles and plates in the dining room. Expecting sherry and sandwiches, they were delighted to find hot soup, chicken salad, French bread, dessert, cheese, coffee and plenty of wine, both red and white. Marian and the porter's wife got busy serving out the food while Dave did the drinks. Conversation became loud and cheerful. It was more like a birthday party than a wake.

Charles ate quickly and drank two glasses of wine, then said he must get back to the City. Dave saw him out to the forecourt, where they stood talking. Marian watched them from the window. Charles had opened the Bentley's bonnet, and Dave was looking inside. Then Charles got in and drove away. Dave came back upstairs.

He helped himself to wine and food. They stood together by the dining room table, people all round them, alone in their secret. She felt affection for him welling up from a source deep inside her.

'I couldn't have done this without you,' he said, lifting his glass. 'Cheers. Here's to another lunch one day, and kisses to follow.'

'Dave, someone might hear.'

'Did you like the Donne sonnet? Rather pious, one of the Holy Sonnets. Next time I'll read you one of the naughty ones. Private performance for wild Marian.'

She would never forget the way he talked, his voice, his smile. She knew him so well, although they'd only met a week ago. He was a dear

96

friend now. The more she got to know him the better he was. No disillusion, no feeling of having misjudged. He knew how to read poetry, and he'd sung with the choir.

'You're just so talented,' she said, meaning good at reading poetry, and singing. And being her lover.

Then they went round together, like the bride and groom at a wedding, saying something to each of the guests. How kind of you to come. Yes, Mimsy was a character. Dave talked for a long time to Uncle Harold and his wife, and then to Emily, who was in a surprisingly good mood. Poor Mummy, a funeral was quite a party for her.

The time passed too quickly. It was four o'clock, and everyone had gone except Dave's friends, who would be taking him back to Pimlico, and John Keble the solicitor. He said that he would be getting in touch with her, since she was a beneficiary. They would have to wait for Probate. Marian said, 'Of course,' though she wasn't quite sure what it meant. She should send him a bill for the lunch, to be paid from Mimsy's estate. Then he took off his jacket, rolled up his sleeves, and helped the rest of them with the clearing and washing up. The porter's wife took the leftovers, thank you very much.

Time to say goodbye.

'I'll come down,' Dave said. They took the lift and he held her in his arms all the way. Outside it was getting dark, and freezing again. He stood with her by the Renault, friendly and cheerful, not wanting her to get upset. She kept smiling, to please him. They told each other that they would write occasionally. She had his address. They kissed, distant foster-cousins saying goodbye after a family funeral. She urged him to go in and not get cold. And he went.

As she drove away she cried and cried, but only because it had been such a happy time.

There was a telephone message for Charles when he got back to his office. It was from Boo, in an agreed code. Dr Carey would be unable to see him this evening, he should telephone tomorrow for another appointment. He was annoyed, because this would have been the occasion for a little talk about the future of their relationship. He might also have mentioned that people were gossipping about her. Was there any truth in what they were saying? All this would have to be done in the friendliest possible way, because Boo was a sensitive little thing.

During the afternoon he forgot about her, concentrating on his assessment of the merging firm's Foreign department. He'd spotted some dead wood there, older men who were listed as employees but probably were not operative in the real sense. Their salaries were certainly out of proportion.

He worked until six-thirty, then started home. Coming out of Knightsbridge station, he thought it might be worth seeing if Boo was at home. If it was just the curse which made her put him off, no matter. She would give him a drink, and they could talk. From the far side of the road he could see that there was a light in her window, in the romantic little Victorian gable at the top of the building. He decided to go in.

There was an entry-phone, but he was able to by-pass it. An elderly resident, clutching a bulging carrier bag, was struggling to open the door. He had seen her several times before, and she seemed to think he lived here too. He held the carrier bag while she opened the door, and they went in together, into the lift and up to the third floor where she tottered out. Politely he held the metal gate back for her, said Goodnight, and went up to the fourth. This was as far as the lift went. He ran up the narrow flight of stairs which ended in Boo's front door, puffing slightly, and rang the bell, his usual signal. Pom-tiddly-om-pom, pom, pom.

He waited, thinking that this would be a nice surprise for her. Perhaps he should have brought flowers. He knew that she must be there because he could hear her moving about, perhaps putting on a negligée. And he could hear voices, which meant her television set was on as usual. She watched the thing practically non-stop.

The door opened and he got the fright of his life. It really was a nasty shock. It was not only surprising, it was horrible, disgusting and unseemly. Quentin Jones stood on the threshold, naked except for Boo's Japanese kimono which he was wearing round his lower half, sarong fashion.

Charles was so angry he could hardly speak. 'What the hell, what the bloody hell are you doing here?'

'I might ask the same of you,' said Quentin, folding his arms on his naked chest.

'How dare you!' Charles fumed. 'I've a good mind to hit you, you swine!'

'Please do.' Quentin, deadpan, dropped his arms limply to his sides. He was pathetic, all skin and bone, totally helpless, not even trying to defend himself. 'Wouldn't you like to take your overcoat off first?'

'There's no need! Put your fists up, man!' Charles caught a glimpse of Boo, wrapped in the pink eiderdown, peeking round the bedroom door, and that heated his anger to boiling point. God, what a squalid situation! Undressed, the pair of them, hardly decent, and it was Wednesday, his special day, a long-standing arrangement. Not that there were rights in

98

this world, nor any justice, when a perfectly sweet girl had to become a tart due to economic privation, to be pawed about by pathetic weaklings like Quentin Jones. How utterly sickening, poor little Boo dragged down to such depths. 'Your fists, you ninny! Come on, for God's sake!'

Slowly Quentin raised his hands and bunched them in a loose fashion. Christ, the man didn't even know how to punch, his thumbs were inside. Charles narrowed his eyes, looking for a target, choosing the middle of the fellow's chest because he didn't want to hurt him too badly. He swung, a powerful swaying back on one foot, then forward with all his weight, full force.

Pow! It should have been a contact which bruised his knuckles but at the last minute something went badly wrong, he didn't know what. He must have slipped. He'd certainly hit his head on something as he fell. The next thing he knew he was sitting on the floor.

'I'm terribly sorry about this.' Quentin Jones was kneeling beside him, wiping his face with a wet towel, while Boo looked on big-eyed. 'I should have allowed for your being so near the table. I am most frightfully sorry, I haven't had much practice with this particular throw. Here, let me give you a hand.' Gently he lifted Charles up, put him in a chair and ran a hand over the back of his head. 'There's a bump coming up, but the skin isn't broken. I think it's safe to offer you a drink. Barbara...'

'He likes neat whisky,' said Boo, and hurried to get it.

'Barbara?' muttered Charles. 'She doesn't like being called Barbara.'

'She does now that we're engaged,' said Quentin.

Engaged? The man must be joking. Charming, sophisticated, pretty little Boo engaged to this gangling publisher, who wore floppy ties and striped waistcoats, and looked so feeble and gutless? Well, admittedly he had tripped one up somehow. But that proved the point. He wasn't a gentleman. He had no idea of fair play.

Boo came back with a glass of whisky in one hand, the other holding the eiderdown modestly round her shapely little bust. 'Here you are, Charles. Please don't be cross. We want you to be our friend when we're married.'

So that was that. It must be true after all. He was hot, and sweating profusely. He had to wipe his forehead again. He accepted the whisky, lifted it to his lips and took a big swallow. He recognised the brand, poured no doubt from the bottle he'd given Boo for Christmas. 'Thank you very much,' he said. 'So I suppose it's congratulations, Jones, to you and your fiancée.'

'I didn't mean to hurt you,' Quentin insisted. 'Please believe me. I don't usually do this sort of thing, not in anger. But for Barbara.' He put his arm round her and she looked up at him with utter devotion. 'I'd do anything for Barbara. Just anything. And please call me Quentin.'

Charles decided that there was nothing for it but to be generous in defeat. 'It is just possible that there was a misunderstanding. I apologise. I don't blame you for knocking me down. Quentin,' he added.

'No, really, Charles. Let me explain. I didn't knock you down. I allowed you to fall. You see the difference? No force was involved. It's a knack, and if you'll allow me I'll show you how it's done.'

'Thank you, no. Not this evening. I don't blame you for allowing me to fall, as you put it. And I wish you and Boo, I mean Barbara, every happiness in the married state.' He drained the whisky and got up carefully. 'And now I think I'll go home.'

'I would see you out,' said Quentin. 'But I'm not suitably dressed.' He indicated the kimono, which was working loose. He pulled it up, wrapped it more securely, then stuck his hip out in a disgustingly camp way and put one hand behind his head. God, the man was a stupid clown! And Boo, damn her, was laughing out loud.

'I'll manage on my own,' said Charles, with a show of dignity. He shook hands with both of them. 'Goodbye, Quentin. Goodbye, Barbara.'

'Goodbye, Charles,' said the impossible Jones. 'Let's have lunch together one day. At my club.'

His club? Was there a place which admitted people like this? Yes, probably in a seedy back street in Soho. Not the sort of club one would want to be seen in.

They closed the door. He thought he could hear giggling, and a noise of bare feet scampering back to bed. What a humiliating, squalid experience! Slowly and very carefully he walked downstairs, all the way to the ground floor, his strength and self-respect gradually coming back, boosted by the whisky which was now coursing comfortably through his veins. He crossed the hall and went out through the door into the street, where the cold air hit him, a sanitary blast which completed his reinstatement as a civilised human being. What an ass he must have looked, sitting on the floor! That was certainly the end of his affair with Boo Carey, or Barbara as she now called herself. A disgraceful train of events, and he was glad that it was over. Good riddance!

'Hi, Charles!'

No, it couldn't be. But it was, of all people, Celia Chase and her husband Victor. They were immediately in front of him on the pavement. There was no avoiding them. He had to say something. And suddenly he felt very groggy indeed, swaying from side to side, very hot in spite of the weather, and at the same time shivering violently.

'Steady, Charles.' Victor took his arm. Another publisher, but a good friend in spite of that. A gentleman, unlike that creep upstairs. 'Anything wrong?'

'Slipped and hit my head,' mumbled Charles. 'Shock. Think I'd better get a taxi.'

'Lucky we turned up,' said Victor. 'Look, we're going to dinner just round the corner. We'll get a cab and see you home. It's not out of our way.'

'Thanks. Real friend.' Charles, sagging at the knees, leaned on Victor.

'Charles, you're drunk!' cried Celia, suddenly very angry, so that she was unable to think straight and her pent-up feelings about Charles's treatment of Marian came out in a rush. 'You should be ashamed of yourself, you've been with Boo Carey and you promised Marian that it was over, I think it's absolutely disgusting, you're a liar and you're reeling and you smell of whisky. I don't know why she puts up with you, she's been looking after her great-aunt and struggling down to Wimbledon and having her car stolen, and today was the funeral and all you can think about is having it off with Boo, and Marian is worth ten of her! And anyway Boo's having it with Quentin Jones now, and he's in love with her, so there! Serve you right if you slipped, because you're drunk, you're a beast and you're drunk!'

'Celia, please,' Victor said several times. People had stopped to stare, some offering help. 'Let it pass, he's in no condition. Taxi!'

They bundled Charles in. He collapsed on to the seat, Victor on one side of him, Celia on the other. She was crying. He was sorry about that. She'd been quite right about Boo, Barbara that is, and Quentin Jones. She wasn't a gossip after all. Basically a very nice girl. Angry with him, understandably, since Marian was a close friend.

Victor gave the address and the taxi pottered slowly along the Brompton Road.

'Celia, let me explain.' Charles spoke with difficulty because he was shaking so much. 'First of all, Boo doesn't want to be called Boo any more, she's Barbara, and she's engaged to Quentin Jones. I barged in on them by mistake, and I tried to hit Quentin and I missed. I fell down. It was undignified. I learned a lesson. I hope Marian will forgive me.'

'She doesn't deserve this!' sobbed Celia.

They reached the house and Victor paid off the taxi. He said they should see this thing through, explain to Marian, get a doctor. Charles fumbled for his key but couldn't find it, so they rang the bell. Marian opened the door.

'Charles! Oh God, what's happened!'

They came through the door massed together, Celia weeping, helping Victor guide Charles into a chair where he sat hanging his head, a picture of shame and misery. Marian listened to a garbled account from Victor and Celia, making no comment. She looked at the bump on Charles's head, then held his face in her hands and looked at him intently, as if reading his rotten thoughts.

'Sorry,' he moaned. 'Very sorry. Please forgive.' Surely she could see that although he had been a despicable wretch and a liar, he was now penitent and ashamed.

'You've got a temperature,' she said firmly. 'You're ill. Victor, get him upstairs and into bed. I'll telephone the doctor. Celia, darling, please don't cry. Come into the kitchen.'

They went in together and shut the door. Marian gave Celia a stiff gin and tonic and had one herself. They told each other that the affair between Charles and Boo was really over now. And Quentin, Celia said, drying her eyes, was really rather super, he was clever and funny, and one just hoped that Boo would make him a good wife. And Marian said that Charles was also super, in so many ways. He'd been at the funeral and was supportive, absolutely. And if only he could be faithful he would be perfect, wouldn't he, because fidelity is absolutely basic in marriage.

She almost said, so nearly, that she'd been having an affair with the Dave character. So who was she to talk about fidelity? But she didn't say it. She didn't want to share her wonderful romance, not even with Celia. There were no words to explain how it happened, how urgent the need had been. She would rather not try to express it, in case she spoiled the memory. It was over. It was a closed book.

Celia's eye make-up was running so Marian took her upstairs to repair the damage. Charles lay in bed, eyes closed. Marian took his temperature and it was a hundred and three, which explained the shivering and dizziness. She telephoned their private GP, who said he'd be there in ten minutes. Victor, feeling virtuous because he had helped Charles undress and put on his pyjamas, and had hung up his suit for him, went downstairs and poured himself a drink. Marian declared that Charles would have no more alcohol, not a drop, just tea or fruit juice, while she had another gin and tonic, and so did Celia. With that, and Marian's eye make-up, Celia felt much better, and she and Victor said goodbye and went out to dinner.

The doctor arrived and examined Charles. While he was doing that, in a moment of calm, the telephone rang. It was Dave, in Pimlico. His voice warmed Marian all through and soothed her. He said he would telephone again in the morning, from Heathrow.

The diagnosis was that Charles had pneumonia. Antibiotics would clear it up, the doctor said, but it would take a week at least. Would Marian like him hospitalised, London Clinic or similar? Because it was going to be hard work for her, with so many stairs. No, said Marian, she could manage it. Absolutely no problem.

Barbara Carey and her fiancé lay comfortably together in her four-poster bed. They talked about themselves: where they had been to school, what their parents were like, what they liked in the way of entertainment, holidays and friends. As often happens in an intimate conversation, there were several surprises.

People who knew the sexy blonde Boo Carey, said to be an easy lay, had no idea of the real Barbara, her talents, her human qualities, her background. Her parents lived in Cheltenham, she told Quentin, and they were not well-off, her father being a retired Army officer now working as a management consultant. She had a brother who had joined the RAF, defying family tradition. She had been a bright schoolgirl and had gained a place at London University to read English Literature. In the 'sixties this subject, like others, was approached from a Marxist viewpoint, and interpreted according to certain rules. Being an independent thinker Barbara was unwilling to follow the current dogma. Her serious intention to study had been interrupted by marches, sit-ins and other student activities. She admitted that she was not a political animal. Unfortunately she had fallen in love with a fellow student, very much a political animal, who was dedicated to Revolution. He left her, after a brief affair, for a girl whose politics agreed with his. Barbara, believing herself heartbroken, dropped out. She had been studying only a year.

Her parents were disappointed of course, and could not understand what had happened. They were even more dismayed when their gentle, intelligent daughter joined the social scene in London and met Maurice Carey, a wealthy socialite with property in Spain and the Caribbean. Barbara was convinced that she had found the right person this time. He was fun, and good-looking and rich, and they got married after a whirlwind romance and had a luxurious honeymoon in the Bahamas. The parents strongly disapproved of their new son-in-law. They thought he was vulgar. 'Not our sort,' was how they expressed it.

The happy couple were hardly home and installed in Maurice's penthouse in Belgravia when he made it clear to Barbara that he would be carrying on his bachelor activities as before. He was often out late, sometimes all night. His name appeared frequently in the gossip columns. He was photographed with models, singers, heiresses. He was said to be dating this girl, having an affair with another, being cited as co-respondent in somebody's divorce. Reporters pursued Barbara, who was unused to this sort of attention. What hurt her most was that Maurice didn't bother to apologise. He gave her a bigger allowance, as if to make up for his neglect. She was very miserable.

'It had to end,' she told Quentin. 'The trouble with men is that they want all women to be tarts, except their wives. Wives are supposed to be virtuous. And I was so lonely being virtuous. So I took a lover. Then another one. And he found out, and he divorced me. And here I am.'

'And here you'll stay,' said Quentin, folding her tender pink body to his bony chest. 'Now, dearest Barbara, you are quite right in saying that some men have double standards, one for themselves and another for their wives. But I am not like that. You will be my wife and my tart. You will be everything to me. We will live in my flat, because it is bigger than yours. And I hope you won't object to the modern furniture in the main rooms. I found this uncommitted style a suitable background for my single state. Of course our combined chemistry will lead to changes. But what I want to stress is that our bedroom must always be like this.' He waved at the rosebud chintz, the frilled curtains, the pink furniture. 'A thoroughly feminine bedroom. And sometimes I'd like you to leave your cupboard door open, showing lots of dresses, ostrich feathers, hats, shoes with high heels. Or perhaps a drawer pulled out, with lace underwear overflowing. You get the picture, my love?'

'Of course, angel.' They had already settled that she shouldn't call him 'sweetie-pie' any more. From now on it would be 'my love', 'dearest', 'beloved' or 'angel'. 'Sweetie-pie' would be for outsiders, and sometimes used sarcastically, though Barbara was good-natured and hardly ever felt sarcastic. 'Oh, and that reminds me,' she said, getting out of bed and going over to her make-up drawer. 'I wrote this, it's rather silly, my love. But it's for you.'

Quentin read the acrostic she had written especially for him. It was such an unexpected and beautiful tribute that he couldn't speak for a while except to say gruffly, 'Thanks.' To think that she had written it before he had kissed her for the first time, before their first date; to know that it couldn't be for anyone else except him, because it spelled QUENTIN vertically; to recognise that she was an artist, a creator; this miracle made his eyes fill with tears, so that she was dismayed and wondered if she had done the wrong thing. He reassured her with grateful kisses.

Then he told her about himself. He was the youngest of the family and had been spoiled by his four older sisters, who were all married and had devoted husbands and several children each. He was used to being petted and made much of. His sisters always laughed at his jokes, and so did their husbands and his nephews and nieces. His parents lived near Guildford in a very ordinary house. He knew it was ordinary, but he had been born and brought up there and he loved the place. He had been to a boarding prep school, on to public school, and then to Cambridge. He had very much enjoyed all the stages of his education, which he knew was unfashionable. One was supposed to hate being taught.

'Never mind,' said Barbara. 'Nobody's perfect. Tell me what your father does.'

'My father is in public relations. His health is not good, because he was in Burma during the War. He was surrounded by Japs, you know the sort of thing, and he was wounded and one of his mates helped him get away. He goes to regimental dinners so that he can go on talking about it, because we've all heard about it ten thousand times and we're dead sick of it.'

This was a coincidence, Barbara said, because her father had been in Burma too. 'He was quite brave and got a medal. His name is Henry Stonehurst, and they called him Harry Stoners.'

'Harry Stoners! I don't believe this,' said Quentin. 'My father is George Jones and they called him Joggers. He was wounded and Harry Stoners carried him to safety! Your father saved my father's life!'

This was fate, their Karma, a special conjunction of the stars. They were meant for each other. A miracle had brought them together. How happy their fathers would be, and their mothers, and Quentin's sisters and brothers-in-law and nephews and nieces, and Barbara's brother in the RAF! Barbara was overwhelmed. It was her turn to cry.

'There, there.' Quentin kissed her and mopped her face with the eiderdown. 'We're going to live happily ever after. We won't get married immediately because we don't want to forfeit that luscious alimony of yours until my novel is published. Then we will be frightfully rich, because it's going to be a best-seller. But we'll announce our engagement and have a fantastically wonderful party at The Welcome Sole. You don't mind, my darling, do you. He's not a bad sort, Charles Broome-Vivier. We'll invite him and his lovely wife, and Celia and Victor Chase and all our other friends, and our fathers and mothers and families. You can go on working in Harrods if you like, beloved, as long as you don't get too tired for other things.' He gave her a suggestive squeeze. 'Then when my novel wins the Northolt Prize and goes into paperback and is made into an award-winning film, we'll get married and have babies.'

'Oh good,' said Barbara, cheerful again. 'I love babies. Dearest, to continue about your novel, you've told me what it's about, and I understand the structure and the social message. But I don't like the title.'

'*House of Ill Fame*? I had thought of calling it *The Brothel*. Is that better?'

'No, worse,' she said firmly. 'You must call it *Whorehouse*. Just *Whorehouse*, with no article.'

'Brilliant! Why didn't I think of it before? *Whorehouse* it shall be. Dear Barbara, I must be the luckiest man in the world. I'm going to marry a genius, a poet, delightful in bed, utterly beautiful, honest, affectionate and, most important of all, mine.' He had a sudden thought. 'Oh dear, I'm afraid my teddy bear is going to be terribly jealous.'

'I'll be very nice to him,' she said.

'Not too nice,' said Quentin. 'He's a virgin.'

'Quentin! You are a naughty, naughty boy.'

'I love it when you say that. But promise that you'll never say to anybody else. Only to your devoted Quentin.'

'I promise faithfully,' said Barbara Carey, previously known as Boo.

Charles was restless, talking in his sleep, tossing and turning. His sweat and the heat which radiated from him made Marian uncomfortable. She woke up every time he moved. She thought of going into the spare room, but she had to be near him in case he needed anything. At two in the morning he woke up and said he felt much better. Whatever the doctor had given him seemed to be taking effect.

'I'm sorry about this, darling,' he said. 'Such a bore for you. I'm sorry about everything.'

'It absolutely couldn't matter,' she said. 'Just a minute, you're soaking with sweat. I'll get a towel and a dry pillow.'

He slept peacefully after that, and she lay awake next to him, thinking. She loved him more now, because he was ill and he needed her, and because she understood him better after what had happened in Wimbledon. She had been wild Marian, just as he was sometimes naughty Charles. It would probably never happen again, and she was certainly not going to upset him by telling him about it. It was over, a one-off occasion. She must try and forget that it happened. Oh Dave.

She fell asleep at last, and suddenly it was morning, far too soon, and there was a noise which meant she must get up and do something.

Telephone! She grabbed it, half asleep. It must be Dave at Heathrow. She'd been dreaming about him, something about being in St George's, Wimbledon, with no clothes on. Oh Dave.

'Hallo?'

It wasn't Dave. It was the police, in Croydon. They'd found her Mini, no wheels, no engine, no seats. It was empty, just a shell, a write-off. They advised her to get in touch with her insurance company. They could contact a scrap metal merchant on her behalf and have the remains removed. There would be a charge, they would need payment in advance. A cheque would be acceptable. No, it was not causing an obstruction, since it was not on a public highway. It was in a waste area behind a housing estate, but it still constituted litter. Presumably it had been towed or driven there before it was vandalised. They could provide her with details, for insurance purposes, of the condition of the vehicle and where they found it. This type of theft had become all too common. They sympathised. She thanked them.

It was half-past eight. Dave's flight would be leaving in twenty minutes.

Charles was awake. He said he felt cooler, had a bad head and a burning thirst. Could he please have two aspirins, and tea, orange juice, water. Whatever was easy, no trouble for her.

'Yes, darling.' Putting on her dressing gown, she hovered near the telephone. It rang again almost immediately. Her heart jumped. 'Hallo?'

But it wasn't Dave.

'Hallo Marian, my dear. It's Ted. I've been trying to get you, the line has been engaged. Now, I don't want you to worry, but...'

'Ted, what's happened?' This was agony. Only fifteen minutes left. Charles turned over and said, 'Tell him about me. I'll talk to him when you've finished.'

'I've had an accident,' Ted explained. 'Quite ridiculous really. I was out in the garden with Morgan, tidying up the avenue, and I fell off a ladder. You may well say that I shouldn't have been on the ladder in the first place, but there I was, and thence I fell. Morgan bundled me into the car and took me to the hospital. Very efficient emergency unit, x-ray and so on. Have I broken anything? Yes, my dear, I have.'

'Trouble?' asked Charles, sitting up. Marian gave a tell-you-in-a-minute nod, while Ted went on with his story. 'My right forearm, in two places, now encased in plaster, which makes life difficult. Ordinary things such as getting dressed and having a bath. The point is I'm going to need assistance. Morgan and his missus put me to bed last night, but I can't ask them to do it for the next six weeks, can I?'

'Of course not. Poor Ted, I'm so sorry. I'll get you somebody, I know a good agency.'

'I don't want a starchy nurse, Marian. Not like that woman Dolly had. Just someone practical who doesn't mind seeing an old man in his birthday suit. And who will help him cook his breakfast, and perhaps an evening meal.'

'Don't worry. I promise you it won't be a starchy nurse.' The seconds sped away. Oh, why didn't Ted telephone last night! Why did it have to be now! 'I may not be able to come down myself for a day or two. As it happens Charles is an invalid too, such a coincidence. He's got a chill, in fact a chest infection.' She knew that the word 'pneumonia' would alarm Ted because it was that, with complications, which had been the cause of Dolly's death. 'He's not seriously ill, I promise you. He's here, he wants to speak to you.'

Charles took the telephone. 'Father, tell me what's happened. Good Lord, I'm sorry. Very painful, I'm sure. Don't worry about me, I'm on antibiotics and Marian is a first-class nurse. She'll organise somebody for you, on the Abbey Mead network.'

Five minutes left. Four. Three. Ted and Charles stopped talking at last, but it was too late. Dave would have boarded by now. She got dressed, staying near the telephone. But no call came.

She would have to try and forget about it. There was a lot to do. To organise Charles, get his breakfast, give him his pills. To telephone Beatrice about a Kiwi type for Ted. To get in touch with the insurance company. To send a cheque to the police in Croydon for removing the remains of the Mini.

Briggsie would be arriving any minute. Celia would telephone. The doctor would come.

Oh Dave. It all happened so quickly. I am going to miss you, your voice, your smile, your love-making. I wish we could have spoken this morning, to say one last goodbye. But life goes on, doesn't it. Just another busy day.

'Will Mr David Mason please come to Gate 13, where his flight is ready to depart.'

He went on dialling, again and again, until he had been called three times. He wondered if she had left the receiver off the hook as a sign that he should not telephone. Or there might be a fault. He dialled once more and the number was still engaged. He replaced the receiver and turned away, past a line of people who had waited fifteen minutes. They glared at him as he passed. One said, 'Bloody well took your time, didn't you.'

He went to Gate 13 and hurried on board, like a business man unavoidably delayed. The in-flight staff fussed over him. He apologised, took his seat in Club Class, and closed his eyes, listening to instructions for getting out in an emergency, use of life-jackets and oxygen masks.

Marian, Marian. The plane taxied away from the terminal, revved up with a shuddering roar, accelerated down the runway and took off, wheeling south and then east, further and further away from her, the pain like wire stretched almost to breaking point.

My singing bird, my slave. And yet I am your captive. Night and day, you are the one.

He asked for a whisky when breakfast came round, and followed it with two more. The edges of his misery blurred by alcohol, he told himself that nothing unusual had happened. This was simply a sexual involvement, by no means his first. Sentiment had no place in an adventure like this. What was required was pragmatic good sense. Unfortunately he had lost control of himself, and had allowed a pretty girl to break through his shell, his personal armament. He had fallen in love with her, to use a commonplace expression. She had changed him. He was not what he had been before.

In time the adventure would fade into its proper perspective. There were other women in the world, lots of them. There was Robyn, his Australian girlfriend, waiting for him in Riyadh. But he didn't want to bed her any more, not since Marian. The affair would have to wither away. It would be a difficult thing to manage.

He would write to Marian. He imagined a letter with a message cunningly hidden. I love you always. But she wasn't that sort of girl, not one for puzzles. Not cerebral. Just someone he loved and couldn't have. He had nothing to give her, no life, no home. She had Charles, and was his loving wife. She had said so.

He recalled each of his meetings with her, how she had looked, what she had said, what they had done together. How happy he had been. The memory of her kisses made him groan out loud, so that the man next to him, a heavyweight in highly coloured leisure wear, said sympathetically, 'All right then. What's the trouble?'

Dave scowled at him. 'Nothing, thanks,' meaning, 'Mind your own bloody business.' Then he slept, sprawled over his seat. He must have been snoring because later, half-awake, he heard his neighbour talking to the stewardess. 'Excuse me, gorgeous. My friend here is making a hell of a noise. Is there somewhere else he could sit?'

Dave was wearing a well-made tropical suit, and was sitting on the aisle. He looked respectable, and could be moved without disturbance. The stewardess asked him to follow her and led him into First Class, where there was room to spare. He settled in, got out Mimsy's copy of Donne, and began to read, by chance finding advice, and some comfort:

So let us melt, and make no noise,
No teare-floods, nor sigh-tempests move,
T'were profanation of our joyes
To tell the layetie of our love.

He wished that he could read this to Marian, just in case she, too, needed consoling. No tears, no tempests. No one must know. He had not fully appreciated this poem before. Now he knew what love was.

By the end of the day Kiwi was installed at Broome, met at the station by Morgan, warmly welcomed by Ted. It was just luck that she was free, and hoping for a post outside London. Mrs Morgan was upset at first because Kiwi behaved like gentry and had her meals with Colonel Broome-Vivier. In the old days a nurse would have eaten separately. But Kiwi was a nice type of girl, she had to admit. Pity more English girls weren't like her. All they thought about these days was pop music.

2   Dates Don't Matter

Charles enjoyed a leisurely convalescence, having breakfast in bed, getting up for lunch, sometimes having an afternoon nap, enjoying his dinner and television in the evening. He kept in touch with the office. People brought papers for him to work on, and the whole Mer/FCE sub-committee came round one day for a working lunch. This had marked a substantial step forward in the pruning of the Foreign departments, not just a re-statement of policy. They had drawn up a definitive list of those who would have to go. Now it would be up to the Board, to confirm or reject.

Marian had provided first-class service on this occasion. He noticed how his colleagues eyed her as she brought coffee in and discreetly cleared away the plates, her long legs in pale tights, liked naked flesh, below a leather mini-skirt. And she'd done something to her hair. Titian colouring was the latest thing, she said, so she'd had a henna rinse. She looked stunning. He was proud of her, her looks, her manner, the way she organised things.

With restored health came a surge of sexual activity. After one particularly adventurous session, in mid-afternoon, he lay exhausted, aware that he had seen a new side of her, something he had not noticed before.

'You're wonderful,' he said. 'Just wonderful. And I was beginning to think you didn't fancy me any more.'

'Of course I fancy you, darling. I've never stopped. The thing is that you are free again, I've got you to myself. And that's how I like it. I can let my feelings go. That's what it's all about, isn't it. You remember my ex-boyfriend Jeremy? I could never let my feelings go with him, I just couldn't. He was always trying to impress. It seemed so forced, as if he wanted to try everything in the book just to satisfy himself.'

'Was I forced this afternoon?'

'Absolutely not. It just happened, it was natural. You see, darling, the difference is that I love you. I've never actually put it into words before. But I want you to know. I love you, whatever happens.'

His eyes filled with tears. She was so honest, so trustful of him. Weakened by pneumonia, not to mention sexual exertion, he buried his face in her Titian hair and said shakily, 'I love you too. Darling Marian, my own beautiful wife, my love. '

Energetically she embraced him, her body strong and slim, like a lovely young tree. God, she was gorgeous. 'Don't,' she said. 'I can't bear to see you crying, darling. I just wanted to make sure that you knew.'

They laughed, Charles through tears. It was ridiculous saying that they loved each other when they'd been married for years, and for some reason hadn't got around to it sooner.

Charles gave private thanks to Quentin Jones, who had taken his place in Barbara-Boo's bed. What a fool he'd made of himself! Why bother with extra-marital activities when one could have such a good time at home? Marian was sexually mature, an imaginative and energetic partner. And what a wonderful wife, nursing him, finding someone to look after Ted, going down to Broome in her Renault to check on his progress. She really was amazing, a great girl in a crisis. And so devoted.

They had got into a routine of having breakfast together upstairs. Charles had the invalid tray, and Marian had her own tray on an occasional table brought in from the landing. He said he liked having her near him. She was touched. It was super how he wanted her company now.

The following Saturday, when he was really well again, 'Just being lazy,' he said, she went down to get the breakfast as usual, quickly looking through the letters on the way. Yes! One was Air Mail, with a Saudi stamp. Holding it filled her with nostalgia, a sudden assault on mind and body. Oh Dave.

She opened it quickly and read it twice through. His writing was a firm, regular script, three pages of it. He thanked her for everything she had done, making Mimsy's last hours comfortable, and the funeral a friendly and memorable occasion. He told her what would be written on Mimsy's headstone, just the simple facts, the style the same as Cecil's. The flat would be put up for sale after Probate. John Keble would be getting in touch with her about the other bequests. It was still cool where he was, quite cold at night. He hoped the Renault was performing well. The Japanese would probably dominate the car market in a few years' time. Charles's Bentley was a wonderful machine. He hoped to see something of them when he was next in the UK, which might not be for a while. Love Dave.

There was no secret message for her, nothing that Charles shouldn't see. She took it upstairs with the newspapers and other letters. Charles read it and said, 'Good letter. Here, this one's for you too.'

She hadn't noticed, because she'd seen the Saudi stamp before anything else, but there was another letter for her, from a firm of solicitors, at first unfamiliar. John Keble was getting in touch, as promised. He was writing to tell her that Mimsy had left her some pictures and pieces of furniture, her clothes, jewellery and silverware.

'Darling, this is fantastic! Do read.' She passed the letter back to him.

'Mimsy's left me all sorts of things, and I can't even thank her. Oh dear.'

Charles was reading the list. 'I say, this is very generous. And you deserve it, darling. You were there when you were needed. And you gave everybody lunch after the funeral, though she wasn't to know that, was she. Dave Mason will probably inherit the bulk of her estate. Fostered, wasn't he?'

'Yes.'

'Probate takes time. It means the Will has to be proved before you can take possession of what is bequeathed. But Keble might let you into the flat to see what you're getting.'

'I'll ask him, darling. Perhaps next week, when you're back in the office.'

The thought of going to Wimbledon again was disturbing. Not Wimbledon in summer, for the tennis. Wimbledon in winter, where she had secretly embraced an engineer who was on a brief visit, for family reasons, from Saudi Arabia. A man of forty, tanned all the year round, with greying hair and a friendly smile. Such a smile.

For the past two weeks she had been so busy looking after Charles and Ted that she had hardly thought about Dave. Only sometimes. Strangely enough it was he who had brought Charles back to her. He had aroused her appetite for sex, and Charles knew this by instinct, without her saying a word about it. There was no need. The animal in him had scented a rival, unconsciously, and now he was claiming her back.

They had so much to talk about now. They discussed his chances of being selected as a Tory candidate. He would probably be asked to fight safe Labour seats to begin with. Experience at the hustings was important. She said she would support him in whatever way she could.

He told her about his last visit to Boo's flat, when he wasn't wanted, stressing the funny side. How she laughed when he imitated Quentin wearing the kimono! Celia and Victor had been round to see them several times. It had been fun, talking with them about something that was now safely over. They hoped there would be no bad feelings, they wanted to patch things up so that all of them, the three couples, could be friends. Quentin, Victor said, was not just a publisher, he was writing an extraordinary novel. He was intelligent and sociable, a member of the Congreve Club. That surprised Charles. The Congreve was a good place, some very interesting people were members.

They were invited to Dearden House for the weekend. Lord Dearden was still alive, but Patrick had the run of the place. The other guests were all involved with the Conservative Party in one way or another, MPs, bankers, right-wing journalists. The weather was almost spring-like, clear and dry. There was shooting for the men. The women were not offered weapons, but were allowed to trudge along behind.

Clarissa, finishing a piece for a Sunday newspaper, didn't arrive until late on Saturday night. None of the guests seemed to be surprised at this. The furnishings, service and food at Dearden House were the same as they had been for the past twenty years. Clarissa had no brief to make changes as this was still her father-in-law's house, run by a butler and a housekeeper, with a substrata of employees from nearby villages. She was said to be more in her element in London, in Patrick's flat in Belgrave Square, where she gave large drinks parties and buffet dinners. Charles and Marian had been to some of these. 'All-Party affairs,' Patrick called them. Media people came, many of them friends of Clarissa's and not necessarily Tory supporters. Patrick regarded this as a challenge. He said she provided him with a useful platform.

Marian took another look at Patrick and wondered how she could ever have thought him attractive. He had obviously forgotten about their conversation at her party, and hardly spoke to her, except to tell her to take the hostess's place at dinner. The table was laid with Georgian silver, including a pair of candlesticks so massive that she could hardly see Patrick at the far end. But Lord Dearden, eighty and proud of it, was next to her.

They liked each other immediately, talked about music, art and antiques. After dinner he took her to see Patrick's collection of firearms, early sporting guns finely tooled, revolvers with pearl inlay. Then they walked the length of the gallery, where family portraits hung against dark oak panels. So many Patrick-like men, and so many women of the same physical type, dark-haired, rosy-cheeked, swathed in glowing satins, decked with frills, ruffs, embroidery and jewels. Many Deardens in uniform, serving their country, including a Dearden nephew who had died in the Battle of Britain. Many children gathered round their mothers, in the background the formal gardens, a distant view of the house, the park where sheep were grazing.

Clarissa made an appearance at lunch on Sunday, leaving early because she was on television that evening. Patrick confided to Charles that he hoped to get her pregnant soon, and put an end to all this gallivanting. Charles said that he, too, was hoping for a family. Marian had been tied up with her boutique, she should give it a rest now.

'Silly bitches,' said Patrick. 'What do they think we married them for?'

They laughed uproariously.

Marian's father, William Foster, was briefly in London. He had an open invitation to use the Broome-Vivier spare room, but he preferred to stay at the Savoy.

'Thank you all the same,' he said. 'But it's better for business. People know where to find me.'

He came originally from Lancashire, and had kept his accent, also a no-nonsense attitude to financial problems, particularly those concerning British industry. He pronounced 'industry' as he always had, with the accent on the second syllable. In his late sixties, he was still active as an investment consultant, with clients in Europe and the United States. Charles, apart from being grateful for the hard cash which Marian had brought with her, enjoyed his father-in-law's company and valued his advice. He persuaded him on this visit to leave his hotel suite for a business lunch in the City, where William spoke forcefully on the need for Britain to keep up with her European neighbours and to curb inflation before it was too late.

Marian had a separate date with him, for lunch in the Grill Room at the Savoy. She hadn't seen much of him as a child. Her mother had custody. Later he used to appear occasionally at Abbey Mead, to see how his little girl was getting on. As a teenager she had several holidays with him and her stepmother in Spain, of which Emily had very much disapproved. As soon as she was independent, Marian had made a point of seeing more of her father. They got on well together because they shared a keen interest in money, and what you could do with it.

On this occasion, eating *filet mignon* and sharing a bottle of red wine, she consulted him about her new project, still a gleam in the eye, which was to create a Marcellina label, her own line in special occasion clothes. These were to be designed by Terence Gray, who was straight from the Royal College of Art and looking for an opening. William Foster was enthusiastic.

'That's my girl,' he said. 'You've hit the nail on the head. This is a period of growth and diversification, believe me. Make it a separate company, put some shares in Celia's name to save tax when you want to sell. You'll have a good ten years' worth, into the mid-'eighties. But no further.'

'Why only ten years, Daddy? Women aren't suddenly going to stop buying clothes. What you wear is your image, your status. And it's such a strong market. You've no idea what it's like. Sometimes the racks are getting positively empty, and we're in a panic in case the new consignment is held up.'

'That's today. Tomorrow is going to be different. We're entering a boom time for consumer goods. So you set up your workshop, float your line with some little publicity stunt, get concessions in the department stores. Perhaps you'll go into the High Street shops. There's lots of money there. But keep it classy, like Jaeger and those French labels. In the 'eighties you'll do fine. Then sell. The boom won't last.'

'I can't believe it. There's so much money around. People want something, and they are prepared to pay to get it. It's like gazumping in the housing market. And with clothes in the higher price range people don't want things that last, like good suits and overcoats. They want excitement. They want ideas expressed in what they wear.'

'Won't last,' he repeated. 'I'm getting on, but I'm not getting stupid. By the beginning of the nineties you'll be in your recessionary period. To use plain words there'll be a slump, a depression. There will be small businesses all over the place, and service industries, people paying mortgages they can't afford, borrowing money, prices soaring all the time and nothing to create wealth. Where's your heavy industry? Where's your manufacturing skill? All going down the drain. You wait and see, my girl. Some fool said small was beautiful, but that's a lot of bollocks, excuse my French. This country will go downhill in the nineties, the Europeans will be way ahead. Sterling won't be worth the paper it's printed on because there's nothing behind it. So you start your own line now, create a few jobs, develop in the next five years, build it up with all you've got. Then get out before the rush starts.'

'So what about my portfolio? You'll have to make changes, won't you.'

'Trust me,' he said.

They went up to his suite for coffee. He had a telephone call to make. 'How's your mother?' he asked, busy dialling. 'Give her my regards.'

He finished his conversation, then started arranging his papers because he had engaged a secretary for the afternoon. Marian realised that her time was up. She thanked him for the lunch and his good advice, and kissed him goodbye.

He said, looking at her with pride, 'You're a fine lass. Remember, it's end of the eighties, end of the boom.' The telephone was ringing. He picked up the receiver, smiling with satisfaction. 'You see? They know where to find me.'

When she got home she settled in the living room with a clipboard and ballpoint pen, meaning to make a plan for publicity, staff and premises. By mistake she fell asleep, and woke up feeling dazed and heavy. She'd been suffering from an odd lethargy the last few days. Her period was possibly a few days late. It could be delayed shock, from

116

seeing Charles when they brought him home that night. He had looked so awful, poor darling.

Anyway there was no need to worry about dates. The Saturday, when she and Dave had had their first kiss, hadn't been ovulating day, she knew for sure. She was feeling guilty, that was all, because she had misbehaved. A one-off occasion, out of character.

Mimsy's flat looked strangely different. The rooms were cool, clean and lifeless. There was no smell of neglected old lady. The French furniture had gone. It was already in store, John Keble said. Friendly but unsmiling, he showed Marian round, pointing out the things she was to inherit and checking them on his list. She'd noticed before that he had an anxious look, as if he were worried about something but didn't want to make a fuss.

'I don't now how you are off for space,' he said, drawing the curtains back and letting in wintry sunlight. 'The side table and wardrobe are in another warehouse, separate from the French stuff. Mimsy had no room for them here, as you can see. The bookcase doesn't show to advantage with this low ceiling, does it.'

Side table with classic decoration, carved and gilt, by Robert Adam. Inlaid side table of Sheraton period. Bookcase of carved mahogany. Dining room table and eight chairs, Chippendale, unauthenticated. Desk in walnut, Georgian. Mirror in Rococo style, probably Chippendale, carved and gilded. Oak chest to the design of William Morris, by Ernest Gimpson. Mahogany card table in the Adam style. Pair of ladder-back chairs of Sheraton-Hepplewhite school. Wardrobe in Continental style, maker unknown.

'Absolutely fantastic,' Marian said. 'My husband has this family house, you see. It's huge, and some of the rooms badly need more furniture.' Loyally she didn't mention that Dolly had sold some large pieces at ridiculously low prices because they were 'not her style'.

John Keble consulted his list. 'And the paintings. These two are Samuel Palmer. I'm told they're sought after. The Moreland, that's fragile, painted on wood, and has to be kept cool. So that's in store. I remember seeing it, a little thing about this big.' He drew a small rectangle in the air. 'View of a stable or similar, with a couple of cows. Said to be very valuable. And here we have a Seascape, Dutch, seventeenth century. And two Piranesi prints.'

'I can't believe it.' She looked at each piece of furniture, each picture, walking from room to room. These things had been obscure, shadowy. Now, with the curtains open, they were revealed as treasures.

'These water-colours are by Frederic Walker. And this crayon drawing is Downman.' They were in the spare room. She hadn't bothered to look at the pictures when she was here before. She'd been looking at Dave. The single bed was flanked by two chairs from the dining room set. There was a chest of drawers painted white, the sort of thing that Mimsy would have thought good enough for her resident maid.

Then the dining room, where they'd had lunch after the funeral. Table and six more chairs, two of which had arms. Marian thought of Charles sitting at the head of the table, herself at the far end.

'And the silver,' said John. 'We've put that in the bank with Mimsy's jewellery. We have to have an up-to-date valuation, I'm afraid, for Probate. This is part of your bequest.' He indicated a Crown Derby tea set in a glass-fronted cabinet. 'And these, three Persian rugs, a Turkish carpet nine foot by twelve, two Afghan rugs, four Kelims.' Folded and rolled up against the wall. 'The French furniture is going to the V and A, as part of the Cecil Jeffries collection. We've been advised to put everything in storage, we'll get that done this week. The insurance premium is astronomical in a building like this.'

They went into Mimsy's bedroom. 'Her clothes,' he said. ' I don't know what an old lady would have that would be of any interest to you, but here they are.' He opened the built-in cupboards which filled one wall.

She remembered the shelves with underwear and nighties. The rest was new to her. Velvet, heavy silk, chiffon and net, bits of fur, things on hangers crumpled and pressed tightly together in a motley of colours and fabrics. A smell of mothproofing and stale perfume. She fingered a lace blouse, looked at a braided suit which must surely be Chanel, and a dress pleated fan-wise from neck to hem. Another dress, draped in a sheet, turned out to be emerald green, beaded all over. There was an overcoat in black and white tweed, with fur collar and cuffs. This must be the coat Dave had described, which Mimsy wore when they went for walks in Richmond Park.

On the shelves above were hats in felt, feather and straw, mixed with belts, bows and fake flowers, grotty old handbags in crocodile skin, leather and canvas. At floor level, lots of shoes jumbled in heaps, patent leather pumps, sandals, side-buttoning boots with curved heels, lace-ups with pointed toes, dirty tennis shoes, satin evening shoes, sensible walking shoes.

'John, I wonder.' She stood gazing into the Aladdin's cave of clothes, thinking what fun it would be to take everything out and look at it carefully, to see if there was anything worth copying, even wearing. That beaded dress would suit her, she knew. 'Do you suppose I could take these things, just the clothes, before Probate? They can't be worth much.'

'I can't see any objection. It would save us trouble actually.'

'How super. Well, obviously I can't do it today. Next week? I could bring my partner from the boutique, she'd help me pack it all up.' How Celia would love it! They would give the rubbish to Oxfam and have the good things cleaned. Terry might be inspired to base some new models on these old ones. 'Thank you so much. I hope I haven't taken too much of your time.'

'Pleasure. You'll come back to the office for a cup of tea, won't you.'

She looked at her watch. 'I can't, but thanks. It will be dark soon, and I want to go to the church and look at Mimsy's grave.'

They closed the curtains, and he locked up and walked down the road with her as far as the High Street. He said he was moving to another firm soon, in Chancery Lane. He'd found a flat in South Kensington.

'But that's so near us,' said Marian. 'You and your wife must come to drinks.'

'We're getting divorced,' he said, grimacing. 'Her new involvement is my neighbour. Hence my eagerness to leave Wimbledon.'

'Goodness, I'm sorry.' Embarrassed, she realised that she must have paired him with one of the guests, not his wife at all. 'I had no idea. Anyway, Charles and I would like to see you. You've been so kind, really helpful. Please let's keep in touch.'

His gloomy face lit up briefly. 'I'd like that. Thank you.'

They said goodbye and she went on to the church. Mimsy's grave was a quiet heap of damp earth, the Victorian posy and other family offerings lying withered on top. She gathered them up to throw away. The gravestone was ordered, to match Cecil's, a scroll in white marble. The scroll of life. *Here Lies Cecil Jeffries R.A.* And by his side, resting peacefully, *Here Lies Mary Isabelle Mason.*

She could hear music coming from the church, so she went in. The organist was practising, the lights on at his end and the rest in comfortable darkness. She sat down in a pew near the back. The music flowed deep and sonorous.

I am pregnant. My little dream daughter, Teresa or Sue, is on the way.

The heavy feeling is a regular thing now. Sleep, how I sleep! All night, and sometimes in the afternoon too. Soon there will be morning sickness, and swelling breasts. My skirts and jeans will be too tight. Celia got big very quickly, both times. I am longing to tell her about it, when I've told Charles. I don't want to tell him too soon. It is such a long wait before the baby comes.

There is absolutely no problem about this pregnancy. What happened in Wimbledon is nothing to do with it, because this is going to be my baby, and Charles's. I am so happy now. It is as if a curse has been lifted. We will have lots more after this one.

I'll go on with my Marcellina project, of course. One must have some sort of interest, not just one's children. It was so useful having that conversation with Daddy. The arrangement means that Celia won't be tied to the boutique forever, there will be opportunities for her in the concessions we hope to have. She said was it fair to me, putting some of the shares in her name, and I said, of course, it was fair, it would be oafish not to. She deserves it. I couldn't have done any of this without her.

Dear Celia, she works so hard, and Victor isn't very nice to her, rather cold and distant. Marriages do sometimes have a cool time, which passes away leaving the relationship better than before. I know, because it happened to me.

Terry Gray will be our designer. He has such wonderful ideas, he believes in good workmanship and detail. He'll adore that beaded dress of Mimsy's. The only thing he didn't like, when I suggested he join us, was the Marcellina label. I'd come to think of it as my business name, and I really didn't see why I should change. We argued about it, and he said it was too long, and so I said, 'How about Marcel, then?' He said, 'Marian darling, that is just super inspirational. Perfect. Like Marcel Proust. So decadent.' He knows a good seamstress, she is young and looking for an opening, she will help us find more people when we expand. So now it's up to me to find premises, somewhere not to far away. Ideally I would like it to be in Fulham, two or three workrooms plus a really impressive fitting room. That's so important.

I feel full of ideas, in spite of the pregnancy. Daddy mentioned a publicity stunt, something to launch the project. If Barbara and Quentin have a wedding, or some sort of celebration, I'll offer her the first Marcel dress. She really is so pretty, and I want us to be friends. I want to forget the past and the bad time Charles and I went through.

I think about Dave sometimes. The other day I was pretending to myself that I was going to join him in the oasis. I sent him a cable saying, 'I am coming. I love you. I am carrying your child.' The dam has an airstrip, so I flew there and Dave met me and took me to a little white house with a fountain in the courtyard. There is only Arab food. I will have to learn the language. It will be a hard life, especially with a child.

Such a silly day-dream. I don't think I would like Dave as a long-term lover, nor as a husband. His way of life is not mine. We wouldn't be happy. And anyway I adore Charles. We have such a special life together.

I am not worried about dates. There's no need. I'll go and see the doctor, and really I can't remember when my last period was. Teresa, or Sue, will arrive when she wants to. I feel full of love for her.

Charles, to his great satisfaction, had been invited to stand as a Conservative candidate in a forthcoming by-election. The constituency was in the Midlands, a safe Labour seat, but never mind about that. What mattered was that Central Office had decided to try him out. It was a challenge, an initiation into the world of politics. He was busy reading his way into subjects of local importance, such as unemployment caused by the dismantling of heavy industry. On this particular day, to add to the not disagreeable burdens of life, he was going to the City an hour earlier than usual because the Merger negotiations had reached a crucial stage.

Marian suddenly left the breakfast table, rushed to the downstairs loo, and came back looking slightly pale.

Charles looked up briefly from his newspaper. 'Upset tum, darling? Bad luck. That seafood thing they gave us last night was slightly off, I thought. Take a couple of aspirins.'

She filled the kettle and made herself some tea. It was the smell of coffee which had upset her. She wondered if this was the right moment to tell him. Perhaps not, because he had other things on his mind. But she did want to share the news with somebody, and he should be first, of course.

'Charles.' How to say it, to put into words this absolutely extraordinary event, which would change their lives completely and forever. 'I think, that is I hope you are pleased. I've been feeling so sleepy and no period, and my jeans are tight already. I'm pretty sure I'm pregnant. Darling, actually I've been to the doctor and she says it will be in October. Everything's normal.'

He put down the paper, accidentally pushed his cereal bowl off the table so it fell to the floor and broke in half, and came to embrace her as she leaned against the custom-built worktop.

'You wonderful, clever girl,' he said, carefully hugging her not too tightly, so that she laughed and said it was a natural condition, it didn't mean she was suddenly delicate. He made her sit down while he poured tea for her. She'd be having breakfast in bed from now on, he said. She only had to tell him what she wanted. Lucky they'd got the invalid table.

'No really, darling. I'd much rather be downstairs with you.' Dear Charles, he was absolutely glowing with happiness. He must have been wanting it just as much as she did, though he'd never said anything.

'Actually I don't really enjoy meals in bed. Not like you, darling! And I'll only be having tea and toast. I've gone off coffee, isn't it strange. Oh, look at the time! I should have waited till this evening, but I did so want to share it with you. '

'But you've made my day!' He collected *The Times* and *Financial Times*, leaving her the *Telegraph* and *Daily Express*. 'Sorry about the broken china, darling. Put it down to shock. It's the most wonderful news, and you've timed it perfectly. The merger and a by-election, and a baby as well!'

She followed him into the hall and helped him with his coat. 'Darling, I had thought of a little girl, called Teresa or Sue. But perhaps you want a boy.'

'I don't mind, darling. Broome Hall came through the female side, remember. Teresa or Sue, Edward if it's a boy, after Father.' He looked at himself in the mirror and found he was grinning, his face contorted with pleasure. 'God, this is wonderful.' He kissed her several times. Then, suddenly anxious, 'Darling, be careful of yourself. Don't lift anything, get Briggs to do it. Put your feet up after lunch.'

'Of course.' She stood in the doorway and waved. He turned at the corner to blow her an extra kiss, and she blew one back. She could hardly wait to tell Celia, to compare notes about the early stages, to discuss disposable nappies and breast feeding, and whether to have a proper nanny or a series of foreign girls.

Dates didn't matter. She was pregnant, that was the important thing.

Barbara and Quentin's engagement party took place at The Welcome Sole on a fine Saturday in early summer. It began at midday, with champagne, followed by lunch with wine and more champagne. There was music and dancing. Well-known people were there, writers and actors, models, television stars. Passers-by stopped to stare through the windows, so that the pavement was blocked. Quentin's self-defence instructor mounted guard on the door to keep out gate-crashers.

Barbara was wearing an exquisite beaded dress in pale pink, a Marcel model designed by Terence Gray. Terry was fantastic, everyone was going to him now, including one of the Royals. You had to make an appointment weeks ahead. You could buy Marcel clothes ready-to-wear at Marcellina, the boutique where it all started. Now they had a studio workshop near the World's End. The label would be available in some big stores soon, just the top of the market of course.

Marian Broome-Vivier was wearing another Marcel model, pale gold silk organza pleated from neck to hem.

'This is not, repeat not, a copy,' said Terry. 'It is *après* Fortuny. It is in the style of. I am his humble admirer, his disciple if you like.'

Marian's hair gleamed with blonde highlights, reflecting the colour of the dress. Her precious bulge, her baby, hardly showed. Little Teresa or Sue, curled up inside her. Or Edward.

Among the guests were Quentin's parents and Barbara's. Henry Stonehurst, known as Harry Stoners, and George Jones, otherwise Joggers, sat together deep in conversation. They talked about the Burma campaign, the current trend in politics, the extraordinary rise in the value of property, the trouble in Bangladesh, and the amazing coincidence which had brought their children together. They could see that Barbara and Quentin were very much in love, in modern parlance 'having a meaningful relationship'. And they were living together, 'in sin' as one used to say. Now they called it 'shacking up'. Young people are very strange.

The two old soldiers enjoyed the party, but found it noisy. Music and dancing, not like the regimental dinner, ha-ha! And some of the young people showed a lack of respect for their elders. The Brigadier would have dealt with them severely, wouldn't he!

Barbara and Quentin were driven away in a pink Rolls Royce, though only as far as Quentin's flat, where they lay down together and made love. They were flying to New York the following day to meet the American publishers of *Whorehouse*. The English edition would be out in time for Christmas, paperback to follow a year after. Quentin was working on another book, temporarily referred to as *Go To Jail*. He was relying on Barbara to find him a better title. Eventually she came up with *Prison Bars*. She said *Go To Jail* was too jokey, it suggested a game of Monopoly.

Talking about his work before *Whorehouse* came out, Quentin described himself as a social novelist, a humble follower of his idol, Charles Dickens. Like Dickens, he said, he hoped to expose social evils without suggesting remedies. Improving society was not the prerogative of fiction.

'I am a story-teller, that's all,' he was to say in a television interview, the first of many, since he was articulate and interesting to look at. 'If I have an aim it is to reach out and touch my readers, to move them to tears and laughter, to show them pictures and scenery. Why do I write? Because I have to. I am driven by a demon. You could call it a lunatic compulsion. Fiction springs fully armed from the head of a madman.'

His words were quoted in tabloids and literary reviews. 'Madman Tells Whorehouse Story' ran the headlines. 'He's Mad for Whores Galore'. Clarissa Dearden wrote an article, 'Fiction or Lunacy?' praising the book as a parable of modern life. She came briefly to The Welcome Sole before going on to a film première with a well-known left wing journalist. People said that this friendship, among others, was much disapproved of by her husband, the Honourable Patrick Dearden, a pillar of the Conservative Party.

Celia Chase was at the engagement party, of course. Her Terence Gray dress was a twenties model in lime green georgette with handkerchief points to the skirt. She wore gold earrings and choker necklace, and her dark hair was braided high on her head and ornamented with a Spanish-style comb.

During the celebrations, which went on late and continued in pubs and restaurants up and down the King's Road, Celia and her husband Victor had a serious quarrel in which they said unforgivable things to each other, overheard by many of the guests. Victor left The Welcome Sole with an attractive woman, also a publisher, simply dressed in blue jeans. She was a strong-minded person, unlike Victor, and had persuaded him that his marriage was destroying him. He should make a break for freedom before it was too late. They had been having an affair for some time, an open secret in publishing circles, but Celia only found out that evening.

'The worst day in my life!' she cried. 'I don't know what you see in her, she's just a boring Women's Lib tart! And I feel so let down, Victor, because you kept saying that you were too tired for sex and all the time you were having it with someone else! You're a cheat and a liar and I don't know why I married you! You disgust me!'

After he had gone she had several drinks too many and her hairstyle came apart, the Spanish comb falling out and being trodden to pieces on the floor. Charles and Marian took her home and sat with her till one in the morning, dispensing orange juice and good advice.

Marian had heard rumours of Victor's infidelity but had rejected them out of loyalty to Celia. She was furious with Victor now that the truth had come out, and spoke for instant divorce, the whole works. Victor had been absolutely feeble, he'd put up no resistance, just swallowed all that nonsense about breaking the mould and finding himself. And telling Celia in the middle of a party, when his whore was there to protect him, what an absolute oaf and coward he was. He deserved what he got. Celia should get the best divorce lawyer in London, immediately.

Charles said that caution was essential, and understanding of a basic male weakness. He didn't tell Marian and Celia, but this weakness had shown itself earlier, at the party, when he had given way to an irresistible urge to caress Barbara's little boobs, so lightly covered in pink beaded chiffon. No harm meant, and no one was looking. She slapped his hand, saying, 'Stop it, sweetie! Or I'll set Quentin on you!' Then she had laughed merrily, and he had to pretend that he thought it funny too.

Now he tried to alleviate Celia's distress. 'From time to time men have a regrettable urge to misbehave,' he said. 'Put it down to a sense of insecurity if you like. The animal is only just below the skin. Hopefully this only happens once or twice in a normal happy marriage.'

'But yours was only an affair!' wailed Celia. 'You never left home!'

'Victor will come back,' said Charles. 'Of course he will. Forgive him if you can.'

'I might have to,' she said, weeping and blowing her nose. 'Because of the Adorables and because I care for him so much. And why should men misbehave and not women? Why don't they just control their horrible animal urges and be civilised and then everybody would be happy! I just don't understand it and I don't know what I'll do without him!'

Victor did come back, the next morning in fact, but only to collect his clothes. He said he was sorry about what had happened, and he wanted a divorce. It would be the only solution, as their marriage had broken down. He was ready to admit that it was his fault. He hoped that Celia would let him see the children occasionally.

She said, with admirable self-control, 'Of course you can see them, Victor. You are their father after all. I'm afraid they're not back from the playground yet, or you could have seen them today.' Then the misery of the situation overwhelmed her, so that what had started in a calm and rational way ended up in a storm of tears. 'Rupert's too young, he won't understand what's happened until later, and then he will absolutely loathe and detest you forever and Emma's going to be terribly upset and I can't bear thinking about it, I don't know how you could do such an awful thing to your wife and children, and I will never forgive you, never, never!' she howled. 'And that fucking tart in blue jeans can bloody well stay away from my children, I won't have her touching either of them, so there! And Victor, I still love you!'

His resolve faltered, but only for a moment. His mistress had told him that it would be like this, his wife would weep and make a scene, she would try and win him back with protestations of affection. But he must be firm. This was his life, he couldn't go on being an emotional slave, imprisoned by domesticity. This was the twentieth century. He must break the chains and be free, fulfilled, reborn. To stay with Celia would be utterly despicable, it would be hypocrisy, it would be self-castration.

'Goodbye, Celia,' he said, grabbing his suitcase and heading for the door. 'Try and accept it. You'll have to get a lawyer. I'll be in touch.'

He stumbled down the front steps and into the taxi which he'd kept waiting. Another minute, he knew, and he would have taken her in his arms and begged her to have him back. As it was he was so afraid that he might change his mind, and lose his new love, that he stayed away until the divorce was through.

Marian acted as go-between. She arranged for the rest of his possessions to be packed and forwarded to him, at his expense. She made sure that there was no injustice, no claiming of articles which were not his. She vowed that she would never speak to him again once this was done. If she met him in the street she would cut him dead.

Poor Celia, this really shouldn't happen to such a nice person.

A few weeks later a small package arrived for Marian from Saudi Arabia. She smuggled it into her desk and opened it after Charles had gone to the City It was a book of poetry by John Donne, leather-bound, with gold lettering. The fly-leaf had an inscription in faded ink, in a fine Italic hand. 'To my beloved Mimsy from Cecil. Thy firmness draws my circle just.' With the book was a letter from Dave.

Dear Marian,

Thank you so much for your letter and for clearing out Mimsy's cupboards. I am returning this book, which she kept always beside her bed. It belongs to you. When my contract ends in January I am going to proceed to India, to join a survey with the possibility of constructing another dam. The control of available water is a problem which interests me very much. During the monsoon crops are often washed away and valuable soil is carried down to the deltas of the big rivers. The dry season brings failure of those crops that survive, and subsequent famine. I very much hope that we will meet again one day. Meanwhile best wishes to you and Charles.

Dave

She opened the book and turned a few of the thin pages. The marker, a narrow red ribbon, lay beside a poem called *A Valediction: Forbidding Mourning*. She read it slowly. The archaic spelling confused her at first. But the meaning was clear. She understood that Dave loved her, and that the poem was to tell her so. No noise, no tears. It would spoil their love to tell anyone about it.

She wrote to thank him. She said she was reading all the poems and beginning to understand them. She told him about the Marcel project,

126

and how the designer was inspired by some of the beautiful clothes from Mimsy's cupboards. She had taken the books and photograph albums, as arranged. Her mother would be interested in the photographs. When they had Probate she would be able to show Charles the various pieces of furniture which Mimsy had left her, so valuable and interesting. She hoped that Charles's father would agree to having them at Broome, which would be a fitting background.

She didn't tell him that she was pregnant.

The merger, a marriage between a humble High Street bank and a powerful name in the City, was complete. 'Prosperous Merchant Weds Girl From The Suburbs' said the *Financial Times*. Charles's chairmanship of Mer/FCE and his presentation of the final report were highly commended. The Foreign departments were to be slimmed down less dramatically than he had proposed, the argument being that some of the extra personnel could be absorbed in planning for Britain's entry into the Common Market, which now seemed inevitable.

Addressing a meeting of the Board, Charles allowed that one or two people on his list could be kept on as strategic reserves. But computerisation was on the way and would certainly lead to reduction in staff. It would be a mistake in the circumstances to create extra posts. Speaking of staff reductions, he himself would in future be working on a part-time basis, as a consultant, because he was going into politics. Yes, Central Office had work for him to do, and in the very near future he was to fight the by-election at Underwood, a safe Labour seat. This would be a valuable experience. The Directors had been kind enough to wish him well. It had been a privilege, he said, to work with such splendid people.

They gave him time off to go up to Underwood and make himself known to the local Conservatives. 'If it's worth doing, it's worth doing well,' he told Marian. They stayed in a hotel overlooking the market place, now the depressed centre of what had once been a thriving manufacturing area. Marian rested as much as possible, reading magazines and knitting, while Charles addressed meetings in draughty halls, spoke on street corners and drank beer in pubs. She went out canvassing with him. Wet and windy weather seemed to be typical of the place, but they kept smiling as they trudged along rows of shabby houses, ringing bells, knocking. Many doors remained shut, or were slammed in their faces.

'Fuck off, bleeding Tories,' one man said.

Charles was not often given a chance to explain what the

Conservative Party had to offer. He would say his piece from the doorstep, usually rebuffed.

'Sorry, we're Labour. Always have been.'

Occasionally they were invited inside and given strong tea. Housewives particularly noticed Marian's natural ways, her pretty face and her bulging front. Rehearsed by Charles, she said that women would have a better deal with the Tories. There would be more nurseries, mothers would be able to go back to work. Yes, she worked herself, she ran a dress shop with a friend, a mother of two. Yes, she would go on working right up to the birth. She did the buying and the accounts, her friend was the manageress. They were starting their own label, Marcel. They had a workshop, their own designer, a cutter and two machinists. Yes, this was her first baby. She would go on working afterwards.

Charles felt like hugging her every time she started on this routine. She was perfect, no one could have done it better. One could almost hear the votes dropping into the ballot box.

On election day he ferried voters to the polls while Marian rested. There was a long night ahead. Most of the evening they watched television in the Conservative headquarters, where they were offered drinks, sandwiches and fruit cake. She wore a blue smock and matching jacket, looking as pregnant as she could. It was only six months. Her hair was brushed to one side and anchored with a big blue bow. `

'You look smashing,' Charles told her. 'I'm so grateful, darling.'

She said she'd loved every moment, and drank to his success in orange juice. She'd gone off alcohol. Charles reinforced himself with a couple of whiskies followed by red wine. He was glad that these were available. He'd been obliged to down many pints of beer, which he didn't like, in the past two weeks.

He felt calm and resigned when they went over to the Town Hall. They'd worked hard, done their best. He was chatting with some Labour people when he and Marian were summoned to the platform. It was one in the morning. The results were ready, and the Returning Officer was holding his piece of paper in one hand, gripping the microphone with the other. 'Ladies and gentlemen.'

Incredible triumph! They'd snatched over three thousand votes from Labour, in their heartland, an indicator for the seventies and beyond, and a personal triumph for Charles. He held his head high when it was his turn to speak, to thank his supporters and promise them that the fight would go on.

'The Conservatives will one day bring prosperity back to Underwood, and that day is not far off. Just give us a chance. My friends...' He knew that it would be a mistake for him to call them 'Ladies and Gentlemen'. 'Friends, all of you, I thank you for making this possible!'

The local Tories raised their voices and cheered as loudly as they could, though not enough to drown Labour's boos and catcalls.

Marian embraced Charles for the cameras. 'I'm so proud of you, darling.'

'But you did this,' he told her. 'You won me those votes, every single one. I couldn't possibly have done it without you.'

The place was noisy now, people joining the candidates and officials on the platform, others gathering in groups in the hall for the inevitable post-mortem. In that single moment he foresaw many such occasions, Marian by his side, smiling, perfectly composed, the two of them working as a team for his political career. One day it was going to be an overwhelming vote in his favour, and a seat in the House of Commons. Charles Broome-Vivier, MP.

The telephone calls started early. The first was Charles's agent, to make sure that he was awake and getting ready for the triumphal reception at local headquarters. Then Central Office, the press, television interviewers. Then Ted.

'Your very proud father,' he said. He had stayed up for the results, wouldn't have missed it for anything. He was bearing in mind Charles's suggestion that he should get some better domestic help. Mrs Morgan was off sick, she had strained her back. And the boiler, which was old, inefficient and expensive to run, had packed up again, so he had no hot water. Fortunately the weather was warm enough to dispense with central heating, but he was treating himself to a fire in the living room each evening. His arm, incidentally, was much stronger now, thanks to the physiotherapy he was having twice a week.

'I'm glad to hear that, Father. Thank you very much for telephoning. Just a minute.' He turned to give Marian a brief résumé of Ted's news..

Marian finished fixing the blue bow in her hair and took the telephone. 'Ted, you absolutely must get a new boiler. Yes, yes, I'll organise it for you. I'm so glad your arm is doing well. We're absolutely thrilled about the results. See you on Sunday. Goodbye, dear Ted.'

Breakfast arrived, brought by the hotel manager in person, a loyal Conservative. Labour attitudes were old-fashioned, he said. They were trying to bring back the cloth cap.

'God, that's marvellous,' said Charles. 'Can I quote you? You've hit the nail on the head. Their thinking is still cloth cap, isn't it. Us and them, the great divide.'

The telephone rang again. It was Clarissa Dearden. 'I'll see that you get plenty of coverage, Charles. I know the right people. And by the way, there's been a crisis in my private life.' He listened, frowning, while Marian poured coffee for him. 'Patrick won't have said anything, but it will be in the papers any day now. He's been fucking his secretary, so I'm leaving him. I'll divorce him, of course. Who cares? I've got my work. And I've got my flat. See you there, I hope.'

He knew exactly what she meant. She needed him, emotionally and physically. They would be lovers again. Ironically Patrick had been one of his strongest supporters at Central Office. 'I'm sorry,' he said. 'Very sorry. Patrick's been a good friend to me. See you in London, of course. Thank you, Clarissa. Goodbye.'

'What's happened?' Marian asked.

'The Dearden marriage is on the rocks. Clarissa is going to divorce Patrick. Adultery, I gather.'

'Heavens. But then I can't imagine why she married him in the first place.'

'Insecurity. He was rich, he knew a lot of people. He offered a background. We'd better get going now, darling, if you feel up to it. '

'I feel wonderful.' They kissed affectionately, left their room, took the lift down to the lobby and emerged smiling, arm in arm. They were greeted by a milling crowd of photographers and well-wishers, who accompanied them along the street to Party HQ. Miraculously it wasn't raining. Grey clouds moved away so that the sun could shine on them.

They were at Broome that weekend. On Sunday Marian called on Mrs Morgan and spent an hour with her, hearing a tale of small woes which added up to the fact that she didn't want to do housework any more, and she didn't want to do the beds. She would cook for Colonel Broome-Vivier, and she would wash his shirts, underwear and handkerchiefs in her own washing machine and iron them the way he liked them. But no more cleaning. There were younger people in the village, just waiting.

'Tell me their names,' said Marian, and made a list. She told Mrs Morgan how wonderful she had been all these years. It was difficult, of course, now that the Colonel was on his own. Something must be arranged.

She drove down twice that week, first to interview prospective cleaners. She persuaded Ted to engage two, who would divide the work between them. She took them round the house, pointing out what should be done, and how often. She said she would see to it that they had cleaning materials, brushes and brooms, vacuum cleaners in working order. She settled their hourly rate.

Then there was the plumber. Once it was established that a new boiler was to be installed as soon as possible, before the weather turned cold, he became enthusiastic, working out cubic capacities, suggesting this model rather than the other. And what about new radiators, to replace the bulky old ones?

'Your streamlined rads give better performance,' he said., 'You should consider it, with a grandchild on the way. There's the initial outlay, then you're all right for twenty years, give or take. Same with your pipework.'

'The boiler first,' Ted decided. 'And perhaps in the New Year we'll have a major review of the heating situation.' He was beginning to feel exhilarated at the prospect of being a grandfather. One shouldn't say so to the mother-to-be, he knew, but he was hoping for a boy, someone who would take on the property after Charles. Someone worth putting in streamlined rads for.

He was delighted with the arrangements Marian had made. He telephoned her a few days later to say that the boiler was installed and working satisfactorily, and the new domestic helps were very efficient. Most important of all, Mrs Morgan's back was better and she was enjoying feelings of superiority now that she no longer had to clean the dark, dusty corners of Broome Hall. 'I couldn't have managed all this without you, Marian,' he said. 'You are a dear girl. And Charles is a lucky man.'

'I am lucky too,' she said.

In fact she was feeling unsettled, not lucky. Charles was seeing Clarissa, with a plausible excuse. She was working on a series of articles about the City, and he was giving her advice and introductions. He had dinner with her one night, to go through the subject matter, he said. He came back very late. She pretended sleep. She didn't want to know about it, to protest and have him tell lies. She knew by instinct that they were having sex. She recognised the signs, all too well. But what could she do? Heavily pregnant, she wasn't exactly a sex symbol.

The revival of interest in Clarissa would be temporary, of course. Things would be all right after the baby, when she got her shape back. Only two months to go.

She decided to give a fun dinner party, with Clarissa as special guest. Charles liked the idea. 'That's just what she needs, darling. She's lonely of course. And upset about Patrick.'

'I'll organise it, then. I'll find her an attractive man. We'll have small tables, bistro style. Music upstairs afterwards. Maybe dancing.'

'Sounds wonderful,' said Charles. He couldn't help smiling. Attractive man? No need to find one for Clarissa. He was the lucky one. She was finding him so attractive that she couldn't keep her hands off him. They had done no work. The old flame was burning as brightly as ever.

3   How To Be Happy

John Keble was an intelligent young man and a successful solicitor, advancing from a small firm in Wimbledon to a more prestigious one in Chancery Lane. His appearance and general style were restrained, in keeping with his profession. He wore unadventurous clothes. His dark hair was neat and well cut. He had regular features, giving an impression of calm reliability. Superficially conventional, he was a romantic at heart. In limbo, waiting for his divorce, he fell in love with Celia Chase.

He first saw her in Mimsy's flat when she came with Marian to clear the cupboards. He noticed her neat legs, her large hazel eyes, and her friendly smile. After that he might have forgotten about her, except that his move to South Kensington brought him on to the Broome-Vivier invitation list. He was that essential element for a hostess, the unattached male.

Marian tried him out first at a drinks party, where he showed that he was a good choice. In company he abandoned his gloomy manner and became sociable, and quietly amusing. He was polite, had the right sort of accent, and could talk about almost anything. Once he'd passed the initial test, she started asking him to dinner. Not only an extra man, he turned out to be a true friend, someone you could depend on. He wasn't the sort who got drunk, started arguments, or monopolised the conversation. He remembered names, and was respectful to older people. Charles agreed that he was a likeable fellow, and no fool.

Celia had been at that drinks party with her husband Victor, and introduced him to John. Victor talked at length about publishing while John listened, deciding that the man was probably out of his depth in that trade, which was said these days to be very much cut-and-thrust. He's not interesting, John told himself. He might be what women consider handsome, but he lacks sparkle. He seems to be insecure, to be in need of support. Is he weak and indecisive? Has he got something on his mind?

Once again, John might have gone on knowing that Celia existed without having any particular feeling for her. But one evening, coming home on the Piccadilly Line from Holborn, he saw her waiting on the platform at Knightsbridge, and then getting in to the far end of his carriage. It was the height of the rush hour, the train was packed, and he couldn't possibly make his way through the dense crowd to speak to her. However, when he got off at South Kensington he hurried along the platform and managed to attract her attention by knocking on the window. Her big eyes looked at him vacantly for a moment, then she saw who it was and smiled. The train began to move. It rumbled away, taking her to her destination. But her smile lingered with him on the platform. It followed him to the barrier. Absent-mindedly he handed in his ticket, thinking the smile might go with it. But it was still there. By the time he got home he was in love.

That was how it started. He did not recognise the symptoms at once, because he had never really been in love before. He was vulnerable, being on his own, starting a new job and a new life, so her smile warmed him right through. He treasured the warmth because he needed it so much. It was as if she had said to him, 'Don't despair. Life is still good'.

He remembered the first time he had seen her, in Mimsy's flat, folding and packing Mimsy's old clothes. He thought about the drinks party, and her husband the publisher. He wondered where they lived. He found, in the telephone directory, 'Chase, V. M.' with an address in Fulham. He already knew that she worked in Marian's boutique, which was in the Harrods area, so presumably she travelled home by tube from Knightsbridge, changing at Earl's Court for Fulham Broadway. On second thoughts, and after consulting a street map, he decided that she would probably get out at Parson's Green.

For the next few weeks he looked out for her at Knightsbridge on his journey into work, and again in the evening. There wasn't much chance of seeing her, because there were so many trains at peak times. His pre-occupation was foolish, he knew, but he enjoyed it. It was a private game called Hunt-the-Celia. One Saturday, daringly, he drove his car to the bottom of the King's Road, found the street where she lived, found the house, Victorian with bay window and artificial gabling, and idled gently past.

There was a big pram at the bottom of the steps. A Nordic blonde was hauling it up to the front door while a toddler made his way up the steps independently, in considerable danger from the wheels, and a little girl tried to help by pushing the pram from below.

Children! He hadn't thought of children. Two of them, and a nanny. This was a nasty shock.

He and his wife had no children. She hadn't wanted them at first, and two years later the marriage was on the rocks anyway. Children would have complicated the divorce, so it was just as well. But Celia and Victor had passed the stage of uncertainty. They were securely married and were raising a family. So she was out of reach, unavailable, forever belonging to someone else. There was no hope, although her smile, seen through the murky glass of a train window, had told him that there was.

Now he knew that he was sick with love.

134

Another drinks party at the Broome-Viviers, and Victor Chase was there but not Celia. That was painfully disappointing. Then better luck, a dinner party for literary people. Victor and the enchanting Celia, a man called Quentin Jones, also a publisher, his blonde girlfriend called Barbara Carey, two other couples and a lone woman, a redhead, who had been at Oxford with Charles. She was Clarissa Dearden, a journalist. Marian told John in advance that she too was in the process of getting divorced, so he should be kind to her. John made a show of polite interest, but Clarissa, intent on renewing her friendship with Charles, ignored him.

Drinks were upstairs in the living room, then they went down for dinner. The kitchen and dining room were opened into one big room, cunningly lit so that the cooking area didn't show too much. There were two tables, one for six and one for eight, and a help-yourself buffet. Casually hovering, John saw Celia put her handbag on a chair, telling the blonde Barbara to sit one place away from her, then tapping the intervening chair with her little hand and saying, 'Who shall we have?'

This was an opportunity not to be missed. 'Me,' said John, stepping forward. Celia and Barbara burst into girlish laughter, obviously approving of him. He helped them get food and drink, seeing Clarissa Dearden settled next to Charles, with Victor on her other side.

Passing Marian at the buffet, John said, 'Too bad,' pretending that he had tried to sit next to Clarissa and failed. He had the most wonderful evening, happily sandwiched between two pretty girls who seemed eager to make a fuss of him. Later they went upstairs for music and dancing. He loved dancing. He offered himself to Clarissa, but she wasn't interested. Marian was too pregnant. He danced with Barbara for a while. Then he saw Celia dancing by herself, and grabbed her. She was bliss, a born dancer. They took off together and became a spectacle, so that the others stopped to watch and cheered them on. When Celia said goodbye he knew that he hadn't done badly. At least he had danced with her.

He treasured his memories of that evening. It was the first time he had held her close, smelled her perfume. And years later, in sharp relief, he remembered how Clarissa and Charles had been together most of the time, sitting on a sofa talking intimately, while Marian poured coffee and drinks and put records on. He remembered that she had looked strained and tired when he said goodnight. It was very late, and she was pregnant. Charles had behaved in a selfish way.

After that night, a milestone in his secret love for Celia, he found he was settling in to his new life and beginning to enjoy it. He invited people to drinks in his flat, including the Chases and the Broome-Viviers and Quentin and Barbara. The Chases invited him to dinner. He invited them back, with the Broome-Viviers and a partner from Chancery Lane with his wife, and a single girl he'd known for some time just as a friend. He agonised over the menu and whether his guests would get on together. His cleaning lady had come to help, and this soothed his nerves a bit. All went well. He was congratulated on the food and wine. Celia knew the partner's wife's sister. The single girl worked in advertising and showed keen interest in the Marcel project, which was about to take off. She was attractive and intelligent, and Charles paid some attention to her. Then John's partner and Charles got together and discussed the budget, the first Tory budget for many years, while Victor tagged along with various conversations, making general remarks which John thought were hardly worth listening to. Taken as a whole it was a successful evening.

John told himself firmly that he had got over his infatuation. In his loneliness it had been a distraction. Now things were different. He was enjoying Chancery Lane, and his social life was busy. In particular, he had become friendly with Quentin Jones and was advising him about certain aspects of his next novel, to be called *Prison Bars*. This was not going to be the sort of book that John liked to read, being largely symbolic, a prison sentence being seen as a state of mind. But it did involve some legal situations, such as a scene in court, on which he had given advice.

This was how he came to be a guest at Quentin's engagement party, which was also a launch for the first Marcel collection. He spoke to Celia early on, and kept his eye on her as the fun accelerated. When the despicable Victor told her, in the middle of a crowd of merry-makers, that he was leaving her for another woman, John was within earshot and heard the subsequent row. He could hardly bear it. Conventional as he was, he felt like hitting Victor. But he knew it wouldn't help.

Then the Broome-Viviers moved in, took charge of Celia, and hustled her away. John could only look on, sharing her agony. Her face was red and streaming with tears, her hair was in disorder, and she had spilt wine on her dress. It was awful, a shocking scene in which she had certainly lost control. But who could blame her? How right he had been about Victor! What a wretched, despicable man! What a swine!

At the back of his mind he nursed the thought that she was now free, though badly wounded. Patiently he waited. He saw her occasionally, at the Broome-Viviers. He noticed that she was losing weight. Her face was pale, her eyes big and sad. She probably still cared for the horrible fellow, and was suffering the pain of loss. John knew that feeling. He longed to console her, to telephone, to take her out to a restaurant. But he knew it was too soon. She must have time to recover.

Meanwhile his own divorce was reaching its final stages. By an extraordinary coincidence, just one day before the court hearing, he was going home a little later than usual, in very low spirits, thinking about the mess which had been his marriage, when Celia got into the train at Knightsbridge. At that moment he had forgotten about her. So the uplift was violent, sensational. As usual the train was full. Suddenly there she was, pressed tightly against him, holding on to the same stainless steel upright.

'John, hallo! Golly, it's worse than ever this evening, isn't it.'

'Yes. Pretty bad.' At first, distracted by her proximity, he couldn't think of anything to say. When she moved her hair delicately brushed his chin. Then he started talking rapidly, to fill the gap, telling her that his divorce was almost through and that he'd been feeling sorry for himself, even if one was a solicitor and knew the ropes the emotional strain was pretty ghastly. So he rambled on and saw her eyes, so close, getting bigger and then filling with tears.

'Oh God,' he said, and put an arm round her so that they swayed, close together, as one. 'Celia, I'm so sorry. I wouldn't have hurt you for anything. I'm a tactless fool.'

'No, no. I'm happy. I always cry when I'm happy.' She sniffed and tried to get into her handbag for a tissue, but there was hardly room to move. He managed to dry her eyes for her, and her nose, with the handkerchief from his breast pocket, fortunately a clean one, which she said she would give back when she had washed it. By that time they had passed South Kensington and were slowing up for Earl's Court. In the most natural way she said that he should come home with her for a drink and something to eat, she would try and cheer him up. And she needed company.

The blonde *au pair* was going out for the evening. Celia went to say goodnight to her children and John went with her. He liked children. He read a book to the little girl, who had big eyes like her mother's. The boy was too young for stories, but enjoyed a mime show which John put on, using a glove puppet. Then he and Celia had several drinks, followed by scrambled eggs, bacon, toast, cheese, chocolate ice cream and a bottle of white wine. They talked, like old friends, and after a while went up to her bedroom. She was wonderful in bed, warm and responsive. He was relieved to find that she wasn't one of those liberated women who talk all the time, telling you what to do and when. They got on beautifully together, by instinct.

Later, lying in his arms, she said, 'You're an absolutely super dancer.'

And he said, 'Save me the next waltz, then!'

After that first time they met often, sometimes in his flat, sometimes in her house in Fulham. They prepared meals for each other, they made love, and they talked. One evening, over drinks, Celia said, 'So what was the Dave character like? Do tell.'

'Dave Mason? A loner, unsettled. Very bright.'

'I couldn't help wondering if he and Marian...'

He smiled, which he did frequently now. He was so happy. 'Like us, you mean? Good Lord, no. I would say he must have found her frivolous, because he is rather bookish. And she probably found him anti-social and eccentric. Wouldn't fit at a dinner party. Personally I like him very much. It's a pity he's so seldom here. I knew him first as a client, now I think of him as a friend. Marian is a very different sort of person. Kind, thoughtful, charming, deeply conventional. Powerful when it comes to organising. She took over completely after Mimsy died. Dave just had to do what he was told.'

'Yes, that's absolutely Marian.' But still Celia felt that Marian had been evasive about the Dave encounter. Usually they discussed everything.

John, reading her thoughts, arranged them for her and summed up. 'You're such good friends. I suppose it might happen that one of you might think, mistakenly, that the other is holding something back.'

'Absolutely. I'm not really worried about it. And I love you, John.'

'I love you too, so much.'

Deeper down, in his mental filing system, John remembered clearly what he had overheard on the day of Mimsy Mason's funeral, when Marian and Dave stood at the dining room table, raising their glasses. 'Here's to another lunch one day, with kisses to follow.' And her reply, 'Dave! Please.'

Yes, he knew that they must have had an affair. It was not only what they said, it was the way they looked at each other, their passion making a beam of light which he had accidentally intercepted and understood. It was warm, like sunlight. It was made of the same magical material as his love for Celia. He would have liked to tell her about it, to share it with her. But he was Dave's solicitor, after all.

He continued working on the disbursement of Mimsy's estate, sold her flat, deposited the proceeds with Dave's stockbroker, and wrote to Dave to tell him that it was done.

Marian had known Celia since they were thirteen-year-olds together at Abbey Mead. She felt sure that something was going on She noticed that

John attached himself to Celia at parties, and stayed with her. Sometimes they arrived and left together.

'He dates me for dinner sometimes,' Celia admitted, looking very attractive with her dark hair cut short, showing some new pearl earrings. A present from John? Marian longed to ask. But if Celia didn't want to confide, that was that.

She decided to ask them down to Broome one weekend. They came, in John's car, with Emma and Rupert, and behaved so discreetly that Marian wondered if she'd got it wrong. John spent Saturday afternoon out shooting with Charles, bringing back dead pigeons, to Emma's distress.

On Sunday they walked in the woods, where the leaves were turning from green to gold, and beginning to fall. Emma had taken a fancy to Ted, and was walking in front with him, holding his hand. John, with Rupert on his shoulders, was striding along deep in conversation with Charles. Marian and Celia followed slowly, Marian's bulge now so low that her usual walk had become an ungainly waddle.

'Oh, do tell!' she said, suddenly exasperated. 'I mean, are you?'

'Am I what?' said Celia vaguely.

'Are you or are you not having an affair with him?'

'With John? What an absolutely super idea. He is rather attractive, isn't he. Actually...' She stopped and stood in the middle of the path, her big eyes alight with happiness. 'I can't keep it in any longer. We're going to get married as soon as the divorce comes through. We're going to have children. And I absolutely adore him. Don't say a word to anybody.'

'Cross my heart and hope to die. But I mean to say, very quietly, absolutely yippee.'

'Absolutely,' said Celia. 'You've no idea what he's like, he's so quiet outside, and when you get to know him it's a revelation. He's the most wonderful person, so strong and efficient. Not a single bit of oafishness. I could go on for hours. Just stop me, talk about something else.'

'Oh, double yippee.'

The others had stopped and were waiting for them. Smiling with the beauty of it all and the shared glow, they quickly changed the subject and talked about Marcel and the workshop, now busy with special orders and the spring collection.

What a lovely wedding dress they would make for Celia. Registry Office, because they had both been divorced. Emma would be a bridesmaid and Rupert a page-boy. And if it hadn't been for Mimsy, John and Celia would never have met!

That weekend Charles had raised with Ted the question of living-in help.

'Not an old-fashioned housekeeper, Father. You don't want to upset Mrs Morgan and the cleaners. An *au pair* is what you need, like Kiwi but not a nurse. The girls who take on this sort of job are visitors to England, perhaps not staying long. They want a chance to travel, a modest wage. They could be Australians, or New Zealanders. Jolly nice people.'

Marian had coached him in this and provided back-up arguments in case Ted put up resistance. But he didn't need much persuading. Since he fell off the ladder and broke his arm, which he knew was entirely his own fault, he had been thinking seriously about old age.

'The time has come,' he told Charles. 'One must accept help, if available. Send reinforcements. And while we're on the subject, I've been thinking of other changes, perhaps overdue. Here, for instance.' They were standing outside the house, facing the pseudo-classical porch. The columns were stucco, not stone, and the plaster was flaking off. The brickwork on the west tower needed repointing, and so did the main chimney stack.

'Repairs, certainly,' said Charles. 'Yes, I can see several things which need attention.'

'More than repairs,' Ted insisted. 'I met a most interesting young man at a dinner party recently, lives locally, an expert in the Gothic Revival. I must confess that I knew nothing about it until he spoke to me. He has kindly given me a very interesting book on the subject, in which our architect is mentioned. Very much influenced by Pugin, you know, who assisted Barry with the House of Commons. My new friend, whom you must meet, Charles, because this is your inheritance after all, tells me that we can get a grant from some ancient monument fund or other to help restore Broome Hall to its original style. A new Broome, ha, ha! No disrespect to dear Dolly, but it would mean taking out her windows and putting the old ones back. Mullioned, and so on. Remove the porch, an eyesore the fellow says. Remove the mansard roof, which was apparently put there because the old roof didn't drain properly. Taking a sledge hammer to crack a nut, of course. With modern materials that problem can be solved without altering the style of the building. Fascinating, don't you agree. I am trying to find the original plans, which must be somewhere in the house. What do you think, Charles?'

'It sounds splendid, Father. And I know Marian will be keen. She's very good at dealing with people, fixing up houses, decorating and so on. And when I get Upweston, say eighteen months from now, I'd like to spend a lot more time here.'

Upweston was a fairly safe Conservative seat with an elderly sitting member who might soon retire. Thanks to his good performance at Underwood, Charles had been asked to make himself known to local supporters. It was expected that the present incumbent might go before the next election, as his health was not good. Charles naturally wished that it would take a sudden turn for the worse. He was longing for the day when he entered the House. Upweston, conveniently, was only forty miles from Broome.

Feeling that he might have been disloyal to Dolly's memory, Ted now made up for it by talking about her at some length as they walked round to the back of the house.

'She was always such a support to me. I was a young man when we married, only twenty-eight. I had to get my Colonel's permission, that was the form. Dolly was twenty-one, a pretty girl, full of fun. We knew how to enjoy ourselves in those days, dances, cocktail parties, theatres. I met her at a hunt ball, as a matter of fact.'

Charles had heard all this before, more than once. 'Yes, I remember your saying what a good dancer she was.'

'Indeed. She was lively, and had an ear for music. When the War came I was away a lot, of course. We were separated, like so many. But she buckled to. This place became a hospital, she organised all that. Every bed was full after Dunkirk, and again after D-Day. We lived in one of the cottages, you may remember.'

Dolly had been devoted to Ted in her way, but after the birth of Charles she was unable to have more children, and lost interest in sex. Ted was devastated by this at first. Then he found himself a mistress, a widow whose husband had been a wartime comrade. She lived in London, so it was convenient to visit her when he was in town on other business. To his annoyance she had married again in middle age. He would have asked her himself if Dolly had gone sooner.

'I was lucky enough to be Military Attaché in some out of the way places,' he rambled on as they reached the back door and went in to take off their boots. 'Dolly was adaptable, fortunately. You remember Turkey, don't you. We went to Lake Van, in a jeep. Bulgaria was interesting. And Peru. I mean to write a book one day, about our travels. I only regret that during my tours of duty abroad this place was neglected. Now at last we are going to put it right.'

Marian was delighted when Charles reported that there were to be improvements at Broome. She wrote to Ted, thanking him for the weekend and saying that she wanted to help, all the way. She wanted to put money into it, because it was a family house after all. And it was the sort of thing she loved doing. She did hope that Ted would let her be in on the planning stage.

She was already thinking what fun it would be to arrange Mimsy's furniture and pictures there. She had heard of air-duct heating, said to be better for antiques. She would find out about it. The whole place would have to be re-wired and the plumbing overhauled. They would keep to the Victorian style with the newly-available reproductions, baths with claw feet, flowered loo bowls, taps which looked like brass. She would have blinds with Victorian fringes, and heavy curtains to keep out draughts, fitted carpets in the bedrooms. A nursery on the top floor, Nanny's sitting room with television set. A new kitchen, Victorian in style but efficient to work in, a big Welsh dresser full of blue and white cups and saucers, plates, gravy boats and meat dishes.

She imagined wrapping her tiny child in a soft blanket, tucking it up in a basket. Lucky that the new boiler was already installed, it would make such a difference. She'd engaged a baby nurse from Queen Bee for the first few weeks, then an English nanny, Janice, straight from nursery college, would take over. They would spend Christmas at Broome as usual, with good heating and plenty of log fires. Last Christmas had been miserable because Dolly was ill and dying, refusing antibiotics, which she said were 'dangerous drugs', until it was too late.

As usual Marian would ask her mother to join them at Broome, and Emily would refuse. She would prefer to come to London in January, for the sales. There were always lots of parties in Gloucestershire at Christmas time, and she didn't want to miss them.

Marian staggered in to Marcellina that Monday, with three weeks still to go. 'It seems like a year,' she groaned. 'The days are so long!'

'There's one good thing about pregnancy,' Celia said. 'It doesn't go on forever.'

'Thank goodness for that.' Marian collapsed into the nearest chair and spread her legs wide, trying to get comfortable.

'Having children changes your life. You'll never be lonely again, there's always company, day and night. Sometimes they are adorable and sometimes they are absolute hell. They make you laugh and cry.'

'Like Quentin's books. I just wish it would hurry up and happen.'

It happened sooner than expected. Charles had gone to Upweston for a few days, planning to be back in good time for the birth. Marian telephoned him as soon as she went into labour, and he hurried back to London. By the time he got to the hospital she had produced a miracle, a healthy, red-faced eight-pound boy. What wonderful good fortune, what happiness! How proud he felt as he sat at Marian's bedside looking at his newborn son and heir, Edward Montague Broome-Vivier!

'You're not disappointed, darling?' he asked several times. 'I know you wanted a girl, but he's a lovely little fellow, isn't he. Look, strong hands.' Edward, with his eyes closed, gripped Charles's finger and held on tight.

'Disappointed, of course not. He's just what I wanted. He looks like Ted, don't you think.' He had straight fair hair and a thoughtful expression. She knew that he was Dave's child.

'Put him down for Eton.' Charles could see the years unfolding in a rapid scenario, getting the early stages over and then on to the interesting part, seeing the child grow into a man, his companion and friend. 'I think one has to take an entrance exam these days, so choice of prep school is important. He looks intelligent, doesn't he.'

'Super brainy, darling, like you. We must try not to spoil him, but it's going to be difficult. He's just so special.'

She felt strong and well. Edward seemed to be satisfied with her milk, although she didn't much like feeding him. The greedy little animal tugging on a bit of her flesh was so primitive. She knew that breasts were for milk, but until now she had thought of them as mostly decorative. And erotic, which was confusing. She remembered how Dave had looked at the opening of her shirt that first time, before they kissed.

Charles spent that night with Clarissa, in her flat in Chelsea. Their love-making was, he told himself, no more than an extension of their long friendship. No harm could come of it. They were responsible adults. No childish endearments passed between them, no Boody-doo. He was Charles, she was Clarissa.

He enjoyed her lack of sentiment, her sophistication. He loved her pale skin and her body, more shapely now than it had been when they were lovers at Oxford. She had been a plump girl, now she was fashionably thin. He remembered that she had not looked her best in a bathing costume, her flesh soft and colourless, harsh sunlight robbing her of her beauty. In that way she was the opposite of Marian, who tanned easily and showed to advantage on a hot, sandy beach. A different sort of woman, not subtle like Clarissa, not mentally stimulating. But a good wife to him and now, at last, a mother.

Clarissa was non-commital about the birth. She seemed withdrawn, not as pleased as she should be that he was in London unexpectedly and free to spend the whole night with her. He took her out to dinner first. She talked in a depressed way about herself, her work and her divorce. 'Perhaps I expect too much. I envy you your moderation, Charles.

You've got just enough of everything, without extremes.'

'I don't like extremes, never did.'

'Your moderation with my intolerance. A state of balance. We should have married. I should have had that baby.'

He knew that she had had an abortion in her last year at Oxford, after he had gone down. 'It wasn't my baby, Clarissa. You were being a very naughty girl at that time, if I remember rightly.'

'Emotionally it was your baby. I should have had it.'

'Nonsense. It would have ruined your life, held you back. And you're not the maternal type.'

'Patrick wanted children. He wanted an heir. Then I discovered that the abortion had sterilised me. That was the beginning of the trouble.'

Back in the flat she gave him a brandy, but said she wouldn't have one. She'd had enough alcohol, the way one mixed was important. He said, 'You're on some sort of pills, are you? I've heard one has to be careful. Tranquillisers and so on, they don't go with booze.'

'You're very innocent, Charles.'

She went through to the bedroom and came back undressed, wrapped in a sheet which trailed behind her. She looked fantastic, like a pre-Raphaelite painting. And her mood had changed. She was animated, passionate, her green eyes glittering with a savage light. She began to pull his clothes off, tearing his shirt open so that he spilled brandy on his bare chest.

'Moderation, Clarissa! For God's sake.' She grabbed him round the waist and they collapsed together on to the floor. He felt undignified, his buttocks bare, trousers constricting his legs, but he managed to penetrate and get a good rhythm going. He thought he was doing very well when she suddenly shoved him off and ran to the bedroom. He got his trousers and underpants off and followed, mounted her, thinking she was almost ready, but she teased him, held him off.

'Clarissa, have mercy!' he groaned. He was only just able to satisfy her.

Then he slept, to be woken in the early hours by her snoring. She was still beautiful. He wondered about drugs, whether he should warn her to be careful. It was not a subject he knew much about. People reacted differently, they said. Whatever she was taking, stimulant, anti-depressant or whatever, obviously didn't suit her. These things could be dangerous.

He dressed and went home, and slept again, got up refreshed at seven. He was going to visit Marian at nine, and get back to Upweston by midday to keep a few more appointments.

Marian brought Edward home in triumph after two days in hospital. It was wonderful to be back in her own room, organising Briggsie to cook meals, getting food from Harrods by telephone, writing thank you letters. Friends came with flowers, knitted boots, woolly toys. Ted was driven up from Broome, stayed an hour and admired his grandson, peacefully sleeping. Her mother came, by coach which was cheaper than the train, and stayed three nights, three too many as far as Marian was concerned, fussing about all the wrong things. Edward shouldn't lie on his front, he might suffocate. He shouldn't have wool next to his skin, a cotton vest would be better. Marian shouldn't go up and down the stairs so much, there was no need. She had the nurse and Mrs Briggs, she should rest for a fortnight at least. She knew of someone who'd had a haemorrhage.

'Mummy, these days one doesn't stay in bed. I must get my muscles back, I need the exercise. I have breakfast in bed and I rest all afternoon. That's enough, absolutely.'

'You know best, pet. I'm only trying to help.' Emily felt that she wasn't going to enjoy being a grandmother. It put one in an older bracket and she liked to think of herself as being young for her age.

William Foster telephoned from Spain offering financial guidance. His grandson should have the best education that money could buy, and a decent amount of capital carefully invested. Marian should take out insurance for the school fees and redraft her Will. Her money should go to Edward in trust. 'I'll let you have it in writing, all the details. He's a healthy lad, is he? Good. Takes after his grandfather. I'll come and see him next time I'm in London.'

The next day Edward decided that he needed a lot more food. He was having a bottle when he woke in the middle of the night and was otherwise breast-fed. He grumbled mildly at first but when nothing was done he took to yelling between feeds, getting red in the face with anger and frustration. Marian knew it was colic, but the baby nurse disagreed.

'I'm afraid he's still not getting enough,' she said. 'He's a big boy.'

Marian took this as an insult and burst into tears. 'I'm doing my best!' she sobbed. 'I only fed him an hour ago!'

'Feed him again, dear. It will stimulate the flow.'

Marian held him to her breasts, which had been briefly swollen and were now back to their normal size. Her tears dropped on his face. He swallowed air, stopping to glare at her, shaking his head and searching for a source of food.

'More, more!' was the message. 'I'm starving!' He yelled furiously as soon as he was put down. The nurse took him away and gave him a bottle, brought him back satisfied, full up, already asleep. Marian went on crying.

'Sorry,' she wept. 'So sorry!'

'It's the baby blues,' said the nurse, offering paper tissues. 'It happens to everybody. There, there.'

Marian telephoned Celia, who left the shop and came at once, by taxi. She talked away Marian's tears, told how she'd cried for days after Emma, for a week after Rupert. There was no harm in bottle-feeding, she mustn't worry.

Charles, who was feeling a stirring of interest in the new arrival, came home early, heard the story, took Marian in his arms and kissed her tenderly.

'You're so good to me, Charles! And I want to be a good wife to you, and a good mother to Edward, I wanted to feed him for six weeks to give him his immunity, and I really love you! Oh, oh!'

She was on the sofa with her feet up, her lace negligée open down the front showing the cleavage between her beautiful but milkless breasts. She looked so vulnerable, unlike her usual self. He was touched.

'Darling, you are my wonderful, adorable wife. You're tired, that's all. You're so strong usually, it comes as a surprise. Darling, my own darling.' He kissed and kissed her. 'You've produced a simply splendid baby. He's got a big appetite, that's all. Nothing wrong with that.'

'Darling, you're so good. I hope you like Edward. I hope.'

'Like him? I adore him, and I adore you. Let's have a drink. Champers, why not?'

That evening, encouraged by the nurse who said that fathers were important from the beginning, he fed Edward four ounces of milk from a bottle. It was the first time he had handled a baby. He loved doing it, soon became an expert, realised that looking after a small animal was something he'd missed. He hadn't kept pets as a boy, Ted and Dolly being so often abroad, and Broome more or less empty. There had been no continuity there, no rabbits, cats, friendly dogs. Now he had Edward, his own human pet. He found caring for him fascinating, rewarding, a source of pleasure. At weekends, wearing an apron, his sleeves rolled up, he would give Edward his bath. 'Edward's *levée*,' he called it.

He couldn't help telling Clarissa what fun this was. It was a mistake of course.

'You're in love with your baby,' she said. 'Silly Charles.'

He realised that he would have to stop talking to his mistress about his son.

'You won't let me get pompous, will you.' Quentin Jones leaned back in his chair, the first complete draft of *Prison Bars* piled high in front of him.

146

Barbara, working for a degree with the Open University, looked up from her books. 'Why do you ask, my love?'

'I'm afraid that fame is going to my head. I'm beginning to think that I have unusual powers. I can see into the future. Crystal gazing you might say.'

'Divination is a science rooted in antiquity,' said Barbara.

'Lo and behold,' said Quentin, pretending to be the High Priest who had just looked at the entrails. 'Some of our friends will live uneventful lives, thereby avoiding divine retribution. Some will defy the gods and suffer terrible reverses. Seriously, beloved, looking at them as a group, I don't think they give a tuppenny damn about suffering and political mismanagement.'

Quentin and Barbara were planning to vote Liberal when the day came. They felt proud, isolated, and yet part of a sweeping movement that might change many things, among them the voting system. Proportional Representation was an issue at the time.

'Biafra and Northern Ireland,' said Barbara. 'Power cuts, three-day weeks, Brixton. They don't care. Their tiny minds are otherwise occupied.'

'Exactly. They just say, "How simply ghastly" and go on voting Conservative. There they are, actors on the human stage, playing their allotted roles. What do I see? Celia Chase, not yet divorced, is having a passionate affair with John Keble. Later they will marry and live happily ever after. They are decent, orderly people. They don't cock a snook at heaven and risk getting slapped down for it. How fortunate for Celia and her children that Victor pushed off! He is deeply flawed, a stupid fellow. He will die of drink and despair. He will keep trying new remedies in his search for happiness. He will be permanently uncertain, while Rome burns.'

'He is a weakling,' Barbara agreed. 'What about Charles? He's the wrong party, but he does try and do something. He assumes responsibility.'

'Every inch a politician. He's attractive, ambitious, quite clever. But he doesn't know what really matters. The Gods will punish him. I see Furies waiting in the wings.'

'If you mean Clarissa Dearden, she isn't waiting in the wings, she's having him right now.'

'So they say. Though I wouldn't touch her if I were Charles.'

'I'm so glad. Why not, particularly?'

'She's unstable. Involved in the drug culture. Half zonked most of the time.'

'And Marian?'

Quentin was thoughtful for a moment. 'Barbara, what is the matter with that beautiful girl? The glass is clouded. I see unhappiness, tragedy.'

'Go on! That's ridiculous, beloved. She's just a very pretty, normal woman, who never reads a book. Her husband is a male chauvinist pig. She loves him and believes in marriage, so she bears it. And I like her, and I'm sorry I borrowed Charles, briefly.'

'Never, never do it again,' said Quentin sternly.

'I promise. I've got you, I need no one else. So what about us, Mr Clever Quentin Know-All?'

'Ah! Let us duly thank the gods for their benevolence. We'll have a lovely baby.' She was already four months pregnant and they were planning to get married, quietly, as soon as *Prison Bars* went to the publisher's. 'Barbara, why are you giggling?'

'Hallelujah!' she cried. 'It's going to be twins!'

Mr Clever Quentin was dumbfounded.

Charles's affair with Clarissa dragged on into December, on both sides with a loss of enthusiasm. He considered he had a duty to her, as an old friend. She was going through a difficult time. She needed him. But she was often evasive about dates, making excuses for not seeing him, sometimes changing her mind at the last moment.

A time came when they were hardly ever alone in her flat. He met magazine editors there: writers, photographers, rock musicians. A rackety crowd, he thought. Most of them smoked marijuana. He supposed they might also take hard drugs. Clarissa seemed perfectly at home with these people.

Then she told him she had a new lover, one of her musician friends, younger than she was. 'He renews me, Charles. You understand, don't you.'

Charles understood. This was typical of Clarissa. He felt no jealousy, he was positively relieved. He saw her less often, in other people's houses, never alone. He could see how much she had changed since her marriage broke up. Her behaviour was sometimes odd, her clothes unbecoming.

He wished he had kept intact his memory of their earlier time together, in Oxford, when they were young and the world belonged to them. He saw himself twenty years old, carefree, driving his sports car, Clarissa sitting next to him, red hair blowing like a flame. Or taking a punt up the river, Clarissa trailing her hand in the water. Clarissa in a black lace ball gown. Clarissa arguing, reading, dancing, making love, against a background of dreaming spires. A poetic beginning, now disenchantment.

Christmas at Broome, a festival centred on Edward, now plump, satisfied, settled on to four bottles a day. His proud parents had total care of him as Janice, the nanny, was on holiday. The new boiler made the house warm and welcoming. Baths were hot. The rooms were clean.

There were local parties, to which Edward was carried in his basket. Ted wanted to show him off and have him get to know his neighbours. After all, he would be master of Broome Hall one day. Mrs Morgan, it turned out, was good with babies. She fed, admired and cuddled Edward, washed his clothes and acted as baby-sitter when he wasn't out socialising. She swore that he had smiled at her, a proper smile, not just wind.

'He'll be talking soon,' she said. 'One of the cheeky ones.'

Marian had bought a new mattress for the spare room bed. How comfortable it was, how firm! While Edward slept in his corner they made passionate love, inspired by happiness and parental pride. She had told Charles, frankly and without fuss, that she knew about Clarissa. And he had told her, truthfully, that it was over for good.

'I know that things will be altogether different now, darling,' he said. 'I'm a father, I have a responsibility. I hope you don't despise me for the way I behaved in the past.'

'Of course not, darling. I don't despise you at all, I just love you.'

Six weeks later, when they came back from their ski-ing holiday, she knew that she was pregnant again. Charles swore that it was the bed at Broome, because that was where Edward had been conceived, on the night of the blizzard. She laughed. Yes, of course, it was a lucky bed, which brought fertility.

The truth about this second pregnancy was that she had been careless. Subconsciously she had ignored the possibility of insemination by Charles. It was rather soon after Edward, but never mind. She would go ahead and have her whole family now, before she got too far into the thirties.

She had sent Dave one of their Christmas cards. To other friends she had written something about Edward's progress, but on Dave's she just put 'Love from both of us.' He had sent her a photograph of the dam, still unfinished, with a short note. 'Five years' work, ten to go before it's fully operational. I'm staying until February, will let you have my new address. Happy Christmas. Dave.'

Clarissa had her first breakdown in January, brought on by the stress of her impending divorce and a mixture of drugs unwisely taken, hallucinogens, pep pills, barbiturates. She had attempted suicide and ended ingloriously in hospital, being stomach-pumped. The tabloids made much of this. 'Tory Chief's Wife Takes Overdose.' 'Journalist's Bid for Death.'

A new man came into her life, an American, some years older than she was, saw her through hospitalisation, helped her return to normal life. She went with him to the States and started writing again, articles, short stories, then a novel.

'I feel desperately sorry for her,' Charles told Marian. 'But I don't want to see her. She's a different person now. Not the one I was in love with when I was at Oxford.'

He was grateful for the fact that someone else was taking care of her, and on the other side of the Atlantic. Unfortunately that relationship did not last long. She came back to London six months later without her lover, apparently in good health, and started working for a newspaper whose policies and style Charles deplored. She mixed with Labour politicians and the extreme Left, 'Trots' as he called them. This was not his sort of crowd, so he didn't see her often. He was relieved when she made no effort to renew their intimacy. He found her physically unattractive now as well as politically alien.

To Marian's surprise Mrs Briggs suddenly gave notice, her explanation being that her back was giving trouble, and with another baby on the way, not that Edward wasn't a nice little boy, she couldn't be expected to give service as usual, not with the stairs, she'd always done her best, she wasn't as young as she used to be.

The truth was that Mr Briggs, still her husband since her Church did not countenance divorce, had had a massive heart attack and died, leaving his mistress with two young children and no money to speak of. Behold, the Lord shall smite the Ungodly.

Mrs Briggs had reported this on a one-to-one basis to the Pastor at the Church of the Holy Word. He advised her to leave her employment and devote herself full time to the Lord's Work. Furthermore, since she was now a widow and himself a single man, should they not enter into a state of Holy Matrimony?

This invitation, just what Briggsie had been hoping for, was graciously accepted. She had considerable savings in the Post Office, but these wouldn't last forever. The Pastor, she happened to know, was a man of independent means. Her future with him would be comfortable and secure.

Marian, who knew nothing of Mrs Briggs's private life, offered a rise, shorter hours, and a new Hoover, but it was no good. Briggsie went, grateful for the farewell bonus, and was seen no more. She was difficult to replace. Domestic agencies said that it was always like this in the winter, as if cleaners, like swallows, would be back as soon as the weather got warmer. Janice, good-natured and energetic, took on a share of the housework as well as looking after Edward.

Marian tried using contract cleaners. They were unsatisfactory and expensive. She decided that the house looked run-down, she would redecorate in the spring, get a new stair carpet, change the drawing room curtains. In the early stages of this second pregnancy she was often sick, and felt gloomy and irritable.

February was a dark, miserable month. A wave of political unrest brought electricity cuts and petrol shortages. Street cleaners and refuse collectors were taking industrial action. London quickly became squalid, littered with rubbish, paper, plastic bags, rotting food. It was grim and depressing.

'Like my mood,' Marian thought. 'I feel so strange. Something bad is going to happen.'

She braced herself, waiting for it.

She went early one morning to the local *patisserie* to get something for dessert. Celia and John were coming to dinner. It was a cold damp day, the sky heavy with clouds of a grey-brown colour, as if they had sucked up dirt from the unswept pavements. When she got to the shop she found the door locked, no lights inside, empty shelves and a notice in the window, 'Closed on Account of Miners Strike'. There had been power cuts twice that week, so presumably their ovens weren't working. She'd have to think of something else. Luckily she had gas at home, for cooking and central heating.

She was turning away from the shop when she realised that Beatrice King was standing next to her.

'Oh Beatrice, hallo. Isn't this absolutely vile. No electricity, and rubbish everywhere .'

'It's ghastly,' said Beatrice. She wasn't Queen Bee today. She was pale, wearing no make-up, and there were rings under her eyes. She stood for a moment looking lost. Then she said, vehemently, 'God, I'm glad it's closed. Take me away from here, please. Just let's go for a walk or something, do you mind? I'm in a bit of a state.'

Marian said, 'Come home with me. We'll have coffee and talk.'

They were there in five minutes, taking off their coats, settling in the kitchen, Beatrice silent, Marian chatting and getting out mugs, boiling a kettle. She felt guilty because she hadn't made much of an effort to include Beatrice socially, except once, when she'd invited her to come for drinks and bring her fiancé. Beatrice had made an excuse, they were busy that night. Now, over black, sugarless coffee, she told her story. Derek, the fiancé, was back on the booze. They had been living together in her flat and she'd turned him out, broken off the engagement, told him not to come back until he could behave like a civilised human being, The loneliness was the worst thing, and the longing for sweets, cakes, pastry. She was fighting it, it was awful, as bad as alcohol. And she still loved him.

She began to cry. 'I gave back the ring. It was so beautiful, a symbol of everything good, and I was so happy, so confident. I thought I could keep him on the rails, but something went wrong. Perhaps I expected too much. He started drinking again, I just couldn't bear it, we had a row and I told him to get out.' She stopped to wipe her eyes. 'That's why I didn't accept your invitation, we'd just broken up. And I'm miserable without him, miserable. And I'm being a bore, and I'll just have to fight my trouble, and leave him to fight his.'

'He'll drink more than ever, because you're not there,' Marian said. 'He needs you. And I'm not unsympathetic, but if you really love a person you have to take the bad with the good. Absolutely.'

'But when he's drinking he's someone else. He's not the Derek I love. He goes downhill, he talks in an oafish way, he doesn't wash. He smells dirty and disgusting and he can't - you know what I mean. He can't consummate.' More tears. Her face was bloated and plain, all self-assurance gone.

Marian moved in. 'Do you want him or don't you, Beatrice? If the answer is Yes, then for God's sake give him another chance. Look, I know exactly what you mean about a man smelling bad, and this is confidential, but before I had my baby Charles was having an affair, and he used to come home sweaty and worn out, smelling absolutely horrible, like a stranger. Then I'm glad to say he came back to me, and we had Edward, and actually I'm pregnant again.' The telephone rang. 'Bother. Won't be a moment.'

Just a telephone call. Doors and windows open and close. It was John Keble, his voice adjusted for a special circumstance. 'I hope this isn't a bad moment, Marian. I've had some distressing news. I'll tell you straight away, no beating around the bush. You are family, after all,'

She knew at once that something had happened to Dave. No need to cry out in anguish. She remembered the poem. It was a valediction. They had said goodbye. There was never to be any more.

The Foreign Office had been in touch, John said. A light aeroplane, which ferried people from the dam to a place where they could get a regular flight to Riyadh, had crashed during a dust storm. Dust storms were not unusual in those parts. There were only two of them in the plane, Dave and the pilot. There was no chance of survival.

She heard herself saying, 'How absolutely awful, John. He was your friend, and you were such a help to him with Mimsy's affairs. I'll telephone Mummy, to save you the trouble, and she'll pass it on to the other relatives. And there's his wife, ex-wife I mean, and his daughter. And his friends in Pimlico.'

'Yes. I've been in touch with them. Distressing for the daughter. I gather that she was fond of him although there wasn't much contact.'

'Poor girl. How sad.' Vividly she remembered. He talked about his daughter. Always wonderful seeing her, and hell at the same time. 'Anyway, thank you, John. See you both this evening.'

Beatrice got up to go. 'You've got things to do. You've been so kind, Marian. I feel stronger about this oafish guzzling thing. And the other.'

'Please stay a few minutes. I need you. This works both ways.'

They sat together in the designer kitchen, Marian explaining that someone, almost a relation, had been killed in a plane accident abroad. Beatrice's turn to give comfort. Then Marian got back to the Derek problem, urging Beatrice to make peace with him even if it meant putting up with the occasional binge. Once he was sure he was loved, there would be fewer binges, just moderate, enjoyable, social drinking.

'Love is so important,' she said. 'Nobody can do without it.'

Beatrice relented. She would telephone Derek before he left his office and suggest that they meet for dinner. To tell the truth, she was longing to see him.

Just as she was leaving Edward and Janice came back from their walk and were introduced. Edward was wearing a woolly cap pulled down to keep his ears warm. He gave a toothless but sociable smile.

'He looks like a little pirate, doesn't he,' said Janice proudly.

'He's the nicest little pirate I've ever seen,' said Beatrice.

After lunch Marian went upstairs to lie down. No tears came.

'Never again,' she reminded herself. 'I'll never see him again.' Still no tears, just an understanding, an acceptance. He had been her lover and given her Edward. Now he had gone.

She wondered if she would miscarry. But strangely she felt better now that the news had come. 'I'm strong,' she told herself. 'And I'm so lucky. I have this house and Marcellina-Marcel, and I have Charles, so involved and affectionate now. This is the life I've chosen, to be with him and love him. With Dave it was different, something other. It was elsewhere.'

She fell into the heavy sleep of pregnancy, her body demanding consideration for the work in hand, feeding the unborn, sheltering it from the outside world. She woke up sweating under the eiderdown, struggling back to reality from an overwhelming dream. She was driving the Renault across a wide expanse of sand, the desert where Dave had died. The sun was rising. She felt so happy.

The lights went out again that evening so they had dinner by candlelight. With Charles, Celia and John, Marian talked about Dave's death in an unemotional way. It was the closing chapter of the Mimsy involvement, she said.

John noticed her self-control. He had hesitated before telephoning her, wondering if he should ask Celia to break the news for him. Then he decided that this might hint at a special relationship, more than friendship, between Dave and Marian.

It had occurred to him that Edward might be Dave's child and not Charles's, a thought which he quickly rejected. Marian was worldly-wise and practical, not a woman to make mistakes. There had possibly been a brief sexual involvement, and why not. Speculation was not something that interested or amused him.

Celia's divorce would be through in June. They meant to start a family as soon as they were married, her second, his first. He was longing for this new beginning as her husband, hopefully the father of her children.

Most of the conversation that evening centred on the power crisis.

'The miners are holding the country to ransom,' Charles said. 'Some of us think Heath should get tough with them. It's all very well getting into the Common Market, but at this rate we'll have nothing to sell. Someone's got to bring the work force to its senses. Industrial strife is the road to ruin, and Labour doesn't want that more than we do. And it's humiliating. It makes the government look an ass.'

Spring came. Marian swelled modestly, a bulge not as big as Edward. A girl perhaps, a little Sue or Teresa. The sickness went away. She felt healthy, enjoyed life, found a cleaner almost as good as Briggsie. Problems, as they used to say at Abbey Mead, are there to be solved.

III

This Way Out

1   The Twister

The elderly twin-engined plane, affectionately known as The Crate, did a regular run to the dam and back, transporting personnel, supplies and mail. The weather was clear and windless that day, deceptively as it turned out. Dave, the only passenger, sat up in front with Mike, the pilot. He had done this trip many times before. This was to be his last, his goodbye to the place where he had worked for five years. His possessions, mostly books, had gone ahead by road, a circuitous journey which took two weeks, sometimes more. Now just himself, one suitcase and an overnight bag for the first stage of his transfer to Delhi.

They were tail-heavy, carrying two electric motors back to the depot for repair. The machine clattered and wobbled along the airstrip, finally leaving the ground with a rush of air, like a sigh of relief. Mike pushed the throttles hard forward and they climbed slowly into a clear sky, getting a good view of the site before they headed north. The retaining wall of the dam, which would one day hold a sizeable lake, looked ugly from the air, the bare concrete a scar on the delicate skin of the desert. The *wadi* had been providing a trickle of water over the years. There was now a blue-green pool in the deep shade of the wall. Compared to this massive structure the purpose-built village of white houses surrounded by palm trees looked small and flimsy. He picked out his own house, saw his Arab boy standing outside, waving. *Allah selamet.*

 He was going to spend a couple of nights in Riyadh in the flat which Robyn shared with two other nurses. The relationship had become difficult because she gone on hoping for marriage, which had been a possibility at one time. He'd told her that he'd thought about it very carefully and decided against. It wouldn't be fair to her. There was no possibility of a domestic set-up in India. He was a wanderer by nature, he'd messed up one marriage already.

Robyn had taken this badly, been disappointed and hurt. Suspicious too, not without reason. Her idea was to take him to Australia, he'd love it. There was plenty of space there. They would have a farm, maybe grow pineapples in Queensland.

No, he didn't want to grow pineapples in Queensland. He didn't want Robyn. A nice-looking girl, good-humoured, practical. But no magic to her.

He thought often of Marian, though he never spoke about her. His love, his enchantment, was a private matter.

They had been flying almost an hour when a reddish-brown patch appeared on the horizon, straight ahead. Mike shouted above the engine noise, 'Don't like the look of that,' and took a more westerly course. Dust storms, coming across the land-mass from Oman, were not unusual in the area. With them came violent gusts of wind, not dangerous to airliners but very risky for a light twin. At first it seemed as if they had successfully avoided this particular cloud of dust then, surprisingly, it reappeared directly below them. 'No threat,' Mike announced.

The cloud seemed to be dispersing, a thin film widely spread against which their own shadow flew small and dark. Ten minutes later, keeping pace with them, it had gathered itself up into a ball maybe five hundred metres across. This meant another change of plan. Flying in a gale-force wind, dust-laden, would be no joke, the Crate being in a fairly terminal condition.

'Taking evasive action!' Mike shouted cheerfully, climbing at a steep angle. He'd done this often enough before, with a bigger load than he had today, and knew that there was nothing to it. So when the port engine began to splutter he couldn't for a moment think what had gone wrong. It couldn't be oil pressure, because the feeds had been changed at the last service. Incredulous, he tapped the gauge. It was way down. Looking across to the port wing he saw a rivulet of oil running out of the cowling vents, and wisps of smoke dispersing in the slipstream. That said it all. They were halfway to their destination. In a few minutes time the port engine would fail, and they would have to fly asymmetrically, with the starboard only. Or come down.

'Christ!' he called to Dave. 'Oil pressure's gone, we may have to ditch!' He'd hardly finished putting out a May Day call when the port engine gave a final cough and cut out. They were losing height and airspeed as he struggled to compensate, applying heavy pressure on the right rudder.

'You're doing fine!' Dave shouted back, checking his seat-belt. 'We'll be okay!' They both knew that the desert landscape, which looks so smooth from a distance, is full of rocks, ditches, hills, alternate stretches of hard and soft ground. Not the ideal terrain for a forced landing.

'Bugger, bugger,' muttered Mike. Oil pressure zero, manifold pressure dropping. Dead engine, dead foot. For a moment it seemed as if they could glide on a more or less level course, the cloud of dust to one side and well below them, possibly moving away. Or was it?

Now the turbulence hit them, rattling every piece of the old machine, trying to tear it apart, tipping it up and down, while Mike tried to bank away and higher, to distance himself from the storm centre. But the wind was stronger, and faster, clinging to their tail, overtaking, rising to a thundering roar. The cloud solidified, gathered itself together and took a new shape, swirling upwards into a huge red pillar.

'Great scenery!' yelled Dave.

'A twister!' cried Mike. 'It's a twister!'

They were laughing because it was so beautiful. This was a rare phenomenon, something you read about in your schoolboy magazine, illustrated with a picture of white-robed Arabs and a train of camels, watching the spiralling column from a safe distance.

Laughing one moment, the two of them. Then they yelled with fear as the wild, tawny-haired thing turned a fiery orange, stretched out its arms and embraced them, pulled them into its flaming heart. Millions of grains of flying sand twinkled in the sunshine, a universe of mini-stars. Sand came spitting in through every crack, every joint. Sand choked the remaining engine.

A sudden hush, only the wind whistling round them.

'Oh God,' Mike moaned. 'Oh God.' He had a girlfriend in Riyadh, a wife and two kids in Cyprus.

'Get ready,' Dave muttered, as if they were going to crash-land. 'Heads down.'

This was nonsense, play-acting. They were finished. More cruel mockery when the starboard engine picked up, gave a brief burst of power which threw them off their axis, then died. Left wing down, they dipped into a deep stall, accelerating through the whirling mass of golden sand in an anti-clockwise spin.

Losing consciousness Dave hallucinated, saw them flattening out, floating to land on a smooth surface, helping each other, bruised, shocked, but alive. We made it, Mike. Just luck. Might have been curtains.

Then he knew nothing, felt nothing.

A final twist, and the Crate smashed belly uppermost into the ground, scraping along with one wing aloft, the other broken off and left behind. The men inside were crushed to formless meat. There had been no time for pain, for screaming agony.

No time to recognise Death.

2   Elsewhere

There was a darkness greater than the blackest night, nothing to see, no sound, no movement. Then came a little light, like a torch beam, searching. Finally it settled, expanded, filled a great space.

Dave knew that he was dead, disembodied, sightless, deaf. And yet he could see and hear. He could move. Thought was there, vocabulary, a sense of withdrawal from one existence, a curiosity about another. Something would happen now, or later, or had already happened, at a time running parallel and therefore unconnected, where past, present and future were only words. Yes, that was a useful concept. They were only words.

In one of these dimensions he walked on Wimbledon Common. He remembered this place. As a schoolboy, during the life now over, he had played football here. He remembered this bench, where an old pederast used to sit watching. The orphanage boys knew his weakness and mocked him as they went past, safe in their solidarity.

The man sitting on the bench now was someone else, a stranger, a thin, elderly man in a tweed suit. He looked up, saw Dave, got to his feet, tottered forward with open arms..

'At last!' he cried. 'My beloved son!'

'Get off!' cried Dave, pushing him away. 'Who the hell are you?'

'I am your wretched father, and as you so rightly say I am in Hell. It was I who left you on the steps of the orphanage. Oh, the pain I have suffered, on earth and in this non-life, the shame, the self-reproach!'

'My father? All right then. You've got some excuse, I suppose.'

They sat together on the bench. The man spoke slowly, stopping often to wipe his eyes. 'Believe me, I regretted that action for the rest of my life. Your mother was a beautiful German girl, of good family. We met in London at a concert. She was a gifted singer. We loved each other passionately. She became pregnant, and I could not marry her. I was already married. I found her lodgings, gave her money. When you were born I told her that I was in touch with a married couple who were childless and wanted to adopt a baby. They were cultured people, I said, and well-off. She believed me. As soon as she was strong enough she sailed for America, where she had introductions to musical agents, teachers, opera singers. She kissed you goodbye. Ah, that farewell kiss!' He wept noisily.

'Less of the self-pity, if you don't mind,' said Dave coldly. 'What happened to my mother?'

With an effort the man controlled himself and went on. 'I betrayed her trust. There was no adoption, nothing arranged. I told the nurse who looked after you that your new parents lived in Scotland. They had come to London to fetch you, to take you home on the night train. She fed you and dressed you warmly. I paid her and said goodbye. I put you in my car, in your basket. I drove to the orphanage and left you there, turned round immediately and went home to my wife. I was a liar and a traitor to two adorable women. Oh merciful God, forgive me! I am so unhappy!'

'My mother. Did you ever see her again?'

'Never. We had agreed before we parted that we should try to forget what had happened. But in my present form, if you understand me, I was able to see her. It was a few days ago, or a year, perhaps a week. I don't know. Yes, she is alive and well, living in New York. She has had a successful career as a singer. She is married, has children, a happy family.'

'And were you a singer, a musician?'

'No. I was an engineer in radio and television in the early days, and made major contributions to technical developments after the War. I had a successful career. My personal tragedy was that my wife and I had no children. I tried to forget that I had fathered a son, whom I had abandoned. I am so glad to have found you at last. Forgive me if you can.'

Forgive? Dave disliked the man, despised him. What sort of a father was he who dumped his child, lied to the woman he'd seduced, went back to his wife as if nothing had happened? A lying sod, a hypocrite.

He said, getting up to go, 'If it's any comfort to you, I had a good life. I was fostered by intelligent people. Books, paintings, good food, a comfortable home. I went to university, travelled a lot.'

'This is a weight off my mind,' said his father, rising slowly, his knees stiff with age. 'I'm sorry I can't come with you. That's the way things are here. You don't have the choice. I've asked for God's forgiveness but I haven't heard yet. There's a long waiting list.'

They shook hands and said goodbye.

Dave walked away, heading for his old home in Albert Gardens. He would find Mimsy and Cecil. He would thank them.

And yet he couldn't get there. His surroundings changed. He was somewhere else, at a different time. The light faded. He was in the dark.

He was alone in a room with flowered curtains, a large sofa and comfortable armchairs, an antique desk, reading lamps, fitted carpet. He sensed rather than saw these things, feeling his way round the room, finally reaching the window, looking out between the curtains.

It was a cold, wintry night. He saw a busy street, London taxis, red buses. The street lights were on, but the shop windows were in darkness. He knew, from news in his recent life, that this was a time of industrial disputes in Britain, resulting in power cuts. Now knowledge came to him that he was in a block of flats in Kensington. He waited, wondering why. Though perhaps in non-life there are no reasons.

There was a noise in the hall, a key being turned. The front door opened. A couple came in, hastily embracing, not bothering to put the light on. The woman, tall, plump, good-looking, kicked off her shoes, helped the man take off his jacket and tie. He was fat and had a big belly, possibly not as big as it had once been because his trousers were loose around the waist, gathered up with a belt. His face was swollen and puffy.

'Beatrice, my Beatrice, I love you so much,' he said between kisses. 'I know it's possible when I'm with you. Just teach me how to do it in moderation, in a civilised way.'

'We'll do it together, Derek,' she said, holding him tight. 'We'll find a way.'

Were they talking about sex, or what? He didn't know these people. He didn't know why he was here, watching them as they passed through the living room, shedding their clothes, shimmering naked in the half-light as they went into the bedroom, their arms round each other.

'Let me wash first,' said the man. 'I'm sweaty. You said...'

'I can't wait,' said the woman. 'Afterwards.'

Who were they? Dave wandered around the living room, hearing them grunting and sighing next door.

Ah, here was a clue. A gleam of light fell on the desk. He saw letters addressed to Miss Beatrice King. He remembered. She was Marian's school friend who ran a nursing agency. And here was a postcard.

'Dear Queen Bee. Just to say thanks for everything. Will be back in UK one day. Hope to see you. Love Kiwi.'

Kiwi, the New Zealander who had looked after Mimi. Dave turned the card over. A picture of a kiwi, of course.

He smiled and faded away.

He was at a wedding. The speeches were done, toasts drunk. He saw half-eaten pieces of cake, empty glasses and bottles. The waiters were clearing the tables. The bride, petite, elegant, with big hazel eyes and dark hair, was wearing a pink suit with matching tricorne hat. Her bridesmaid, a little girl of four or five years old, wore a long pink dress and roses in her hair. A small boy in a sailor suit was hanging on to the bride's arm, looking dazed, sucking his thumb. There was a big crowd there, smartly dressed people, getting up from their seats and beginning to move towards the door, where a pink Rolls was waiting to take the newly-weds away.

Who was the lucky man? Dave followed the crowd. He saw the groom put his arm round the bride's shoulders, turn and smile as if to say, 'Yes, I'm the one!'

Surprise! It was John Keble, of all people. He'd found himself a second wife twice as pretty as his first one, and a lot of new friends as well by the look of things.

'Good luck,' said Dave. 'You deserve it. She's a lovely girl. Don't stand any nonsense this time.'

The bride and her husband got into the car with the bridesmaid and the boy in the sailor suit. The guests stood on the pavement, talking and laughing. Among them, right at the front, Dave thought he saw Marian.

Was it her? The face was beautiful, her face. But the body was bulging in front, as if she were pregnant. Charles was certainly there, flushed with drink, shouting, '*Bon voyage!*' as the Rolls began to move away.

'Marian!' Dave tried to push his way through the crowd but they were already fading, disintegrating. He couldn't find her. There was nobody there. All he could see was the name of the restaurant, swimming in the evening sky.

The Welcome Sole.

Time passed, backwards, forwards. Sometimes it stood still. For many years he found himself studying, reading books, listening to music. He wished that he could see Marian, but he had no choice, no power. He had to accept what came.

He was in a hospital, in an operating theatre. This interested him. At one time he had considered medicine as a career. A young woman, a beautiful blonde, was having a delivery by Caesarean section. He saw the surgeon bring out one small red baby, then another, both girls. They were perfect little creatures, one fair, one dark-haired. The paediatrician took them away, examined and washed them, put them in an incubator. They were small but strong. They would do well.

The surgeon finished stitching the patient and went away. The anaesthetist yawned as he pushed his equipment to one side. He was tired, not through overwork but because he had a new girlfriend. Sex was taking all his spare time and most of his energy.

The patient was wheeled into Recovery. A nurse waited by her side, holding her hand. 'Wake up, dear. You have two lovely little baby girls. Wake up now.'

Dave nudged the nurse's arm. 'Her blood pressure is way down,' he said. 'Do something. She's gone into shock.'

The nurse took the patient's blood pressure and paged Emergency. There was a flurry of activity as help arrived, the duty doctor, oxygen, two more nurses.

'Well done, ' said the doctor. 'Just in time.'

'Not at all,' said Dave. 'Don't mention it.'

In the corridor the girl's husband paced up and down, groaning, running his hands through his hair. 'Agony,' he muttered. 'Agony. Such a long time, I can't bear it. Agony.' He sat down, got up again, stood stiff and motionless, his fists clenched, waiting.

Half an hour, one hour, two hours. At last Sister came, smiling.

'You have two beautiful little baby girls, Mr Jones. Your wife will be coming back to her room in a moment. She is in Recovery.'

The man leaned against the wall, his face as white as a sheet. 'Recovery?' he gasped, fainting, slithering to the floor.

Sister caught him, supported him into a chair, grabbed his head and pushed it between his knees. 'Often happens,' she said. 'You'll be all right in a moment.'

Later Dave passed through the wall and into the patient's private room. She lay on her high hospital bed, her cheeks pink now, her eyes bright. Her husband was having a substantial tea, with biscuits and sandwiches. Dave happened to know that he had been in such a state of anxiety since his wife went into hospital that he had forgotten about breakfast, and lunch. This would account for his fainting fit.

'Beloved Quentin,' the girl said.

Quentin poured himself another cup of tea, added several spoons of sugar. 'Darling Barbara. I'm so proud, so happy.'

'I had such a strange dream,' she murmured. 'I dreamed that I was on a mountain. A man saw me and sent for help, because I was too near the edge. It was a precipice.'

'It wasn't a dream,' said Dave softly. 'I just happened to be there. I'm in Purgatory, if you know what I mean.'

She smiled as if to say, 'Thank you, whoever you are.'

She was so pretty, so young, her husband so devoted. He left them holding hands, murmuring loving words to each other, and flitted across the squeaky-clean corridor to the nursery. He saw the newly-born twins lying quietly together in their incubator, their tiny chests rising and falling in unison. Knowledge came to him of how they would grow, become strong, learn to walk and talk. Their parents, the little blonde Barbara and the tall, gaunt Quentin, would be kept busy feeding them, reading them stories, taking them to school. They would grow into two remarkable young women, clever, beautiful and kind.

Time passed in the hospital, two days or three. Barbara was sitting up in bed. She had just expressed milk from her breasts into a sterile container and a nurse had taken it away to feed to the twins. There were vases of flowers in her room, a bowl of fruit, a bottle of orange juice, two little teddy bears, many other toys, knitted coats, boots, Get Well cards, books and magazines. Her husband Quentin was pacing up and down, deep in thought.

'The title is of the utmost importance, beloved,' he said at last, settling by her bed. 'Not only does it tell the reader what to expect. It is also, in the creative stages, a great help to the writer.'

'You mean, dearest, that your subject matter is already there, but you don't yet know how to present it. The title, when you find it, will define your approach.'

'Exactly. To recapitulate, my story is one of continuing hope in the face of suffering. What is hope? Why do some people go on hoping, looking for light at the end of their particular tunnel, while others give up and descend into a state of despair? Is despair a freak, a disorder? And why do an unfortunate minority reach a state of such utter despair that they no longer want to live? Why?'

'Those last people are exceptions,' Barbara said. 'Yes, their despair is a disorder. For them the tunnel seems to be endless. Or they have struggled to the end only to find that the way out is blocked. Or that they have arrived at a place where the sun never shines.'

'That must be Hell.'

'One sort of Hell. But the norm is to go on hoping. "Hope springs eternal in the human breast. We never are but always to be blest." That sums it up, don't you agree.'

'It does indeed. Hope is the normal condition.'

'Hope-loss can be temporary,' Barbara went on. 'One can be temporarily in despair, and recover.'

'Yes. One can have a mild case, an affliction which can be cured, or which may pass. The patient may make a complete recovery, with for instance psychiatric help, or the help of friends. A belief in God may strengthen a sufferer, enough to get him through the tunnel.' Quentin stopped, thought again, then asked her earnestly, 'Do animals have hope? And plants? Is it hope which makes a caged bird go on singing, and keeps plants alive through the long, dark days of winter? Is it hope, or is it just biology? That's a question I shall have to deal with. And the title. Oh, the title! *The End of the Tunnel.* Or perhaps *The Springs of Hope.* Or, as you just said, *Always To Be Blest*. '

'*Blind Biology*,' said Barbara smiling. 'No, darling Quentin, writer of distinction, television personality, beloved husband, father of twins, I have the perfect title for you. Your book is called simply *Purgatory*.'

'*Purgatory*!' He pulled her towards him for a kiss, hugging her so passionately that she cried out, 'Ouch! My stomach!'

So he kissed her more gently, her lips, her little hands, her shoulders. 'You are ever wonderful, my Barbara,' he said. 'You never fail me. *Purgatory* is the title. It encapsulates everything I have written so far. How on earth did you think of it?'

'It just came to me.'

'That's a lie!' said Dave crossly. Useless, because they couldn't hear him. 'I gave it to you. You damn nearly left your present existence and joined me here. I saved you and gave you the title. Go on, admit it.'

'I mean I was inspired,' Barbara told Quentin. 'The man in my dream inspired me.'

'That's better,' said Dave, turning away, leaving the room not of his own volition, steadily following the Exit signs along corridors, past patients on trolleys or in wheel-chairs, past long-faced relatives and friends, waiting. Some of them were hopeful. Others knew that there was no hope.

He reached the reception area, enquiries desk, main entrance. As he wafted out into the open air a girl carrying flowers and gift-wrapped packages came towards him. She was beautiful, serene, pregnant. It was Marian.

'Marian, I'm here! Come back!' But she walked on and through him into the place he had just left. Desperately he tried to manoeuvre himself back through the swing doors, but it was no good.

It was hopeless. He was never to be blest.

And yet, still human in his thinking, he couldn't help hoping. He could see a glimmer of light at the end of the tunnel. Even Marian was not immortal. She would grow old and eventually die. In earthly terms this would be many years ahead, for him a disorderly mass of time in which he would wander on earth and in other regions, waiting for her. When at last she came their spirits would rest together in peace. They would be in Heaven.

A blissful concept, followed by black despair. What if she died and wandered somewhere else, not with him but with Charles, her children, her friends? What if he never saw her again, in any form?

Yes, he knew what that would be. It would be Hell.

He was in an upstairs room, a nursery. A young girl sat with a small baby on her knee, trying to feed it from a little bowl of milky food.

'Come on, Teresa darling. You can't be on a bottle forever, you know.'

The baby spat and dribbled.

A toddler, a fair-haired boy, was reaching up to the radio-cassette player, pressing the knobs. 'More, more.'

'More please, Edward.'

'More please.'

The girl got up with the baby tucked under one arm, put a cassette in and turned it on. It was *Eine Kleine Nachtmusik*.

'La, la-la!' sang Edward, trying to beat time with his foot. 'La-la, la-la, la-la!'

Dave sang in harmony with him.

He saw Charles, handsome, self-assured, taking his seat in the House of Commons. That must be Marian up in the gallery, smiling down at her successful husband, Charles Broome-Vivier, Conservative Member of Parliament for Upweston.

Marian, so far away.

Another hospital, this one for the care and treatment of the mentally ill. A room with a window high up, a heavy door, a narrow bed, a table, two chairs. A young man in a white coat sat at the table making notes, tapping his ballpoint pen on the page from time to time as if to say, 'That's done. What's next?'

Under the bed lay a red-haired woman. She was wearing a loose nightgown which she had pulled up over her shoulders, leaving her pale legs and buttocks bare. She was silent, motionless. The man talked to her in a kind, quiet voice.

'You're an intelligent and well-informed person, so there's no need for me to over-simplify. You know how your condition is described, and to what extent it can be alleviated with analysis and medication. As the psychiatrist in charge of your case, I am confident that you will one day write again, see your friends, lead a normal life. But we need your energy and co-operation to start the healing process.'

The patient said nothing. She withdrew further into the corner under the bed, pulling her knees up to her chin.

'We offer occupational therapy here,' he went on. 'Many patients are helped by simple activities such as tapestry and basket-work Your talent is a creative one, so you would probably prefer painting, or modelling in clay. There is also group therapy. We know that you will find this tiresome at first, because many of our patients are less educated than you are, and less articulate. You will find their company boring, their problems of no interest. But look at it another way. Your being there, listening, perhaps speaking about yourself, will help them. And this shared experience will in turn help you.'

He tapped his pen on his notes. Then he began to speak with urgency, in a less formal way. 'You've been here for two months and have done very little of anything. No exercise, not much food, sleep induced by medication. No reading. Very little speech. I'd like you to get out and about a bit. Summer is here, the grounds are looking their best, the birds are singing. And the outside world is full of interest, particularly for people like you. You haven't read a newspaper for some time, so you are not aware that we have had a General Election, and that the Conservatives are in power. We have a woman Prime Minister. They ditched Heath, you remember, in seventy-four.'

This was a deliberate mistake. He paused, hoping for a reaction. The woman under the bed moved slightly, pulled the nightgown down over her behind and hid her face in her hands. 'Seventy-five,' she said, her voice muffled.

'Yes, of course. Seventy-five,' he said, privately rejoicing in this small success. 'The new Prime Minister is called Margaret Thatcher. I thought you might be interested. See you tomorrow.'

He closed his notebook, put his pen in his pocket and left her.

Later a nurse came and put food on the table, a sandwich, a plastic mug of fruit juice, some biscuits. 'There you are, dear. It's smoked salmon today, quite nice.'

'I want my clothes,' came the voice from under the bed.

'Of course you do,' said the nurse, and went away.

In his state of non-being Dave found that certain information came to him in a constant stream, without effort on his part, whether he wanted it or not. So he knew that the red-haired woman was the well-known journalist, Clarissa Dearden. She had at one time been married to Patrick Dearden, who had recently inherited the title and now sat in the House of Lords on the Conservative benches. The divorce had been acrimonious. He wanted her to drop the name Dearden, particularly because she had become increasingly Left Wing. His lawyers advised him against pursuing the matter. His wife-to-be was already pregnant when the divorce came through and they were able to marry. She subsequently bore him a son-and-heir.

Due to a deep emotional disturbance, Clarissa had written nothing for the past year. She was now undergoing treatment at Weston Towers, once an Edwardian gentleman's residence. It was one of the best private institutions of its kind in England. The professional care was of the highest order. There were sports facilities, workshops, a chapel, a cinema. The food was excellent. Patients had private rooms with television, but were expected to take part in general activities, to mix socially and to eat in the dining room which belonged to their section, if their state of health allowed. The house was surrounded by extensive grounds which included a kitchen garden and hothouses. Patients were encouraged to have individual garden plots.

The red-haired Clarissa, her hair brushed and tied back, sat weeping on a bench. Her doctor was sitting with her.

'You're doing very well,' he said cheerfully. 'We're particularly pleased with the contribution you've made to the group therapy sessions. If you weren't an outstanding writer you could have been a first-class psychologist. Perhaps the one pre-supposes the other.'

She shook her head, tears pouring down her cheeks. 'For God's sake give me something to stop this bloody crying! It's disgusting, it doesn't help me. I don't want anyone to see me like this!'

'That's understandable. You cry mostly in the morning, don't you, but less each day. This is progress. We'll be giving you a tranquilliser this afternoon because you've got a visitor and naturally you don't want to give a gloomy impression. He's the local MP, isn't he. Charles Broome-Vivian.'

'Broome-Vivier,' she corrected him, mopping her eyes.

'Sorry. Broome-Vivier.' He smiled because he was sure now that she was on the road to recovery. It had been a struggle for both of them.

The bell rang and people wandered indoors to their various dining rooms. The garden was empty.

A few hours passed, in earthly terms. Dave saw Charles coming out of the house, across the terrace, down the steps to the lawn, looking around at the various groups sitting in the sun.

Clarissa had been waiting under a tree. Now she hurried forward and threw her arms round Charles, leaning on his shoulder, murmuring, 'Thank you Charles. Thank you for coming.'

'My dear Clarissa.' Charles gently held her away, took her arm as they walked together down the avenue to a seat in the shade. 'Well, here I am at last. I was late getting to Upweston, road repairs, single lane, you know the sort of thing. Then I had my meeting with the local worthies. They do like to air their views, and have every right to do so. But at such length! I thought I'd never get away. Now, how are you? You look wonderful.'

This was not true. Charles, beneath his hearty manner, was shocked by her appearance. She was very thin. Her face was haggard and pale except for some bright green eye-shadow and lipstick badly applied. She looked like an old actress playing a young woman's part. Her voice was lower than it used to be.

'The worst is over, Charles. They say it's up to me now, to fight my way back to normality, whatever that is.'

'Normality!' Charles spoke in a hearty, cheerful manner to disguise the fact that he had not been looking forward to this visit. It was a duty, not a pleasure. 'Normality is one thing you don't find in the House. The reverse in fact. The place is a...' He stopped just in time. He was about to say 'madhouse.' 'It's a zoo. All the animals chattering, singing, roaring. You never heard such a racket!'

She smiled, showing lipstick on her teeth. 'And what sort of animal is Margaret Thatcher, Charles?'

'Naughty Clarissa! You're teasing me. She is without doubt the best Prime Minister we've had since Churchill. She has what I consider the essential qualities of leadership, patriotism, perseverance and integrity.'

'She knows nothing about the economy and is not interested,' said Clarissa firmly. 'Does not care. We'll be holding out the begging bowl by the time she's finished with us.'

They were soon deep in friendly argument.

Outwardly it seemed that Clarissa was on the road to recovery. She herself was hopeful. She had certainly made progress since the time when she lay, half-naked, silent and withdrawn, under her bed.

But Dave knew, with his special insight, that she would never be really well again. He saw that she would suffer a series of ups and downs, phases of manic activity, writing, socialising, travelling, followed by periods of deep despair. She would become a burden to friends and colleagues. She would take to drink and be dried out, go on drugs and be rescued from dependence. Weston Towers would become one of the few stable elements in her life. She would return there many times to start yet another programme of consultation and treatment.

It was most unfortunate for Charles that Weston Towers was in his constituency He found illness distasteful, especially illness of the mind. How ghastly Clarissa looked, at least ten years older. How embarrassing.

Dave melted away, leaving them in the beautiful grounds, where the flowers were blooming and the birds sang.

He was at sea in a destroyer, the narrow prow cutting through huge grey-green waves, heading south. Prime Minister Margaret Thatcher was sending a task force to drive the Argentinians out of the Falkland Islands.

He saw young men burned, blown up, dying.

In Africa he saw millions dying of hunger and disease. He travelled with countless refugees across dusty soil, where no crops grew. It was hot and dry. There was no food, no water.

An old man dressed in a ragged loincloth said to him, 'The journey of my life is over. Now I will sit and rest. Please sit with me until I am called. You have a ciggy?'

Fortunately Dave had cigarettes and matches in his pocket. They lit up and smoked in peace, while the throng of displaced people walked past them and away into the distance.

He saw a Russian leader, a man of revolutionary ideas. His face was confident, calm and strong, his forehead decorated with a birthmark. He wanted cooperation with other leaders. The Soviet Union would no longer be closed to the rest of the world. There would be *glasnost*, meaning openness, and *perestroika*, meaning reconstruction. Later this man was removed from power by a new leader, who renounced Communism. The USSR began to split into many smaller parts. There were bitter struggles between neighbouring countries, and between central government and dissident areas.

There was war in the Gulf, the Western Allies coming to the aid of Kuwait, which had been invaded by Iraq. Dave knew these places well. He saw tanks, armament and troops massing in Saudi Arabia, where he had worked on the dam. There was a new Prime Minister by this time, an unassuming man called John Major. Margaret Thatcher had been deposed by the Party after eleven years in power.

There was war in Yugoslavia. He saw civilians murdered, old men, women, children, in the name of Ethnic Cleansing. He saw cities bombed to ruins as separate groups struggled for survival.

He was present in his bodiless state at the breaking down of the Berlin Wall. With a crowd of citizens, weeping, rejoicing, waving homemade banners, he advanced through the gap from the Communist side of the city to the democratic West.

He remembered that his mother was German. He looked at the faces round him, wondering if he had a relative somewhere there, an aunt, an uncle, a cousin.

These events and many others came to him in disorder, a later one first, an earlier one somewhere in the middle. In life he had been trained in science and mechanics, in which a result is preceded by contributory factors. So in non-life he was immediately able to sort these chunks of history into their proper sequence.

But it was a sad business, this review of what was happening in the world. So much of it was cruel, unnecessary and wasteful.

He was in England, flying over a damp, green landscape. He was not alone. Travelling alongside, more or less invisible but highly vocal, was a man with a persistent, hearty manner which Dave found intensely annoying. He had tried to get rid of the fellow by pushing, kicking sideways, flying higher, without success.

The man went on talking, as he had been doing for some time, apparently unconcerned. 'I say, lovely view. Nothing like the English countryside, what-ho. Now, I don't think you've been to this particular place before, and it's going to be a real treat, I assure you. We're going to visit your son.'

'I don't have a son,' said Dave angrily. 'I have a daughter. And it's no business of yours. And who the hell are you anyway?'

'Who the hell? That's funny language to use in Purgatory, ha-ha! As it happens I can't introduce myself, because I lost my identity earlier on. They gave me Oblivion by mistake, pretty shocking, what. By way of compensation I'm being upgraded to Heaven as soon as the administrative muddle has been sorted out. Meanwhile they've given me a job in Virtual Reality. I'm a guide, I tell people where they are, and what they are going to see. Very simple really. Now in your case... I say, you are David Mason, aren't you? We don't want any more cock-ups.'

'Yes. I am David Mason. Get on with it, would you.'

'Right. We are now approaching Broome Hall, the home of Charles Broome-Vivier, MP. You can just see it now, between the trees. The eldest child in the family is called Edward, and he is your son by Charles's wife. The boy's parentage is a secret, known only to his mother... I say, are you all right?'

A son by Marian! A sudden lurch in their non-bodily progress reminded him of that other flight, with Mike, when the cloud of orange dust overtook the Crate and smashed it to pieces.

172

'I'm fine. I felt dizzy, nothing serious. This news comes as a surprise. A bit of a shock. I saw a small boy years ago, or perhaps just yesterday. His name was Edward, he liked music. Was that the same boy?'

'Yes. Ever so sorry, and all that. I try to break the news gently, if it's a bit irregular, know what I mean. It's difficult to get the balance right. Anyway, I've got to push off now and get back to the office, what-ho. They promised I would get news soon, my name and what sort of life I had. They think they can get it back through Recycle, but it's tricky, being some years ago.' His voice began to fade, became squeaky and irregular. His words echoed through the non-atmosphere. 'Broome Hall, straight ahead, up the avenue, new, new. You can't miss it, miss it. Jolly good show, what-ho, what-ho. Ta-ta for now, for now. Ta-ta, ta-ta, ta-ta.'

Dave tried to follow him, but in Purgatory you don't have full control. There was no steering, no acceleration. He shouted as loudly as he could, 'I'm sorry! I was unco-operative, bad-tempered! And I'm sorry about your identity, hope they recover it, best of jolly British luck and all that, what-ho! Can you hear me? Please, please, just tell me anything you know about the boy's mother, Marian. Anything!'

Silence, loneliness. There was nobody there, nothing.

He reached a circular room inside a tower. It was full of electronic equipment: a keyboard, headphones, a cassette-player, a player for the new compact discs, a television set, two speakers, a computer. A boy perhaps fifteen years old, fair-haired, blue-eyed, sat at the keyboard playing a tune, replaying, editing, recording. He whistled and hummed.

Edward, my son. My son.

The boy went to the door of his tower room and called down the stairs, 'Sue, come up and listen to my fugue!'

A girl of about eleven came up to join Edward. Like him she was wearing jeans and a tee-shirt. She was very pretty, like her mother Marian. Her hair was dark and curly, cut short.

Edward pressed a button and she listened, smiling, to his recorded fugue.

'Knockout,' she said.

A younger boy came up the spiral staircase, hitting the handrail with a riding crop. He was good-looking, brown-eyed, rosy-faced, the image of his father Charles. He knocked on the open door with his crop.

'Stop it, Jack,' said Edward. 'What do you want?'

'You owe me four pounds fifty and I bloody well want it now because I'm going shopping.'

'Foul-mouthed brat,' said Edward, producing a fiver from his wallet.

'You owe me fifty pence. Get thee gone.'

Jack stuffed the cash in his pocket and went downstairs, slashing his riding crop this way and that. Dave followed, through a hall with a massive stone fireplace and high mullioned windows, up a second spiral staircase to another tower room.

A teenage girl sat at a table, frowning over her books. She was Teresa, the second child in the Broome-Vivier family. Dave had last seen her as a baby. She had grown into a plain, thin girl with pale eyes and mouse-coloured hair. She had extra work to do in the holidays because she needed to get at least three 'O' Levels. She wanted to be a doctor or a social worker. She was serious-minded and sensitive.

Looking over her shoulder, Dave saw that she had been writing a letter, which she covered with a book as the ebullient Jack approached.

> Since we talked together I know that we don't need them except for reproduction and we can be sexually-fulfilled within our own sex and there is no need for the female to be the slave of a male because in society as it is today the female is a slave to his demands to reproduce his own kind and use the reproductive process as a...

He foresaw that Teresa would have a troubled and unhappy life. The other three children had inner strength and resilience. She was the sort who took life's blows very hard. The death of her grandfather Ted Broome-Vivier, for instance, had affected her deeply. The others had wept and recovered. She still nursed her grief. To add to her problems, she was going through an emotional involvement with a girl at Abbey Mead, older than she was and in a different House.

'Do you want any shopping done?' said Jack.

'No,' said Teresa. 'Go away. I'm working.'

Dave roamed around Broome Hall. In the kitchen two girls from New Zealand were sitting at a long wooden table, drinking coffee. The shelves of the old-fashioned dresser were crowded with blue and white china. A dog, a Labrador, got up and growled.

'Shut up, Winston,' said one of the girls. 'There's nobody there.'

'That's what you think,' said Dave, winking at the dog.

In the living room he recognised some of Mimsy's pictures and carpets. Her Crown Derby was in a glass-fronted recess built in the Gothic style. In the library he saw her Sheraton side table and carved bookcase, in the dining room her table, with the extra leaves in place, and twelve matching chairs.

174

There was a study for Charles, equipped with computer, telephone and Fax machine. Marian, in a smaller room, had similar up-to-date facilities, her own telephone line and Fax. She spent most of her time at Broome now, and so did Charles. They would stay in London when Parliament was sitting, to entertain and attend social functions. They went to the theatre and to Covent Garden. In the summer they went to Glyndebourne. Opera had become a special interest for them. A good-looking couple, they were seen at Ascot and Henley and other fashionable gatherings. Their photographs appeared in society magazines.

Broome Hall had been featured in the *Architectural Review* in an article about the Gothic Revival. *Vogue* had written about its tasteful refurbishment. There were photographs of the dining room and the kitchen. Also one of Charles Broome-Vivier, MP, and his wife Marian, standing on the front steps.

Dave understood that Marian had sold her boutique and her share of Marcel Design two years ago. Terence Gray, the designer, had been furious when she told him that she wanted to pull out. He said she was dumping him, Marcellina had been just a little shop behind Harrods selling Italian dresses for a hundred and fifty, and look at it now, Marcel models were never less than eight hundred and his wedding gowns four or five thousand, people just couldn't get enough of them, he'd put her on the map hadn't he, and this was all the thanks he got.

Once the sale had gone through Terry realised how lucky he'd been, and actually thanked Marian. The new investor had useful American contacts and introduced him to Hollywood, where he expanded into television and film design. 'The cream of the rag trade,' he said. He was one of the few British designers who survived the recession.

Marian's father, William Foster, had shepherded his daughter through this operation. 'You're doing the right thing at the right time, my girl. What goes up must come down. The boom is over.' He still telephoned her regularly from his house in Spain with financial advice and details of recent alterations to his Will, which had become a major preoccupation. He had set up a Trust for Edward, who would inherit Broome and have the expense of keeping it up. The other children had small legacies. William adored Edward, his eldest grandson. Edward returned his affection.

All this Dave learned as he drifted through the downstairs rooms. He looked for Marian, but didn't find her. From the hall he sped up the carved oak staircase, across the wide landing and into the master bedroom. Marian's dressing gown lay on the bed, her satin slippers on the floor. Gently he touched these things, remembering her naked body, her bare feet. Next door was the bathroom, the bath very big with claw feet, Victorian-style brass taps, a massive shower fitting.

There were spare bedrooms on the other side of the landing, more bathrooms, and rooms for the two girls. Sue's was chaotic, full of dolls, stuffed toy animals, books, posters, photographs. Clothes lay scattered about. Teresa's was tidy, everything in its proper place. On the top floor there were bedrooms for Edward and Jack, and the resident help. Also a gallery with windows looking west.

No sign of Marian. He skimmed downstairs again and out through the kitchen, the dog Winston following, barking at the back door. 'All rightee,' said one of the New Zealand girls, and let him out. He ran alongside, barking, as Dave hurried round to the front of the house.

A white Renault, the latest model, was waiting in the drive, the engine running, Marian at the wheel. Her mother, Emily Foster, was in the passenger seat, grumbling. Children were spoiled these days, she said. They had too much pocket money. When she was Jack's age she had a shilling a week.

He heard Marian's voice. 'Mummy, it's inflation. The value of money has changed, you see.'

'Don't talk to me about inflation, pet. With my limited income and prices constantly going up, I know all about it.'

'Yes, Mummy. I know it's difficult for you.' Her mother was staying four days, and this was only the first.

Jack came running out of the house and climbed into the back of the car, the dog trying to squeeze in with him.

'Bad luck, Winston,' said Jack, pushing him out and banging the door. Winston gave a last bark and went off to explore the shrubbery. The car sped down the drive and disappeared among the trees.

The scene shrunk to a small space, a tiny green spot on the map of England. A spot inside which there was a house which looked like a castle, with a tower each end, a gallery on the top floor, beautiful furniture, carpets, curtains. A warm, comfortable place, well maintained. The perfect home for Marian, her husband and family.

Dave longed to be with her, to speak to her. He wished that he had taken home leave, just once, before he died, even if it had led to no more than a telephone call. Hallo Marian. It's Dave Mason. I'm in London for two weeks. Can I give you lunch, or a drink? Whatever suits you.

It was too late now.

He prayed often, hoping that there might after all be a God, a Supreme Being, who would help him. In life he had not been sincerely religious, though baptised in St George's, Wimbledon, with a batch of orphanage babies, and confirmed there in his early teens. He had sung in the choir. Later he had joined more prestigious choirs and sung the great oratorios, cantatas and masses. That had been his faith, more musical than spiritual. Any lingering belief in God had been replaced in adulthood by agnosticism, loosely based on science. The Big Bang theory had appealed to him as a plausible explanation of how things started. If God existed, He would have been a Prime Mover, creating the explosion which set the universe in motion, then standing aside. He had been amused at the thought of God as an engineer, like himself. Now he fervently hoped that God continued to care for his creatures and would sometimes answer their prayers.

'Help me find her,' he prayed. 'My sufferings are nothing compared to some. But help me. I want to tell her, because I never did in life, that I love her eternally.'

Sometimes he found that he knew by instinct where she was, although he wasn't there himself. She had bought a house in France, in the Alpes-Maritimes, and spent holidays there with her children, sometimes the Keble family as well, and the Quentin Jones's. She went to Canada with Charles on a Parliamentary delegation, to New Zealand and Australia. She went to Hong Kong on business connected with her boutique. She went several times to the United States.

On one occasion he was at Heathrow and saw her, with Charles, in the Concorde departure lounge. He tried to join them but an unseen force barred the way. Agony, frustration. He had to take an alternative route, flying through the ether, getting lost, landing in Newfoundland in a snowstorm, struggling south to New York. Yes, she was somewhere in the city. All he had to do was to find her. He looked for her in smart hotels, restaurants, department stores. He wandered up and down Fifth Avenue. He went to the Guggenheim and the Metropolitan Museum of Art. At night he haunted Broadway, watching the crowds as they came out of theatres. He had no luck.

Exhausted and depressed, he found himself in an apartment on the West Side, overlooking the Hudson River. He was in a room crowded with furniture, ornaments, books, photographs. An elderly woman sat at a grand piano, playing the accompaniment while her pupil rehearsed his Schubert *liede*. He was a promising young singer, an American. His teacher, originally from Germany, had sung at the Metropolitan Opera House in her youth. She was an indifferent pianist, banging out the chords, stopping frequently to correct her pupil's pronunciation, his phrasing.

Dave knew her at once. He could see that she must have been a beautiful girl, many years ago. Now her fine skin was wrinkled, her body rounded out, her fingers bent with age. Her hair, once pale blonde, was white. He recognised her blue eyes, the set of her head, because he was part of her.

She was his mother.

In the framed photographs standing on bookshelves and occasional tables were his half-brothers and half-sisters, their wives and husbands, and their children, his nephews and nieces. He looked at their faces, the way they stood, the way they smiled. They were his family.

They seemed closer to him, more congenial, than his own daughter, who looked like her mother and wasn't interested in music. He knew that he had failed her as a father. Since the divorce he had seen her perhaps twice a year, no more.

He had failed his son too, except for passing on some musical talent. Fondly he imagined Edward's becoming famous as a composer of operas and choral works, marrying an attractive girl, having several children, inheriting Broome Hall. A proud father's dream.

He turned back to his mother. He understood that she was now a widow. She had been married to a musical impresario, a devoted husband. She had confessed to him, when he proposed marriage, that she had borne an illegitimate child in England who had been adopted. Dave longed to tell her that he was that child, that he had been fostered by an artistic couple and had had an interesting life. That he, too, liked to sing.

'Dein ist mein ganzes Herz!' sang the pupil, and Dave joined in, adding a richness which made the room resound with this confession of love. *'Dein ist mein Herz.'* And on to a triumphant ending, this time accurate in every respect and so full of emotion that Dave's mother said, as she lifted her hands from the piano. 'If Franz Schubert were only here! You know how it happens.' There was a box of tissues on the side of the piano. She took one and wiped her eyes. 'Sometimes you feel you have an extra voice, more than you think, yes? At that moment I heard your extra voice!'

The lesson was over. The singer collected his music, thanked her and said goodbye. Dave knew that his time was up too, kissed his mother's cheek, saw her put her hand to the place as if to hold his kiss safely there. *Auf weidesehen, Mutter.*

No time for more. A sudden force hustled and pushed him out of the apartment, slapped his arms to his sides, jerked his head upwards. Like a rocket he rose above Manhattan, circled over the Hudson and turned east, over Long Island, heading for the Atlantic. He flew higher and higher, reaching an area where all the world's music had been assembled into a dense, cacophonous cloud, for which he was prepared, having earphones, on his non-existent ears, which separated the many components. He heard quartets, symphonies and concertos by Beethoven, Mahler, Mozart, Haydn, Sibelius. He heard the *Messiah,* the *Christmas Oratorio*, the *Passion of St John*. He heard *Otello, La Traviata, Peter Grimes, Akhnaten.* He heard classical music, jazz, *avant garde,* Minimalist, atonal, dodecaphonic, quarter-tone. He sang as Caruso, crooned with Frank Sinatra, chanted Gregorian masses, wept as Pagliacci. *Veste la gubbia!* What grief, what irony!

From this monstrous noise he fell through the stratosphere into the swirling clouds of a great storm, which rounded Cap Finistère and entered the English Channel, sweeping up many devils, goblins, elves and fairies, witches and warlocks, swelling to become a hurricane. Exulting in their combined force this crowd of non-people swept over southern England, uprooting trees, shattering walls, overturning cars, ripping roofs away and flying them for kites. Dave flew with them, his frustration expressed in this orgy of destruction.

'Marian!' he shouted against the solid roar of the wind. 'Marian!' For a brief moment gifted with steering power, he managed to turn the force to one side as they approached Broome, saved the lime avenue, spared the beeches. Sevenoaks got it instead. Trees crashed in Kew Gardens, and in Chelsea. Marian's town house was spared, and so was Marcellina. Windows were broken and tiles scattered in the next street.

'Ah, Marian!' he sighed, suddenly dumped into silence as the storm veered away and left him behind. He began to fall, fast, spread out his arms and legs to reduce speed, and began a spiral flight back to earth. 'Where are you, Marian? Where?'

A voice came to him through the headphones. 'This is Virtual Reality. Please give your name and requirement. We may be able to help you.'

Dave groaned. That so-called guide was back, the fellow who'd been given Oblivion by mistake, who would go to Heaven as soon as they'd unearthed his records.

'It's me again, Dave Mason. Marian must be somewhere here. Can I get through to her, talk to her? Or see her. Anything.'

'Hallo, Mason old boy. Yes, I think there's something in the pipeline, jolly good show. But you've got to do another visit first. Patience is a virtue, don't I know it. Just hang on a minute while I get you on to my screen, what-ho. Yes, you're due on the other side of the river. From where you are, it's turn south at Hyde Park Corner, head for Vauxhall

Bridge.'

'Can't I skip this and go straight on to Marian, if it's in the pipeline?'

'Sorry. I have to access someone else. It's an emergency. Ta-ta for now!'

'Ta-ta, and the best of British luck to you,' said Dave sadly.

He knew this part of London, but it had changed. There were no big buildings, no tower blocks. There were no cars, no traffic lights. The streets were narrow, crowded with horse-drawn vehicles, buses, hansom cabs, carriages, carts and heavy drays. There was a street market, the goods piled high on carts under striped awnings, fish, hunks of meat, mounds of potatoes, cabbages, carrots, trays of eggs. People shouted, drivers swore at each other and cracked their whips.

The noise died away. He drifted into wider streets, past a church and a cricket pitch, floating along a terrace of small houses until he reached a larger one, semi-detached. He soared over the roof and came to rest in the back garden.

There was washing hanging on the line, white aprons, sheets, table cloths, handkerchiefs, babies' napkins. It was a warm spring day, the trees green with new leaves, the air still. He heard nothing at first, then a regular creaking sound, as of hinges which need oiling.

Creak, creak.

A little girl was sitting on a swing, swaying backwards and forwards, pushing herself with one foot. She was wearing a black pinafore over her dark serge dress. Her brown hair was plaited and tied with a black bow. A boy sat on a bench nearby, whittling a stick with his penknife. He wore knickerbockers and a Norfolk jacket. There was a black band on his sleeve.

'Tom, I want to tell you something,' said the girl.

So sad, the noise the swing was making. Creak, creak.

'What is it?'

'I can't love Baby Vincent, you see.'

'He's still small, Mimsy. When he grows big we'll teach him to play Snap and...' He was going to say 'Happy Families' but changed his mind. 'We'll play Hide-and-Seek with him, and give him piggy-back rides.'

'But I don't want to. I don't like him because when he came our Mama went away to Heaven. And I would rather have Mama back.' She began to cry. 'Because Baby Vincent is only a trouble and a nuisance, and I don't want him to be my little brother, so there!'

'Hush, Mimsy, don't cry. Be a brave girl.' He was afraid that he might blub, too, and make a fool of himself. He jolly nearly had at the funeral,

180

which was only last week. What had helped him was thinking about his ambition in life, which was to be a soldier. No blubbing in the Army, only bravery in the face of the enemy. 'We all have to die in the end,' he explained. 'Poor Mama was sick, and she died and went to Heaven, which is very sad for us. But we must bear it, like our Queen, who is an example to us all. You see, her husband Prince Albert died, and she has had to rule without him to help her. She rules England, Ireland, Scotland and Wales, and the whole of the Empire overseas.'

Mimsy wiped her eyes on the corner of her pinafore. 'I think she is happy, because she has a palace to live in, and a castle in Scotland. And she has a crown.'

'Yes, these things are proper for a Queen'

Mimsy felt more cheerful and said, 'I wish I could be Queen then,' which made Tom smile.

Then their sister Katie came out and asked them to help her get the washing in because Mrs Higgs, the cook-general, was busy making scones, and Nurse was feeding Baby Vincent and keeping an eye on little sister Rose. So Tom put away his penknife and helped Katie take down the washing and fold it, while Mimsy collected the pegs. Tom hoped the people next door couldn't see him, because such a task was not suitable for a boy of his age, which was nearly twelve. They couldn't afford a laundry woman, Katie said, not with Nurse as well, because Papa was having trouble with his business.

Then they went indoors for tea. Dave followed them as far as the kitchen. There was a wonderful smell of hot fresh scones. It was strange that one could still appreciate the smell of food, although one didn't need to eat it any more.

Dave started walking, the effort increased by the fact that he had to get forward in time. The early part of the twentieth century was uphill work. But soon he was almost running, through the next fifty years at speed, slowing down as he reached the nineteen-eighties.

He was in St George's Church, Wimbledon. To his embarrassment he was wearing the wrong clothes, a cutaway jacket, velvet waistcoat, narrow trousers, high-collared shirt with floppy tie. His boots were cracked, the soles worn almost through. He was short and plump, had reddish curly hair, and a pink freckled skin.

He recognised himself immediately. He was the composer Franz Schubert.

And yet at the same time he was David Mason, respectably dressed in his dark suit, the one he had worn for Mimsy's funeral. He sat in the back row while the choir practised the anthem for next Sunday, 'Except the Lord Build the House'. The setting was a new one but well within their scope, some of them being experienced singers. With one of the basses conducting, they had rehearsed the individual parts and were now going to run through the whole thing with the organ.

Schubert and Dave were two people, and yet one, forever separate but united. How typical of Purgatorial mismanagement, how pointless, how inconvenient!

Schubert was unaware of his surroundings. He sat at the church's antiquated upright piano, adjusted his spectacles and was soon absorbed in composition. *'Dein ist mein ganzes Herz,'* he muttered to himself, playing a bar or two, humming, busily writing with a quill pen, dropping ink on the keys and blotting it up with a dirty handkerchief. *'Dein ist...'*

The anthem and the *lied* were in different keys and horribly discordant, but Schubert-Mason was oblivious. He went on working away as if he were at home in Vienna, miles from Wimbledon and safely in the early part of the nineteenth century. Mason-Schubert was offended by the sound of the two musical offerings coming together, and became extremely angry when he saw the composer rise to his feet and present the manuscript to a beautiful woman sitting in one of the side rows. She was wearing a raincoat and her hair was hidden under a silk scarf. In her hands she held what looked like a prayer book. He hadn't noticed her before and did not immediately recognise her. But now he knew that it was Marian. He was being given a chance to tell her of his love. He hurried up the aisle and sat down beside her.

The book was not a prayer book. It was a leather-bound copy of Donne's poems, open at *A Valediction*. He read over her shoulder of their two souls enduring not a breach but an expansion, like gold beaten to an aery thinness. This was the book he had sent her from Saudi Arabia, the red ribbon marking the page, his message to her.

'Gnadige Frau,' he said, his voice trembling with emotion. *'Dein ist mein Herz.'* He was speaking German! What a disaster! He had no idea if she understood what he was saying, or if she had heard him. Desperately he tried to speak English, gabbled and stammered and finally gave up.

Schubert-Mason seized his opportunity, thrust his manuscript into Marian's hands and repeated again and again, *'Dein ist mein Herz, dein, dein.'* She looked right through him, thoughtfully listening to the anthem. Passionately he exclaimed, *'Ich liebe dich!'* and tried to kiss her lips.

This was too much. Mason-Schubert was furious, pulled him away from Marian and succeeded in getting him out of the pew and on to the floor. He wanted to punch the fellow's face but found he was

182

pummelling his own cheeks, hitting his own ears, punching himself in the chest. But could he get his hands on Franz Schubert? Unfortunately not. God, what a nerve the man had! He was paunchy, red-nosed and foul-smelling, a figure of fun, a randy sentimentalist. Marian wouldn't look twice at him. *Ich liebe dich!* How dare he!

The choir meanwhile were singing steadily, the parts nicely separated, the words clear. 'It is but lost labour that ye haste to rise up early, and so late take rest, and eat the bread of carefulness.' The altos were filling their lungs, ready to lead into the next section, marked *sostenuto*. 'For so he giveth his beloved sleep.'

At that moment something went badly wrong with the organ. A huge volume of uncontrolled sound spilled out, in howls, wails, squeaks, whistles and moans, followed by a long, slow, elephantine fart. The choir stopped singing. One or two trebles giggled nervously. The acting conductor looked anxiously up to the organ loft, wondering if the organist had collapsed over the keys.

'Trevor,' he enquired. 'Are you all right?'

'Oh dearie me, no,' said Trevor. 'My reservoir has burst. I've run out of wind.'

'Blah! Blurt! Bloop!' The noises gradually subsided until there was only enough air left for a final thin stream, a tiny piddle of sound.

'Wee, wee, wee!' And then no more.

There was a moment's breathless silence. Then laughter swept through the choir-stalls like an equinoctial gale, blowing the singers from side to side in a chorus of unrestrained merriment. They laughed, they stopped, they began again.

Sopranos: 'Oh, tee-hee-hee! Tee-hee-hee!'

Altos & Tenors: 'Ha, ha, ha! Oh, ha, ha, ha!'

Basses: 'Ho, ho, ho! Ho, ho, ho! Ho, ho, ho!'

How they laughed! Marian threw back her head and laughed until tears ran down her face. Dave Mason laughed, and Franz Schubert, and the organist and the conductor, and when they finally stopped laughing the choir practice was abandoned.

Never forget it, they said to each other, still smiling as they packed up their music and put on their coats, looking forward to sharing the joke, telling the story when they got home. One moment pure sound, the next total bathos. What Trevor said about his wind! Can you beat it? And the sound of the organ so rude and loud, just like a big animal doing you-know-what. Ever seen an elephant doing it? Or a giraffe? Ever seen it at the circus? It was so lifelike! You had to laugh.

Except the Lord build the house, their labour is but vain that build it.

Except the Lord keep the city, the watchman waketh but in vain. Services will be accompanied by the piano until the organ is repaired. The anthem will be performed at a later date.

Schubert had resumed his whole identity and disappeared. Marian, with Donne's poems in her raincoat pocket, was going down the aisle with the organist, talking kindly to him so that he smiled and chatted, his morale restored.

Dave tried to follow, but his feet had become intolerably heavy. He could only just drag them along. By the time he got to the door it was locked for the night, and no matter how hard he tried he couldn't get his non-body through and out to the street, where Marian would have parked her Renault. He couldn't get into the passenger seat next to her and be driven to some quiet place, not far away, where they would kiss, copulate, sing Gershwin and Cole Porter.

He wandered slowly up and down the church, seeing the familiar stained glass windows, the font where he had been christened, the red and white bell rope worn soft and fluffy by much handling. He touched it lightly, feeling the bell in the tower above stirring, almost ringing but not quite.

He looked at the marble slabs let into the wall. *In Memoriam. Requiescat in Pace.* There was a new one, grey marble. Proudly he examined it and gave thanks.

IN MEMORY OF DAVID MASON
1931 - 1972
WHO SANG IN THIS CHURCH

It had been put there a year after his death. There had been no funeral because his body and Mike's had not been recovered. Prayers had been said in the English Church in Riyadh, also in Cyprus for Mike, and here in St George's for Dave. His friends in Pimlico had had a drinks party, with some singing, to remember him by.

He was in the south of France on a warm evening in May. Under his ghostly feet the earth was dry and stony. He walked among olive trees, crossed a stream, saw a tennis court and an empty swimming pool with a background of pine trees. A nightingale was singing an aria in the baroque style, with many decorative trills.

The place was called La Pinède. Ahead of him was an old stone

184

building, once an olive mill, now the Broome-Vivier's holiday home. Marian had converted it with the help of a local architect, keeping many of the original features. Through a barred window he floated into the living room, black beams against white walls, parts of the olive press still standing in one corner. He drifted upstairs and found smaller rooms, bedrooms, bathrooms, a miniature office. He looked for Marian. She wasn't there.

He sighed, disappointed again. Apparently the Kebles and the Quentin Jones's were staying, but not the Broome-Viviers. He dropped down into the kitchen, saw Celia Keble and Barbara Jones drinking vermouth and gossipping as they prepared *magrets de caneton*. Their voices were indistinct. He thought he heard them mention Marian, he wasn't sure. Celia had put on weight since her wedding party at The Welcome Sole and Barbara, who had been a slim, frail-looking blonde, was now a sturdy matron. They were no longer girls. They were women.

Many years had passed in earthly terms. Marian must be in her late forties now. And himself, if he were still alive he would be sixty, troubled perhaps with arthritis, a weak heart, delicate lungs.

As an old man, he shuffled out on to the terrace, where John and Quentin had laid the table for dinner and activated a lamp which burned up flying insects. They were enjoying glasses of duty-free whisky with Perrier water.

Quentin's long locks, once thick and lustrous, were receding from his forehead like an outgoing tide. He was wearing blue jeans, a crumpled tee-shirt with a design of spouting whales, espadrilles from the local market. He had the air of an aged hippie, once a style leader, now a reminder of the past. Glass in hand, he stood on the edge of the terrace admiring the view, the dark garden, the lights of a small town perched on a nearby hill, the twinkling stars above.

'But frankly, is there such a thing as Justice?' he said. 'With respect, to use a media expression, meaning I don't care a damn what you think or feel - With respect, is there such a commodity?'

'As your sounding board I say Yes,' said John. 'As a lawyer I do my best to see that justice is done. There is a system of law in our country, democratically achieved. We vote for our government, the government makes laws, the police are responsible for apprehending and charging offenders. Then we legal fellows decide the rights and wrongs of each case. An important contribution, I believe.'

Dave looked at John with admiration. Conventional of course, but that was how he had always been, dressed tonight in white trousers, a short-sleeved shirt, clean trainers, his grey hair neatly cut. How handsome he was, how self-assured. A good stepfather to Celia's children Emma and Rupert, a good father to two boys, Celia's precious gift to him. Happy in his marriage, successful in his profession. A lucky man.

'But the law is an ass,' said Quentin. 'Everybody agrees.'

'Thank you very much,' said John cheerfully. He was used to this sort of thing from Quentin. 'But do you mean to condemn the whole system? Are you prepared to admit that law, even when imperfectly administered, is better than no law? Do you postulate anarchy, the law of the jungle, might is right?'

'No, I don't. Not at all. But let's put your sort of law aside for a moment and consider another sort. What about heavenly justice? If there is a God, why does He let criminals get away with murder, rape, theft? Why doesn't He smite them, on the spot, with His divine anger?'

John was a fairly regular church-goer. This sort of talk was awkward for him. He cleared his throat. 'I grant that there does seem to be injustice sometimes. The wicked go unpunished, the innocent suffer. But I still believe that there is a God and that He is in charge and has a Plan. We can't see the Plan, being comparatively simple creatures, and we therefore presume that it doesn't exist.'

Dave, exasperated, cried out, 'Of course there isn't a Plan! For God's sake, I know what I'm talking about. There's no Plan, I tell you. Just wait till you're dead. It's Chaos out here, and hideously lonely.'

They couldn't hear him. They were oblivious, secure in their friendship, enjoying their holiday, looking forward to a good dinner cooked by their loving wives.

Quentin was thoughtful for a moment. Then he said, 'I think you're right, John. There must be a Plan, a grand design. It's something I want to write about in my next book. A sense of purpose. Celestial purpose if you like.'

'Good,' said John. 'Talking of celestial purpose, just look at that moon.'

A silvery disc had risen above the pine trees, shedding a pale, harmless light.

'Queen and huntress, chaste and fair,' said Quentin. 'And unfailingly beautiful. Time for another drink.'

Dave travelled on a moonbeam into space. The world revolved below him, twice round. He descended into Saudi Arabia and began trudging slowly across the desert towards the dam. It was many hundreds of kilometres. After many years he came to a particular sandy hillock, one among many, and knew that this was where he had died. Nothing

186

remained, no bones, not a scrap of metal. Travellers avoided the place. It was said that an *afreet* lived there.

His own weary spirit howled, shrieked and wailed among the dunes. This was the End and the Beginning. His adventures in Purgatory would now repeat themselves one by one, again and again. He would see his father, his mother, Marian's friends, her husband, her children, Broome Hall, her house in France. He would try in vain to tell her of his love. She would laugh. Oh, how she would laugh!

Despair enveloped him. This was the fate he deserved. He had lived for himself alone. He had fathered children and left them. He had been casual with women, unfeeling, until he met Marian. Now he knew what it was to love and to lose. She would remain unattainable, as distant as the moon, forever.

Was this Hell after all? He lay down in the hot sand under a burning sky, alone and yet not alone. Visions came to him, horrific scenes of human suffering, torture, degradation. Men, women and children were beaten, mutilated, left to die. Some were forced to live when they would rather be dead. He saw road accidents, fires, violent acts of destruction, plunder and rape, storms at sea which broke ships to pieces, scattering crew and passengers on the waves. He would have moved away, closed his eyes to the evils he saw, shut his ears against the screams of the victims, but he was trapped. He had to see, to listen, to share the pain.

In art the ugliness of Hell is transmuted. He thought of Homer, Virgil, John Milton, William Blake. He remembered gruesome mediaeval paintings of monstrous humans, grotesque animals, red devils with horns and forked tails stoking the fires of the Underworld. Now he suffered these things. Saints and martyrs were stoned for him, pierced with arrows, roasted, dismembered. Christ was crucified. Each agony was drawn out and multiplied many times, as if replayed, repeated in slow motion, to make sure that he had seen and understood. He longed for Oblivion, the waters of Lethe. But this soothing drug was not available to him.

At last, after millions of years, he noticed that the procession of horrors was changing shape, sorting itself into categories, as if whoever was in charge had now arrived, apologising for the delay, due to a seasonal increase, staff shortages, the weather, lack of funds and general inefficiency.

'Right, jolly good show,' said a familiar voice. 'Let's get started. War wounded, accidents, this way please. Deformities, handicaps, over here. Yes, you will be made whole, as good as new. Abused children? Don't worry, it's all over now. Virtual Reality has got it right this time, good homes, decent parents. Murderers, thieves, bullies and sadists, I'm afraid you'll have to go round again. Hey you, none of that! Get back in where you belong. You'll get an extra millennium if you're not careful. No, I don't take bribes, wasn't born yesterday!'

Slowly and stiffly Dave got to his feet and brushed the sand off his clothes. 'Sorry,' he said in the direction of the voice. 'I don't want to interrupt your programme. But is there any news for me? Marian, you remember. It didn't work last time, they got me muddled up with Schubert.'

'David Mason, what-ho! We've been looking for you. Found your file, checked it through. Abandoned in infancy, behaved himself in the orphanage, was fostered, worked hard at school and university, cared for his foster-mother on her deathbed. A few bad marks, selfishness, obstinacy, a weakness for women. After many years in Purgatory, he ascended into Heaven.'

'Heaven! Are you sure?'

'That's what it says. Don't just stand there. You're walking, and it's a long way.'

'And you? Have you heard?'

'Yes. Jolly good news, what-ho. I'm flying Heaven Direct!'

'Congratulations. I'm so glad.'

The crowds of sufferers were far away now, treading their appointed routes. He was alone, talking into empty air, when suddenly the voice from Virtual Reality became flesh, taking the shape of a huge Angel, towering many metres high. His wings opened with a fluttering of feathers, casting a deep black shadow on the sand.

'Ready for take-off.'

Dave stretched his neck to look up. He couldn't see the Angel's face because it was so far away, and the sun blazing behind his head gave him a golden halo, too dazzling to look at. Lower in the sky he thought he saw many birds, flying in close formation, but as they approached he realised that this was a flight of babies, many hundreds of little creatures enveloped in a cloud of mist. A few fell out as they passed, and the Angel deftly fielded them, cradling them in his big hands.

'There, there,' he murmured gently. 'Not to worry. Might happen to anyone. Okay, David Mason, get started. I'm going east, you're going west, so this is where we say goodbye.'

'Goodbye, and thank you!'

There was no time for more. The Angel flapped his wings, the noise like the sound of huge waves breaking on a stony beach. He rose into the air, wheeled once round Dave's head and zoomed off into the burning sky. Soon he was no more than a shape, then a small spot, then nothing. He was gone.

Dave began to walk. It was a long way, but he wasn't going to give up.

Marian, Marian.

One of the best things at Broome, in Charles's opinion, was the shower which Marian had installed in their bathroom. It looked old-fashioned, matching the Victorian style of the other fittings, but was completely modern in function, providing a choice of gentle raindrops or needle-sharp spray at whatever temperature you chose.

Soaping himself, shampooing his hair, rinsing first in hot then briefly in tingling cold, he felt full of happiness and well-being. What a relief to be out of London, with three weeks of Recess ahead!

The weighing machine gave good news too. His doctor had sounded a warning about his weight and cholesterol level, so he was on a reducing diet. He regretted this because he had always had a good appetite for what he thought of as simple foods: roast beef, lamb chops, steak and kidney pudding, eggs and bacon, well-cooked greens, desserts with cream. He'd been told to cut down on these things, an exercise in self-denial which took some of the fun out of life. One got very tired of fish and chicken, with only a limited amount of white wine, and he didn't like his vegetables undercooked, which was how they were served these days. Marian said it was *nouvelle cuisine*, and much better for you.

Sometimes at his club or in the Members' Dining Room he treated himself to a good, old-fashioned meal washed down with claret and followed by a glass of port. The occasional indulgence couldn't do one much harm.

Recently he'd had to remind himself that such relaxation of rules did not apply to extra-marital activity. As an MP one was in the public eye and was expected to behave in a conventional way. Sexual intrigues could involve one in serious trouble. He was proud of the fact that since Edward's birth, twenty years ago, he had been almost entirely faithful to Marian. He had lapsed occasionally when he was on his own in London and she was at Broome with the children. And he had once or twice given in to temptation when she went off to Paris, Milan or Hong Kong, buying stock for Marcellina.

It was simply loneliness and a perfectly natural sexual need which had lead to these mini-affairs. They were never serious, little more than an evening's embrace with an old sweetheart, someone he could rely upon to be loyal and discreet. He had given up confessing his infidelities to Marian because they were rare, and of no importance. If she guessed she tactfully said nothing. She was a wonderful, loving and understanding wife.

The last time he'd confessed had been years ago when he'd finally ended his involvement with Clarissa, now diagnosed as schizophrenic, a poor ruin of a woman, an embarrassment to her former friends. Marian had relieved him of a considerable burden by making it her duty to be kind to Clarissa, visiting her during her now frequent stays at Weston Towers Sanatorium, helping her furnish her cottage in Little Weston, sometimes inviting her, when she was more or less stable, to Broome for the weekend.

In front of the mirror Charles rubbed his head with a towel and checked the extent of his bald patch. It didn't worry him much. Hair was worn short now, and possibly the little empty space on top gave him a distinguished look, like a Roman senator. His teeth had given trouble a few years ago and some were now capped, well worth the expense. He brushed them, grinning at his reflection. Not a bad-looking man for his age, energetic, in good physical and mental shape. And still attractive to women.

As evidence of this something had occurred two weeks ago which had taken him by surprise, and which must on no account be repeated. Marian had been in Spain visiting her father, now eighty years old and suffering from emphysema. Charles had gone to Upweston for a Party meeting, and afterwards to a fund-raising dinner in the village hall at Bishops Weston. One of the organisers was Alison Peters, a lively and intelligent girl in her thirties, with whom he had a slightly flirtatious relationship. Nothing wrong with that, in fact it seemed to be what the female of the species expected from someone like him. Alison was married, and lived in a small Queen Anne house on the outskirts of the village. Her husband made films for television and was often away.

After the dinner, a friendly and enjoyable occasion, Charles had offered to help clear the top table where he'd been sitting.

Alison had said, 'No really. You're the guest of honour.' They were leaning together over a pile of dirty plates, and Charles was saying, 'Please let me. They're heavy.'

Suddenly a spark seemed to flash between them. Their hands touched, their eyes met. She said quietly, in the most casual way, 'I want you, I can't help it. Why don't you go away now, and come back later? Park in the lane at the side of my house. The back door is open.'

He should have put her off, said he was too old for that sort of thing. But he didn't. Another helper had joined them at the table, and he said in what he hoped was a natural tone of voice, 'Oh, all right. If you're sure you can manage.' Alison had smiled and disappeared into the kitchen at the back.

So, after acting out a few more good deeds, carrying chairs to the side of the hall and saying goodnight to a few people, he left, got into his Jaguar and drove round the dark, unfrequented lanes for thirty minutes, then back to Bishops Weston. He was half intending to say he was sorry, this simply wouldn't do, they were both married, better if they remained just good friends. But she was waiting for him, fell upon him with hungry kisses, took him to bed and demanded all he'd got, and not just once.

Afterwards, at three in the morning, he'd driven up to London. He'd got appointments in the City that day, so had to set an alarm to make sure he got up in time. Edward and Teresa were using the house, Edward being a student at the Royal College of Music, and Teresa, who had failed to get into university, taking a secretarial and computer course. He'd had breakfast with them, was in time for his ten o'clock appointment, then attended a board meeting, and had a sandwich lunch.

He took his seat in the House for a debate which interested him, but had fallen asleep halfway through and woke up with a start, hoping nobody had seen him on television. He spent the rest of the afternoon on correspondence, then had drinks and dinner.

When he got home both Teresa and Edward were out, so he telephoned Alison. Her husband had answered, which was embarrassing and a shock. He hadn't thought to ask about the fellow's movements, but there he was, back home in his Queen Anne house with his wife and that was that. He'd replaced the receiver without speaking. And he'd heard nothing from Bishops Weston since.

In retrospect he saw that what had happened had been pure athletics with no emotional involvement, no affection. With distaste he remembered Alison's big bottom and bad legs, her slovenly way of walking, the greedy expression in her eyes. How could he ever have found her attractive!

Marian had been back at Broome almost a week, but he'd been in London and they hadn't seen each other. Last night he'd driven down late, and she'd waited up for him. They had gone to bed immediately and made passionate love. He'd told her how much he loved her and how he'd missed her, every word of which was true. He adored her. She was everything a wife should be. She would be hurt, disgusted, if she found out what had happened between himself and Alison Peters.

Dressing in an old pair of cords, checked shirt, sweater, comfortable shoes, he arranged tactics and strategy in his mind. There would be no more embraces with Alison. He was no longer interested, and such an entanglement could harm his reputation. Marian must certainly not get to hear of it because it would certainly damage her trust in him. Nothing must disturb the beautiful balance of their life together. With these

192

thoughts he went downstairs and had the prescribed breakfast of grapefruit, muesli, skim milk and black coffee, then went into his office to read the newspapers, open the letters and see if there was anything on his Fax machine.

Marian had got up early to see the gardener. Her latest idea was to have bulbs and bedding plants in large stone containers, instead of in straight lines in front of the house. The gardener had been sulky about the plan at first, but had been persuaded. Last autumn the front beds had been planted with lavender. Now summer was on the way and the containers had arrived, to be filled with suitable soil. In the greenhouse geraniums, marigolds, pansies, and lobelia were waiting for the right sort of weather, which might be as soon as next week. Several urns for the courtyard on the west side had already been planted with lilies, which were now coming up, promising to look like a detail from a Renaissance painting.

From his window Charles could see Marian admiring two camellias, in full bloom. She looked up and saw him, came to the window and made a kiss-shaped mouth. She'd had her hair waved into a floating, curly mane, the ends lightened. 'To hide my grey hairs,' she'd said, though he wasn't aware that she had any. God, she was beautiful, ten years older than Alison Peters, her body firm and straight, her smooth skin slightly tanned from her visit to Spain, her eyes brilliant with good health. And she loved him.

He opened the window and said, 'Darling, when you've finished, could you help me with some letters? And we'd better check diaries.'

'Of course, darling. Five minutes.' She waved a hand towards the courtyard as if to make the flowers bloom by magic. 'It's going to look good, don't you think.'

When she came into his office a little later he noticed that she was smiling to herself, as if at a private joke. He offered her a penny for her thoughts.

'My thoughts?' She sat down opposite him. 'Funny and serious at the same time. Clarissa invited herself to tea yesterday, a friend drove her down from London and took her on to Little Weston afterwards. We went to look at the greenhouses, just Clarissa and me. And darling, I had to tell her the most awful lie.'

'Lie?' Charles felt a stillness, the sort that is said to come before a storm. Except that Marian never stormed.

'Darling, you really are awful,' she went on. 'You know how Clarissa goes for long walks at night, especially when she's about to go mad again? Well, she said she had walked through Bishops Weston, this was two weeks ago, and seen the Jaguar outside Alison's house. So she presumed, you know.'

'The Jaguar.' He looked away, then sheepishly into her face. 'Yes, I went there for a drink after the dinner, which was very well done, incidentally.'

'It was two o'clock in the morning, darling. Bad Charles, bad!' This was the way she spoke to the family dogs when they misbehaved. 'But I wasn't going to let on. I said, quick as anything, "Oh Clarissa, but it must have been someone else's Jag, because ours is being serviced. Charles had to go in my Renault." Don't you think that was absolutely brilliant?'

He held his head in his hands and groaned, wishing he'd never met the blasted Alison. What a disaster! What a horrible coincidence that Clarissa, on her nocturnal meanderings, had seen the car, possibly seen him getting into it.

'I'm so sorry,' he murmured. 'Ashamed. Alison was at the dinner. I must have had too much to drink. Afterwards, I can't think why - God, what a big behind!'

To his dismay, because he felt very miserable, Marian burst out laughing. 'I know, I've seen it!' she chortled. 'Size twelve above the waist and eighteen below! Darling, you must have been terribly squiffy! But seriously - What's that phrase? Damage limitation?'

'Yes, damage limitation. I mean, never again. Can't face the thought of her. Don't know what to do for the best.'

'I'll tell you, darling.' Her grey eyes, so gentle and clear, filled him with sorrowful love. 'We'll treat it as a joke. Clarissa says Alison sleeps with lots of people, gets lonely I suppose, with her husband away so much. So it's nothing serious. And I'm going to chaperone you until things are normal again. I'll come to Upweston with you on Monday. That means cutting the Bring-and-Buy in the village, and my Yoga. But I don't care. This is more important, absolutely.'

'Thank you, darling. Thank you.' He felt better. On Monday he was to address a public meeting, in Upweston Town Hall, to explain to the locals what the Government hoped to do about the controversial Community Charge, or Poll Tax.

As yet nobody had come up with a satisfactory answer to this problem, handed on by Maggie Thatcher to her successor. So he would have to do a bit of bluffing. Having Marian on the platform with him would be an enormous help, particularly since Alison, as a Committee member, would be there too. 'And you'll come to the wine-and-sandwiches afterwards, and drive me home.'

'Yes. And I was thinking, darling, that Edward will be back, so we

194

might get him to come too. Solidarity, you know. Massed Broome-Viviers against Peters.'

'I was a bloody fool,' he said, relapsing. 'It was her idea. I should have said No, but somehow...'

Marian was wise and impartial, like a marriage guidance counsellor. 'Sometimes a woman goes wild for sex, and the man simply hasn't got a chance.'

'Have you ever been wild like that, darling?' He smiled at the thought.

'With you, often. Otherwise...' She smiled back at him, so loving, loyal and honest. 'Not really, darling. Anyway, let's forget about Alison. It's just that I felt badly about my little lie. I took advantage of Clarissa's rocky state of mind, which was unfair. She's boiling up for another session in the bin, don't you think. Wandering about at night is always a sign. And yesterday she brought up all the old grudges, including that story about her abortion, saying it was your baby, which simply isn't true.' They had talked about this more than once over the years, Marian each time expressing sympathy with Clarissa. It would be such an awful decision to have to make. 'Then she said she saw your car, and I said it couldn't have been. So she's wondering now if she really saw it, or if she imagined it. Poor thing, I do feel guilty.'

'Don't,' he said. 'I'm the guilty one. You did it for me.' He leaned across the desk, took her hands and kissed them.

'There,' she said, pushing him away. 'Now we must get busy.'

They went through the letters together. He gave her those which she could answer without his help, and kept the more challenging ones to deal with later. He would dictate the answers either to Marian or to the secretary, who was coming in on Wednesday. Then they went through the engagements for the next few weeks and got their diaries up to date.

Marian made a mental note to ring Celia, at La Pinède, that evening. She had telephoned the caretaker, responsible for cleaning and general maintenance, before she went to Spain, and had listened to a lengthy complaint about the builder who was supposed to mend the crack in the swimming pool. Already, the caretaker said, the cement which this *bricoleur* was using was shrinking and in consequence when the pool was filled it would leak as before. Her brother-in-law, a good workman, could make a complete repair with a cement which did not immediately retire, since water is not to be wasted, it costs money, and many times in the summer is altogether turned off. It is important therefore to save what is already in the pool.

Administration, long distance! Marian imagined the Kebles and the Jones's in conference with the caretaker and her brother-in-law. Barbara had read a lot of French literature, Proust, Zola, and Flaubert in translation, but didn't know much of the language. Quentin could hold his own in general conversation. John could be relied upon to translate anything to do with machinery or electrical fittings, with the aid of a phrase book. Celia's knowledge of the language was limited to shopping and cooking, but the caretaker recognised her as Madame's deputy and close friend, and would listen to her voice rather than the others.

There was no need to mention the Alison Peters incident to Celia. Such a bore, absolutely. Charles should be more sensible.

Of the four children, Charles privately cared most for Edward. It was that bonding exercise, feeding him when he was only a few days old, which had done it. From that moment Charles had watched every detail of his progress with doting pride. In spite of this Edward had grown up unspoiled, considerate, easy-going. He had been a good-looking child and was now a very attractive young man.

Charles thought that with his natural advantages Edward should have a greater variety of girlfriends. But Edward remained attached to just one, a music student like himself, a soprano, for whom he had written several songs. His teachers at the Royal College said he should certainly go to Cambridge for further study. Charles wished that his mother could have lived to know Edward since she had played the piano as a girl, and enjoyed classical music, especially opera. The boy's talent must have come from her side of the family.

Teresa had been born so soon after Edward that she seemed always to be in his shadow. Charles was fond of her, of course, but found her hard to understand. She seemed not to share his idea of what a nineteen-year-old girl should be. She wasn't interested in her looks, nor her clothes, and she didn't have a boyfriend.

'She will develop,' Marian said protectively. 'She's immature, a little bit shy of her body. Shy of being a woman.' The truth, though she hadn't told Charles yet, was that Teresa had categorically refused to get herself organised with contraception, saying that she was not interested in the male sex and never would be. Marian had found this disconcerting. Teresa would change her mind, of course, when she found the right person. Meanwhile it would be best to let the subject drop. One shouldn't hurry young people into sex if they didn't want it.

Sue, four years younger, wasn't at all shy about being a woman. She had Marian's looks, was female and proud of it. 'You don't have to fight for your rights any more,' she explained. 'So there's less aggro. You're equal, just the other sex.' She adored her father and her brothers,

196

tolerated her older sister, treated her mother with the respect due to an elderly person who used an antiquated vocabulary. 'Ma, must you say "absolutely" all the time! It's so dinosaur!'

'Dinosaur' was the current Abbey Mead word for anything hopelessly old-fashioned. Marian couldn't help thinking how much the place had changed, even since Teresa's day. Sue and her school friends spoke in strange accents, as if they were working-class, or came from Liverpool, or the East End.

'Do you have to talk like that, Sue?' she'd said. 'Really, I don't like it. It's so down-market.' She remembered very well what an effort she'd had to make to get rid of her Nottingham style of speech when she first went to Abbey Mead, all those years ago.

'Ma, there's no rules, not any more. Okay, when you're writing essays and exams you make it formal, like it's the Queen's English. But when you're talking you just relax. As long as people understand. You don't want to create a barrier.'

It's no good criticising one's young, Marian decided. Their standards are different. Sue was said to be academically promising, again eclipsing Teresa, who had found school work difficult. Jack, her youngest darling, so like Charles to look at, had learning problems too. He had managed to get into Eton, but his tutor had reported that he was 'an idle boy' and should have extra tuition in the summer holidays. At his present rate of progress he wouldn't achieve more than two 'O' Levels, let alone 'A' Levels to get him a place at university.

Edward, the brain of the family, was a hard act to follow.

If Charles could find any imperfection in Edward, it was his attitude to politics. He had a grasp of philosophical concepts, but no idea of how the country was run, nor what a burden Members of Parliament carried. That was one of the disadvantages, in Charles's mind, of studying music, a subject well removed from the realities of everyday life. Sometimes, annoyingly, Edward was highly critical of the Conservative Party, particularly of the Thatcher regime.

'Maggie was a despot,' he said. 'She had practically abandoned the Cabinet as an instrument of Government. If Ministers didn't do what she wanted she sacked them, and that was that.'

Charles had to admit that there was some truth in this accusation. 'Well, yes. But she acted in good faith and her decisions were soundly based. And look what she did for Britain. We needed a strong Prime Minister, and she was certainly that.'

'But as soon as Geoffrey Howe spoke up, you all ratted on her.'

Charles winced. The memory of what had happened last October was still painful.

'That was a very testing time. It was a question of where one's loyalties lay, and I decided that mine were with the Party, and my constituency. I still maintain that she was a good Prime Minister and brought us through the eighties with flying colours. Then it was time for a change.'

'The change we need is to the Liberal Democrats,' Edward said. 'Labour's no good at the moment. Dinosaur, as Sue would say. Successive Tory governments will turn us into a one-party state.'

'That's scare-mongering by the Left. People vote for us, the result is achieved democratically.'

'It's not truly democratic until we get Proportional Representation. Sorry to be argumentative, Father. But the Tories have been in power for eleven years, during which time the country has gone steadily downhill. Civil unrest, crime, unemployment, a general moral decay.'

'A sign of the times,' said Charles. 'It's the same all over Europe. You can't lay all the blame on the Conservative Party.'

They digressed into consideration of problems following the re-unification of Germany, and the break-up of the Soviet Union. Edward argued that this was Progress. 'Progress being movement in any direction,' he added. So Charles came back with, 'The old order changeth, yielding place to new, but not necessarily for the better.' This sort of thing reminded him of debates at school, good practice but generally lacking in seriousness. He enjoyed it very much all the same

Edward would settle down politically when he got older. He had Broome to consider, after all. You needed stable politics if you had property.

In spite of his reservations about the Conservatives, Edward said he would like to come to the meeting at Upweston on Monday and sit on the platform with his parents. He made sure first that they would let him drive the Jag.

'Darling, it's a quarter to five.'

Charles stood in the hall, ready to go. The meeting was not until seven, but the route from Broome to Upweston was cross-country, and at this time of day there was more traffic than usual, a rural version of the rush-hour. He wanted to consult several people beforehand, to feel the local pulse as it were. He intended to be so busy doing this that there would be no risk of private conversation with Alison Peters. When he saw her he would be natural and friendly, as if nothing unusual had happened between them. And he very much hoped she would behave in the same way.

'I'm ready, darling.' Marian checked her appearance in the mirror. In the past she had often worn blue for political occasions, but this was now a cliché, and too reminiscent of Mrs Thatcher. For today she'd chosen a black wool skirt with a white jacket. She fluffed her hair out. It made her feel wonderful, the big, soft mass with light streaks.

Edward had brought the Jaguar round to the front door. He was a good driver, but liked to go fast, weaving in and out of traffic, of which his parents disapproved.

'No weaving,' said Marian as she got into the passenger seat and fastened her belt.

Edward gave her a sideways look. 'I'll drive like a Central Office chauffeur.'

Charles got into the back and settled down to think about what he was going to say, the object of the exercise being to convince his audience that things would be put right in the end, although there was a lack of clarity at the moment. The Community Charge was unpopular, voters had a democratic right to make their views known, and politicians were there to listen and take suitable action in due course.

He took a set of index cards out of his briefcase and began to work. His method was to write headings on the cards, sometimes as many as ten, and then all he had to do was to glance at a card, moving on from one to another until they were all used up. Depending on audience reaction he might use a later heading near the beginning, or the other way round. It was a good system.

He wrote down a heading he had just thought of. 'Politics doesn't mean standing still and doing nothing. It means getting things done, moving forward, making life better for all of us.' Then if there was heckling from the Labour louts or fringe lunatics, he would go into the attack. What had the Opposition done except pick holes in Conservative policies? What had they to offer? Nothing. The Conservatives were active, they were in charge, and they were getting things right. More heckling, then he would bring up the subject of high-spending Labour councils, Upweston being a Conservative seat with a Conservative local council, which had set one of the lowest rates in the country before the Community Charge was proposed.

There had been no short cuts either. The hospital had been modernised. Schools and housing had been improved. Local roads had been re-surfaced so that farmers had proper access to railheads and the motorway, as well as to local markets. Not a bad record.

He felt confident that he could deal with the Alison Peters question. She had made no attempt to get in touch with him, which indicated an acceptance of the *status quo*. Both of them were married. They had indulged in a sexual frolic, which was now over, and not to be taken seriously.

The Town Hall in Upweston was good Georgian, facing the market square. The upper floors had been made into offices with dividing walls of plaster board. The Assembly Room, on the ground floor, could hold three hundred, which was more than one expected at the average political meeting. But the Community Charge issue was important and would draw a crowd.

Edward and Marian had drinks in the Tudor Lounge of the White Hart Hotel next door, and went over to join Charles at twenty to seven. The place was filling up nicely. Marian saw Alison Peters and took Edward over to be introduced. She thought Alison was looking worried, less confident than usual. She couldn't help feeling pleased about this. The three of them went up together to join the select few on the platform.

'Hallo darling.' Charles greeted Marian, as he always did before a meeting, with a special look as if to say, 'I'm not nervous in the least, it's just that I'm glad you're here.'

She smiled back at him. Looking round the room she saw that a group of young men were standing silently against the wall down one side. 'Yobboes?' she asked, still smiling. He said, 'Don't know. They might be the Young Farmers. Yes, I think I know some of their faces.' He gave a vague salute in their direction.

Apart from the Young Farmers, most of them loyal Tories, there were other groups who attended meetings at Upweston. There were Labour representatives, Liberal Democrats and Independents, sometimes united in heckling the common enemy. There were sometimes Militants and others from the extreme Left. National Front supporters also appeared occasionally, though their main activity in the area was writing slogans on railway bridges with spray paint.

What happened at this particular meeting was confusing for those who were there. Afterwards nobody could be sure how the trouble started. Whatever the cause, they agreed, it was not entirely political. Some people blamed violence on television. There was so much of it these days that it became part of ordinary life. People accepted violence. Their inclination to break the law was increased by television. Others said television was not to blame, violence being the inevitable result of unemployment, inadequate housing, poor education, and the break-up of the family as a social unit.

A majority, afterwards, blamed the new policy of having mental patients live in the community when really their problems would be better dealt with in decent, modern mental homes. A journalist who happened to be present said the events of that day would remind him for the rest of his life of a Quentin Jones novel. One minute you are laughing because human beings are such idiots, their efforts so futile. Then suddenly you are in tears, overwhelmed by the tragedy of it all.

There were at least two hundred and fifty people in the Assembly Room, the regular Conservative supporters filling the front rows as usual. Behind them there were respectable locals of various political persuasions. Towards the rear there were a lot of empty seats, and the stewards were trying to persuade the Young Farmers and others to sit in them, without success. They made as if to move into the back rows, then edged away again and reformed in their original groups, still standing. On the platform Committee members sat down, in their accustomed order, the more important in the middle. Alison told Edward where to find an extra chair. They sat down together and chatted.

Marian, eye-catching in her black-and-white outfit, waited at Charles's side. She said, as she always did, 'Good luck, darling.' He liked to present her to his audience before he began to speak. 'My wife, who is such a help to me, as part-time secretary and general manager.' This or similar jovial introduction never failed to bring a ripple of laughter from the Party faithful. He felt he needed the warmth of that laughter today, although what he had to say would, of course, be serious. He took a last look at his headed cards and put them away in his pocket.

At this point there was a disturbance at the back of the hall. Two burly men, possibly National Front, were arguing with one of the Young Farmers, and others nearby had become involved. There was some pushing and shoving and voices were raised. The stewards, ready for trouble, were quickly on the spot and were joined by two local policemen who had been on the door. At the same time, adding to the confusion, a new group came in, mostly young women, carrying a banner which said, 'Single Parents Need Your Help'. Marian gave Charles a sweet smile and managed to look unconcerned.

'Whoops,' she said. 'Look who's here.'

'Who?'

'Clarissa. She's with a lot of women.'

'Hell. I'm going to start anyway. I'm so glad you're with me, darling. And so grateful.'

This was not the first time that Clarissa had appeared at one of his meetings. Weston Towers was only five miles from Upweston, and her cottage was even nearer. Both were on a bus route, which she used because she was no longer allowed to drive a car. Excursions, mixing with ordinary people, taking an interest in what was happening in the world, these were all important for patients at Weston Towers. The locals were mostly intolerant of this policy and would rather have the loonies, as they called them, kept securely inside walls, with barbed wire along the top. Clarissa's previous appearances had been mildly embarrassing for Charles because she always made a point of asking a question, about nuclear weapons, or housing developments on what had been farmland, or about the pollution of local streams by industrial waste. The questions themselves were harmless, the sort of thing politicians were used to. It was just that it was Clarissa who was asking, and one was never sure what she would do next, start shouting, burst into tears, lose control of herself.

Today his anxiety was more like terror. He foresaw a nightmare scenario, Clarissa making a public accusation about his moral standards, and naming Alison Peters. Half an hour ago, as it happened, he had had a brief, meaningful conversation with Alison when nobody else was near. Good resolutions thrown aside, he'd found himself saying, 'I tried to ring you.' She had said, quick and casual, 'Next week, Wednesday or Thursday. Telephone at nine in the morning.' And he had said, 'Can't wait!' What a fool he was, what a traitor!

There was no way out except forward. Clarissa, dressed in an old mackintosh and green wellies, her flaming red hair flowing long and loose, was leading her group through the crowd. The Young Farmers and the National Front supporters found themselves separated by the new arrivals, and as they struggled to regain contact several of the Single Parents were pushed about, and one fell over. Several onlookers came to help the stewards. Unfortunately their efforts were misunderstood. Isolated arguments developed and blows were exchanged.

Suddenly, like a spreading fire, there was a general punch-up. People sitting quietly in their seats, waiting for the meeting to begin, turned round to see what was happening, and were terrified. Some got up and headed for the emergency exits. The local chairman, who usually opened the proceedings, urged Charles to leave the platform before things got worse. Charles brushed him aside, glared at the unruly mob and said in a loud, clear voice, 'I've got a lot to say to you this evening, and if you don't want to hear it you are free to go and settle your arguments outside.'

Nobody took any notice. The noise had reached an angry level. There was shouting and swearing, and nervous cries from the Single Parents. Their banner had been taken from them and trodden underfoot. But they managed to stay together, swaying first to one side then the other, gradually moving into the middle of the hall and up the central aisle. Fighting continued, chairs were seized and held aloft. You had to try and protect yourself, people said later. A policeman went down and came up again without his hat. Bodies heaved and struggled while the peaceable members of the audience huddled together in fear. Upweston had never seen anything like it.

Suddenly Clarissa detached herself from the crowd and made her way forward, calling out, 'Justice, justice!' Her voice was high-pitched, operatic in intensity, and she looked ridiculous, poor woman, dirty and unkempt. For a moment it seemed as if her behaviour would defuse the situation. What she was saying had nothing to do with the Community Charge debate, although it might have been an appeal on behalf of the Single Parents, in a general way.

'It's all wrong!' she shouted. 'I had to have an abortion, I had to kill his baby! People like that have no right to live, fucking women and leaving them to decide what to do! It's barbaric, they behave like animals! They treat us like whores!'

Hostilities continued on all sides, the noise almost drowning her speech, while the hatless policeman called on his radio for reinforcements. One of the Single Parents was hit, accidentally, by a raised chair. Her head was badly cut.

'His baby!' Clarissa yelled, pointing at Charles.

My God, she had a gun! Nobody knew at the time how she came to be carrying it that day, whether it was hers or someone else's. It was small, a lady's revolver. Later it turned out that her ex-husband collected guns and that she might have had an opportunity to take it from his house. How did she get it into the hall? She had no handbag. Perhaps she simply brought it in her mackintosh pocket. The two policemen were not on the door when the Single Parents came in. They were trying to stop the fighting. So security had been lax. Surely, everybody agreed, the law should be changed so that mental patients didn't have access to firearms. There should be tighter controls.

She fired and missed. She hit the framed picture of the Queen in Coronation robes, which splintered and fell to the floor in a shower of glass. She managed to fire two more shots before a steward grabbed her from behind and got hold of the gun, but it was too late. She'd shot herself in the head. The steward was covered in blood, a horrible sight. And all this took no more than ten seconds. Bam! Bam! Bam! And then a huge roar of noise from the crowd as people voiced their distress in various ways, screaming, shouting, howling, moaning.

More police arrived and helped the stewards clear a space round Clarissa, who lay crumpled on the floor, her skirt rucked up, bony knees exposed above her boots. Someone said, 'I'm a doctor,' and made his way through to look at her. He shook his head. There was nothing he could do.

On the platform there was a moment of stillness. Everyone had ducked instinctively when Clarissa raised her weapon. Some were lying flat, some crouched down behind chairs. Edward, at the far end, stepped past Alison Peters, who was on her knees, weeping hysterically, and went to his parents. Charles, white-faced, sat on the floor, looking at a patch of blood on his sleeve. Marian was in front of him, leaning on his shoulder.

'Are you all right, Father?'

'Yes, I wasn't hit. Marian...'

She lay quite still. Her eyes were open. A red rose seemed to blossom on her white jacket, a flower which was blood. She looked at Charles and Edward and smiled.

'Better soon,' she said.

Better soon. That was what she said to the children when they were small, if they were hurt or distressed. The doctor abandoned Clarissa, hurried up to the platform and knelt at Marian's side. Ambulance men arrived with a stretcher.

'We're taking you to hospital,' Charles told her. He got to his feet and stood back so that they could lift her and get her into the ambulance, hopefully through the back door. God, what a nightmare! Fortunately the new accident unit at the hospital was now in operation, with all the latest equipment. All they had to do was to get her there. It was only a mile and a half. He and Edward would follow in the Jaguar.

Tensed up, clenching his fists, he said to anyone who was listening, 'For God's sake, hurry. Just get moving. Every second counts.' He'd seen this sort of emergency in a demonstration. They were probably giving her oxygen and blood, and taking a hell of a time about it.

The hall was still full of people, some pushing forward to see what had happened, others trying to get to the door. Another lot of ambulance men were in the centre of the hall now, and plenty of police, keeping the mob away from Clarissa. Blood on the floor, a disaster, a scene of unbelievable horror.

'Come on,' Charles groaned, his voice sounding strange, as if from far away. 'What's the hold-up?'

The doctor detached himself from the group who were on their knees round Marian. 'Mr Broome-Vivier,' he said, his hand gently on Charles's shoulder. 'There is nothing we can do for your wife. She was shot in the heart.'

'No, no.' Charles swayed and felt faint. They led him to a chair. 'Get moving. The accident unit. Intensive care. Just get her to the hospital.'

'It is too late,' the doctor insisted. 'She died, I would say, without suffering. I am so sorry.'

Charles tried to speak but no words came. What he wanted to say was that she was very important to him. He must have her back. She stood on platforms with him, she looked after him and his children, she managed his home, his whole life. He would be nothing without her, just a shell, a shadow. A hollow man.

Edward, the son of whom he was so proud, stood in front of him. He said, without a tremor, still suspended in shock, 'We must be brave, Father.' He did not say, though Charles could read it in his face, 'It was your fault. You did this. You killed her.' His blue eyes were cold, like steel.

'I loved her,' Charles protested. 'So much. If I could have done anything.'

If he could have foreseen what a ghastly liability Clarissa would become, if he could have stopped her coming to Weston Towers for treatment. If Marian had stayed at home. If she had been sitting down instead of standing in the line of fire. If the police and stewards had done their job properly.

Useless thoughts, because the thing had happened. He had been robbed and there was no way of getting back what he had lost, no insurance, no compensation. Somehow he would have to carry on without her, for the children's sake. God, he would have to break the news to them tonight, as soon as possible. Teresa in London, Sue at Abbey Mead, Jack at Eton. He had to do it before they heard it on the radio, or saw it on the Nine O'Clock News. He would get them all back to Broome, which was marginally less public than London. They would face this together, as a family. Oh God. He would have to tell Marian's dreadful old mother. And her father, the best father-in-law a man ever had. And her friend Celia, at La Pinède with John and the Joneses. He would have to telephone the Chief Whip. And write to the Prime Minister.

He would have to make a public statement, fairly soon. The police had managed to keep the media at bay so far, for which he was grateful, although he thought he'd seen some flash bulbs popping when the shooting started. He imagined himself standing on the front steps at

Broome, pale and grief-stricken, perhaps tomorrow evening. He could hear himself saying, 'This tragic event was unforeseeable. A middle-aged woman, a mental patient, suffering severe hallucinations, entered the hall where the meeting was to take place. Nobody knows how she came to be in possession of a weapon. I am not apportioning blame. The stewards had no brief to search people as they came in. The local police were already engaged in dealing with a disturbance. There was some confusion. The woman suddenly fired three shots. The second shot killed my...' His voice would break. He would square his shoulders and struggle on. 'My dear wife, Marian. I didn't realise what had happened until a few minutes later.'

Yes, that was when the real horror of the situation reached him. There was blood on his sleeve. He had wondered for a moment if he had been hit. But he felt no pain. Then he had seen the hole in Marian's chest. She must have stepped sideways to protect him. She died instead of him.

The hall was nearly empty, the noise diminished. The police were measuring distances, making chalk marks on the floor round Clarissa's body. Photographs were taken. Officials stood watching, talking to each other in low voices. The young chap on the platform was their son, only twenty. Yes, a National Front member had been arrested. Two Young Farmers had been taken for questioning. And the Single Parents, all of them, had been asked to make statements. A shocking business, shocking.

Edward was talking to the ambulance men and the police, asking what would happen next, what he should do. They were bringing the ambulance round to the emergency exit, they said, to remove the body. The body, his mother, so quiet, so still, lying covered on a stretcher. A policeman offered to bring the Jaguar round too. Edward thanked him and handed him the keys. Then his control went, as if he had given it away with the keys, and he began to cry, mopping his eyes and blowing his nose. He tried to stop the strange sounds he was making but he couldn't. He sat on the floor by his mother's side and wept.

Charles sat watching as if in a dream. It's better to let go, they say. But I cannot cry. I have no tears. I feel strange, all stopped up. Reaction will come later.

Christ! At that very moment he began to shake uncontrollably, his limbs quivering, his head wobbling. He felt a fool. He couldn't stop. Someone brought him a pill and a glass of water. He took the pill and put it in his mouth. He couldn't manage the glass, his hands were shaking too much. The person held it to his lips. He swallowed.

Alison Peters, tear-stained, came and sat next to him, offering

206

condolence, help, anything she could do.

'Fuck off,' said Charles, shaking. 'That's all. Just fuck off.'

The Kebles were sleeping in the master bedroom at La Pinède. When the telephone rang John woke in confusion, haunted by an embarrassing dream. He and the senior partner were in the swimming pool together, and the water was only ankle deep. He felt terribly ashamed about this, since he had nothing on. If the water had come up to his waist it would have been all right.

With one hand he found the receiver in the dark, with the other reached for his dressing gown, which was on the floor. He was naked, as in his dream. He and Celia had made love earlier. She turned over and mumbled, 'Telephone? What on earth.'

It was two o'clock.

'Hallo. La Pinède.' John listened. He heard Charles, his voice hoarse and low, so that the message was at first unclear. Then he understood. He felt himself standing on the edge of a pit of grief and horror, a huge hole. He said, 'I'm so sorry. So very sorry. What a terrible shock. I must tell Celia.'

She was fully awake by then, had put on the light and was wrapping herself in a bath towel. Her face was contorted with anxiety. 'John, what is it? Emma, the boys, are they all right?'

He said quickly, 'Not our family. It's Charles.' Then he listened for a long time, putting in an occasional word. 'Yes. No. I understand. She didn't suffer.' Celia watched his face, reading the dreadfulness of the news. She heard him say, 'I'm going to ring you back in a few minutes' time. We'll come back, to be with you. To help if we can.' He put down the receiver.

Celia said, 'Marian. An accident.'

'Yes.' He held her in his arms and told her. She clung to him and wept. She was shocked to see that he was crying too, and that helped her stop for a moment. 'We must tell the others,' she moaned. 'We can't keep it to ourselves until the morning. We can't bear it alone.'

'No. We can't.' John covered his face with his hands and saw, as if the years had stood still, Mimsy's dining room on the day of the funeral, Dave and Marian standing at the table. Oh God, he prayed. May they rest in peace, forever and ever. Amen. 'We'll tell Barbara and Quentin. We'll fly back in the morning. Charles will need us.'

Celia wept again. 'Why, why? Why did it have to happen?'

Marian was driving the red Renault across the desert. The road was rough, no more than a track, but she knew that the oasis lay straight ahead. She would be there in a few minutes.

It was very early in the morning, just before dawn. The sky was pearly white, and cloudless. As she drove the sun began to rise behind her, gradually flooding the sandy wastes with a rosy red glow, which faded to pink and then to pale gold, while the sky darkened to blue. What a beautiful day!

She was in Saudi Arabia. The Gulf War had been organised from this area, so she was expecting to see tanks, aircraft, military transport, rows of tents. But there was no sign of them, just an endless vista of golden sand. The road led to the edge of an escarpment, then took a winding course down into the valley. There were palm trees ahead and a cluster of white houses shimmering in the sunlight. The oasis.

She was worried about the stain on her jacket, but when she looked down it had gone, of course. She was young again, only twenty-six. Her hair was long, tied back in a pony tail. She was wearing her blue jeans and a designer sweater.

Dave was waiting for her outside the house, as she knew he would be. They embraced lovingly. It had been such a long time.

He said, 'I'd almost given up hope. It was hard to bear.'

His voice was the same. She looked at his eyes, his hair, his tanned skin. He was just as she remembered.

'I missed you so much,' she said.

He led her through the courtyard, where a fountain splashed into a shady pool, to the spare room. The single bed was there, the white-painted chest of drawers, two chairs. The water colours and the crayon drawing hung on the wall. His zipper bag lay open on the floor, shirts and socks half tipped out.

She smiled, looking at these familiar things. 'I knew it would be like this. Absolutely perfect. I'm so happy. And the war is over.'

'Yes,' said Dave. 'There's only peace here. '

4   Save

This has been a bad winter for coughs, colds, influenza and secondary infections. Quentin Jones considers himself a splendidly healthy man, fortunate in having a sound constitution to begin with, but also wise in that he takes regular exercise, eats and drinks well though not to excess, and doesn't smoke.

It is particularly annoying for him, especially at Christmas time, to have come down with one of the prevailing illnesses. The first sign of this was a runny nose, which he treated with a specific for the common cold available at the local health food store. To call forth his body's full resistance, he went running on the Heath as usual, took alternate hot and cold showers when he got home, drank a double whisky before going to bed, and slept with a woollen vest under his pyjamas.

In spite of these precautions his condition did not improve. Suddenly, to his alarm, he developed pains in his chest which made breathing a major effort. This was surely a heart condition, probably angina pectoris. Barbara took his temperature and announced that it was over a hundred and two degrees Fahrenheit, or thirty-nine Centigrade, and he should have gone to bed instead of running about in the cold.

He felt too ill to protest when she telephoned the doctor. The diagnosis was that he had pleurisy as well as the current 'flu bug and would be laid up for a week at least. Antibiotics were prescribed. Quentin didn't believe in them, and privately intended to take less than the stated dose. With rest and plenty of liquids his system would revive on its own. Luckily Barbara was ready for this, and stood over him while he swallowed the right number of pills at stated intervals.

He spent Christmas in bed, while she went to parties without him. She cooked several festive meals for friends and family, bringing him small helpings which he tried to eat, to regain his strength, but which he couldn't finish. People came to see him, keeping their distance in case he was infectious, not staying too long in case they tired him. All of this damaged his usually positive ego, and made him feel very sorry for himself.

Now at last he is convalescent, his temperature normal, his chest no longer painful. But it will be some days yet before he is quite himself. He has lost weight, and his muscles have shrivelled. Shaving this morning, a week's growth too long to deserve the title 'designer stubble', he noticed that his face looks hollow, his eyes larger than usual. And he is desperately tired. He goes downstairs briefly, sits in his study, turns on his computer, turns it off again and goes back to bed. After lunch he starts reading the first two hundred pages of his latest book, as yet untitled, and falls into a heavy sleep.

When he wakes up it is seven o'clock, and Barbara is getting dressed to go to a New Year's party at the Kebles.

Welcome 1996, the year of the Olympics, elections in the USA and possibly in Great Britain as well. He is sad to be missing the party, which will include a lot of young people, Broome-Viviers and Kebles as well as Harry and Chris. But he doesn't have the energy, so it's out of the question.

'Sorry,' he says. 'Just couldn't keep awake. Book sent me to sleep.'

'Good thing, my angel,' says Barbara. 'How about a drink before dinner? It is New Year's Eve after all.'

Thoughtfully she has prepared a festive dinner for one, a small fillet of turkey in cream sauce with mashed potatoes, mushrooms and green beans, a mince pie for dessert, to be followed by cheese and biscuits. She brings him a martini cocktail to drink while she assembles everything, and then a half-bottle of white Burgundy to go with the meal. Her loving care reminds him that life is basically good and that soon he will be enjoying it to the full again.

She is wearing a blue velvet trouser suit with a ruffled lacy shirt. Her hair hangs round her face in silky blonde curls. 'You look adorable,' he says. 'Gainsborough's Blue Boy. Don't forget to kiss me goodbye.'

As it is New Year, which means having a lot to drink and staying up until after midnight, she has ordered a minicab to take her to the Kebles and bring her back.

Quentin eats his dinner comfortably in bed, watches some television and feels better than he has for some time. He gets up, wanders downstairs in dressing gown and slippers, and admires the way Barbara has arranged the Christmas cards. They are tied into big bunches with red and green ribbons, some hanging, some perched on bookcases, some flying from the ceiling. They look very jolly, individual robins, angels and snow scenes happily obscured in the bulk display. He knows that she will have made a list of who sent them, as she does every year, and will have sent out their own card, designed by their daughter Harry, to all the right people, with suitable messages written in her neat hand. His beloved Barbara is so efficient.

He looks into his study, not meaning to settle there, but turns on his computer and finds himself writing another page of his book, and then several more. The subject is terrorism, non-law, anarchy, but scaled down into novel form. He thinks it may be compared to *A Tale of Two*

Cities, since his readers now expect Dickens look-alikes in everything he produces. The story, the setting and the characters are already in his mind, so that he is in a way transcribing rather than creating. The underlying theme is the Grand Design, the Plan. He remembers talking to John Keble about this, on holiday at La Pinède, when he was still busy on a previous book. This one was no more than a germ, a sperm, the beginnings of an idea. He remembers the moon rising over the pine trees, and how they got the news of the shooting at two in the morning. It was the Year of the Poll Tax.

At midnight he takes a break, gets himself a glass of whisky and looks briefly at television. He goes back to the study, writes fluently and with enjoyment, and is still at it when Barbara comes home at one-fifteen. She is tipsy, pink-cheeked, and her curls are all over the place. She says she has had a wonderful time, and what is he doing out of bed?

'Beloved, I'm cured,' he says. 'Thanks to you, and those despicable antibiotics, and the good dinner you gave me. And I'm writing a book and I rely on you to give it a name. Man's Defiance of The Plan, Down With Celestial Purpose, A Tale of Two Cultures.'

'I'm thinking about it,' she says. 'Come on, it's bedtime.'

He is in fact quite tired now, in spite of sleeping all afternoon. He crawls back into bed while Barbara throws off her Blue Boy outfit and tells him what they had to eat and drink at the party and who was there. Among others the Keble boys, and their step-siblings, Emma and Rupert Chase, the Broome-Vivier children and Charles.

'How was Charles?' says Quentin.

'Better. He brought a woman friend, not young. She seems quite nice, she works with him at the bank. I think they're going steady.'

Charles had been through a very depressing time. Upweston didn't want him any more, not after the Town Hall tragedy. He tried to talk himself back into favour, but it was no good. He was deselected a few weeks later. For a while he kept in touch with Central Office, hoping that they would ask him to stand somewhere else when the opportunity arose. He would have to be patient.

Finally Patrick Dearden, who had been supportive in spite of a general view in the Party that Broome-Vivier smelled vilely of sleaze, invited him to dine at the Carlton Club. Charles thought this must mean good news at last. But Patrick, who was a sportsman and believed that killing, if undertaken, should be swift, told him over drinks that there was no chance of his playing a political role ever again. Upweston didn't want him, and nor did the Party.

Once that was over, they ate a good dinner together, with several bottles of wine. They talked about the prospects of political change and they talked about Clarissa, her intelligence, her instability. Charles got rather drunk. Patrick put him into a taxi and said goodnight.

He reported next day to Central Office that Broome-Vivier had taken it like a gentleman. He knew when he was beaten.

The only thing Charles could do was to go back to the bank. They found a slot for him, at a nominal salary, as an adviser on EEC matters. He was still a member of the board, and attended meetings. But one way and another he didn't have enough to do, and got miserably depressed. Friends were kind, and asked him to dinner and for weekends. He was grateful for this, and gradually began to enjoy himself a little. He found consolation in the arms of some of his previous mistresses when he was in London. At Broome he was often alone. Memories there were very painful.

A solution to his problems came unexpectedly when he had to update his Will. It would be good sense, tax-wise, to hand Broome over to Edward now, and find himself somewhere else to live, the obvious place being Home Farm, once a tied cottage, now empty and neglected. Restoring it to its former Victorian Gothic glory, decorating, furnishing, putting in central heating and good plumbing, finally making a garden for it, kept Charles agreeably busy for several years.

In his new home he felt that he had reached an adjustment, a lessening of his burden of sorrow.

He felt the need of a companion, someone to enjoy with him the good things of life. The woman friend, not young, who worked with him at the bank, would fill this position perfectly.

'Another piece of good news,' says Barbara, slipping on a Victorian-style nightie and getting into bed. 'Teresa's got a job.'

'Didn't she have one before?' says Quentin.

'She's had six in the last six months. She keeps changing her mind. She thought she might go abroad and work with refugees. Then it was do more exams and get better qualified. But now she's settled at last. You remember Beatrice King?'

'Only vaguely, my angel.' Quentin feels so happy lying next to her, watching her punching her pillows into shape with her little fist and switching off the bedside light. He reaches out in the darkness to hold her hand.

'Beatrice King was at Abbey Mead and she married Derek who had a drink problem. She helped him over that, and he's seriously rich and they're going to live mostly in France. So she's been looking around for someone to take over Queen Bee.'

'Buzz, buzz,' says Quentin. 'What is Queen Bee?'

'It's Beatrice King's nursing agency. Just right for Teresa. No men. Goodnight, my darling, and a happy New Year.'

'Happy New Year, beloved Barbara.'

In the early hours of the morning Barbara has a terrifying dream. She is in the Town Hall at Upweston, among the spectators, wearing the blue velvet suit and lacy blouse. She sees Clarissa coming in with the Single Parents, dressed in an old mackintosh and green wellies, her flaming red hair flowing long and loose. Barbara knows she has the gun in her pocket and pushes forward to try and take it away. But Edward is there, an older Edward. His blond hair is turning grey.

'No, no,' he says, holding Barbara back. 'It has to happen. It's part of the plot.'

So Clarissa shoots and kills several people, while Barbara tries to get through the crowd. She can't find Quentin anywhere, nor Harry and Chris. Oh God, where are they? So many bodies, dead and wounded. On the platform a couple are singing *Night and Day*. A man is clapping his hands, saying heartily, 'Jolly good performance, what-ho,' as if this was theatre with audience participation. But Barbara knows that it is real. She screams and screams. Then she wakes up.

'Okay, okay,' says Quentin, shaking her. 'It's only a dream.'

'Sorry, sorry,' she groans, clinging to him. 'Oh, how horrible. So frightening, the gun. People falling down. I couldn't find you.'

'Poor darling. There, there. All over now.'

'Yes. It was the end of the show. They were singing *Night and Day*.'

Fully awake, with a burning thirst, she goes to the bathroom, takes an aspirin and drinks several glasses of water. She settles into bed again, lying with her head on Quentin's shoulder, and is soon asleep.

He listens to her gentle, regular breathing, feeling wakeful now because once again she has produced the perfect title for his latest work, from her clever little subconscious, and this is exciting, and a relief, and a great help. The book will be called *Night & Day*. The dark night of secrecy, lawlessness, cruelty and oppression. The sunlight of peace, understanding, and ordinary life. Happiness.

Long ago, when we were young, Barbara and I took ourselves very seriously. We were pedantic, self-conscious. We asked rhetorical questions. We quoted. We argued for and against. How amusing to remember the way she used to talk, my adorable little wife, pretending to be very grown-up and intellectual. And, of course, I was a terrible poseur.

I only managed to get a First because I have a good memory. I'm not a great brain. Some people think my writing must be based on a personal philosophy. Why don't I reveal it, they say, and let the world into the secret? Because there's no secret, that's why.

My work. That's my Reality.

The End